Mohave Mambo

Colleen Rae

MOHAVE MAMBO
© Colleen Rae, 2009
All rights reserved

Cover art by Colleen Rae
Book design by Jo-Anne Rosen

ISBN: 978-1-931002-78-3

This is a work of fiction. Names, characters, and incidents are the product of the author's imagination and are used fictitiously. Any resemblance to actual persons, living or dead, is purely coincidental. Certain towns and some restaurants and bars mentioned do exist or did at one time.

Printed in the United States of America. No part of this book may be used or reproduced in any manner whatsoever without written permission except in the case of brief quotations embodied in critical articles or reviews. For information, please contact Colleen Rae at raecol@i2k.com.

Wordrunner Press
Petaluma, California

Acknowledgements

I would like to acknowledge and thank my long-time mentor and novel instructor, Guy Biederman, for showing me the way to paint pictures with words. He is and has been a dear friend for many years. I owe a great deal to him and I am most grateful.

I want to thank my good friend, Roberto Haro, for his guidance and for reading the manuscript and making many helpful suggestions. He too, has been a mentor for me.

Christie Nelson, writer extraordinaire, and Grant Flint, published author, also read the novel and gave me some wonderful and creative ideas and suggestions.

Many thanks to Frank Baldwin, editor, and author of *Balling the Jack* and *Jake and Mimi*, for copy and line-editing the entire manuscript. His additions and subtractions and his suggestion of an additional story line helped mold the novel into a presentable piece of prose.

Guy Biederman's novel workshop that I attended for five years was a fantastic sounding board; a completely safe place to read the work over a period of months. The members of the workshop provided invaluable ideas and additions to the manuscript.

My gratitude and thanks to Rosie Sorenson for her many suggestions and help.

Thanks to Annette Cress for her excellent proofreading of the manuscript and to Jo-Anne Rosen for all she has done to enable the manuscript to come alive in a book.

And last but not least, thanks to my wonderful writer's group, The Fourth Street Writers, a group of eight women who uplifted, suggested, critiqued, supported and encouraged me, as we did for each other in all of our writings. Thank you Christie Nelson, Diana Franco, Barbara Toohey, Kathy Rueve, Amy Peele, Betsy Fasbinder, and Linda Joy Meyers. I am very grateful for their friendship.

This book is dedicated to

the wonderful gardener in my life,

Larry Cummins.

He nurtures me to bloom and flower.

Contents

PART 1
In Hiding   *1*

PART 2
Down Hill Slide   *101*

PART 3
Losses and Gains   *189*

Epilogue   *271*

MOHAVE MAMBO

A novel

by

Colleen Rae

PART 1
In Hiding

1979

*L*ola leaned out over the balcony railing and looked up at the Big Dipper. The sky was alive and twinkling with a million stars, trying to compete with the neon splendor a few miles away in downtown Las Vegas. The air was warm, its touch like a feathered kiss on her skin. Her legs brushed against the wrought iron balustrade as she inhaled deeply the luscious aroma of the thick jasmine bush in full bloom, growing alongside the wall of the house. She moved over to the jasmine and buried her face in its blossoms. White star shaped flowers enveloped her, covering her shoulders and bare breasts. She could almost stand inside the bush, it was so thick.

She didn't know why she had awakened. An elusive dream hung just beyond her consciousness. It was something about her and Tony dancing. The image of them twirling across a black and white marble dance floor, her skirt billowing behind like a sail on the wind, suddenly came to mind. She loved to dance with him. Last night he had taken her to a club on the Strip. It was crowded and difficult to move without getting bumped by the other couples. Not at all like her dream.

The night light in the bedroom illuminated just enough that she could see Tony asleep in bed through the vines of the jasmine, like the small aperture of a camera. Through the glass door she saw one arm thrown above his dark curly head, the silk sheet falling across his groin. One minute she was staring at him alone in the bed, the next, two men swiftly came into view. One of them raised his hand and plunged it down toward Tony.

When Tony cried out the first time, Lola covered her mouth, afraid she would cry out, too. She grasped the jasmine bush, embedding herself nearly within its center. Each time he screamed her heart spasmed as if it were pierced. She could hear him thrashing against the headboard, and someone was grunting as the other man held Tony down. Every shriek made her feel faint. Finally the man stopped attacking Tony and looked down at the floor. Lola saw him pick up her nightgown. Both men searched the room and the bathroom. Then the man who had struck Tony walked to the balcony doors and peered out. He opened one of the French doors and stepped onto the balcony. Lola held her breath, willing herself to complete stillness. She must not allow even a vine to move. Lola could not see him but she knew he was only a few yards away. She thought she could hear his excited breathing. A few seconds later she saw him come back into view as he returned to the bedroom. When he turned to close the balcony door she saw his close-cropped white hair and the grim look on his face. A face she would never forget. My God! They had wounded, or worse, killed Tony!

She no longer saw them in the bedroom and then the lights came on downstairs. They had gone from room to room switching lights on and off, searching... searching for something.

Just when she felt like she could cling no longer to the bush, the lights were turned off downstairs and a car door slammed out front and sped down the street. She was sure she no longer heard sounds from anywhere in the house, so she uncurled herself from the jasmine vines and crept to the French doors. Opening one door very quietly she stepped into the room. It was then that she smelled it; the overpowering odor. The smell of fresh blood. She saw Tony stretched out, one arm still flung over his head like he was about to catch a ball. His legs were close together, moonlight illuminating his soft penis. Rivers of black liquid oozed over his shoulders, pooling darkly on the sheet. His chest and neck were covered with open wounds. Lola clasped her hand to her mouth but it was too late as she vomited on the rug beside his dangling hand. She leaned on the side of the bed, wiping her mouth on the sheet. Her eyes were drawn to his arm. Her fingers closed on his wrist pulse. There was none. Her moan was low and primal, like an animal in pain. She couldn't take her eyes from him. Crouching beside the bed, tears poured down her cheeks.

Finally she stood up, realizing she had to get out of there. She grabbed her shorts and tee-shirt from the closet, dressed and slipped on her sandals. Finding her purse on the closet shelf she scooped up her nightgown and stuffed it inside. At the doorway she took one last look, her eyes drawn to the half-digested shrimp marinara on the carpet. She rushed to the bathroom, grabbed a washcloth and wiped up the vomit. After rinsing the cloth in the toilet and flushing it, she threw it on the side of the tub. Taking the stairs two at a time, she bolted for the front door. Glancing up and down the street, she jumped into her VW, and drove to her apartment.

When she closed and locked her door, she began shaking. Sobbing, she slid to her knees and curled up into the fetal position. She cried for a long time until her eyes were swollen and red. When there were no more tears, just dry sobs, she stood and went to her bedroom, pulling clothes from her closet and drawers. Packing quickly, she took only one suitcase and her old Valencia guitar.

It was five a.m. when she drove into Carrow's Coffee Shop. Lola ordered a cup of black coffee, and popped three aspirins. Four hours to kill until she could close out her bank account. Food didn't seem very appetizing this morning when she remembered Tony. Gagging, she managed to swallow another gulp of coffee and started to cry again.

One of the waitresses, a pretty twenty-something, came over. She leaned near Lola.

"Anything I can do? Are you in trouble?"

Lola shook her head. "No thanks, I'll be fine." She looked up into the waitress' friendly brown eyes. "You know, man problems."

The young woman nodded vigorously. "I know, exactly. Want more coffee?"

"No thanks," Lola sniffed, wiping her nose.

"Well if you want anything to eat, just wave at me."

The waitress smiled and walked away.

After some deep breaths Lola settled down into the booth and tried to figure out why Tony was murdered. The most obvious reason would be that he was skimming from the casino he managed. But Lola's gut feeling said he'd been straight with the Mob. He'd always seemed very efficient and took his work seriously.

She saw him every evening because she danced three shows a night, five nights a week, next door at the casino theater. Her exotic-dance act was a belly dancing strip number with Middle Eastern music. She had auditioned for the job six months ago, and had met Tony that first night. He came every night after that to watch her act and finally she accepted his invitation to dinner. She became known as Tony's girl and everyone at the casino and the theater treated her with new respect.

The waitress came over and gestured toward her cup and this time Lola nodded, thanking her.

She lit a Marlboro, leaned her head back against the hard leather and blew smoke toward the ceiling. Jesus! What a mess she was in. They might be looking for her, although there was no logical reason why they would. She'd left no evidence she'd been at Tony's last night. Her car was parked across the street, instead of in the driveway where she usually parked it. But everyone at the theater knew she was Tony's girl and when the police came and started questioning ...it would come out. And they would be looking for her then. Maybe the killers would be too.

Out of the corner of her eye she noticed outside the window a Las Vegas Police car slide into a parking place. Two uniformed cops got out and entered the coffee shop. Lola held her breath as she ground out the cigarette and pulled three dollars from her wallet, leaving them on the table. The officers took a seat in a back booth. Instinct told her to run. Anywhere. Just get in her VW, Betsy, and go.

※

"So long, Vegas," Lola murmured, drumming her fingers on the steering wheel. The morning was still cool; 98 degrees in the shade. Passing the high-rise hotels on the Strip, their glass exteriors flashing like beacons in the early sunlight, she smelled the familiar combination of chlorine and suntan lotion wafting from the pools as early risers made ready for a few safe hours in the sun. Her dark hair streaming from the window, Lola swigged on a can of Bud Lite, and took the first entrance onto the freeway heading south.

She knew that she wouldn't miss this town. The town where everyone was either addicted to alcohol, drugs or gambling. She had been the rare one who wasn't addicted to anything. Unless it was men. She never could seem to spend any time without one. There was always someone she was half in love with, sleeping with, or just dating.

Images of the first few times she and Tony went out together came to mind. He'd treated her very specially and gave her expensive gifts. The ruby ring she had on her right hand, the diamond and gold bracelet and earrings. Oh God! The last image she had of him seared into her brain. Her throat started to close and her eyes watered. Hang on, she told herself. She'd gotten away in time. They didn't know she was there. But she had to disappear, anyway.

Her white shorts rode high on tanned legs, and the red halter top missed her waist by two inches. Clenching the cold beer between her thighs, she glanced at the map on the seat. Her finger found the town — Laughlin, Nevada. She could spend the night there. Lola's '69 VW bug did 60 miles an hour on the straightaway, but on the hills, she was lucky to get it up to 20. She dug in her purse for the Marlboros, lit a cigarette with a Zippo, and inhaled deeply. A total of 1,565 bucks was in her purse after closing out her checking account. One weathered, brown leather suitcase she'd bought at Goodwill rested on the back seat. Her old guitar was propped behind the passenger seat. She'd left all her costumes behind at the theater. Not much to show for two years in Vegas.

Memories of Tony on the bed flashed across her mind like a surrealistic movie. A soft shudder ran across her shoulders and down her spine. She had to put his death out of her mind; escaping was the only important thing right now.

Forty minutes out of Henderson, she pulled into the last casino before the Nevada/California border, parking on the uphill side. She took a pee in the restroom, then bought a cold Bud from the bar. Cigarette smoke circled above the one-arm bandits. The smell of hamburgers grilling drifted from the coffee shop.

"Hey, babe. Where you from?" the beefy bartender said, checking out the long tanned legs.

Lola gave him a cold stare as she paid for the beer.

"If you wanna' hang around til' I get off, I'll buy you dinner. They have a pretty good band here." He brushed a blond wisp off his forehead, licking his lips with a red tongue.

She picked up her change, and turned on a sandaled heel. "Sorry. I'm in a hurry."

"Fuck off," she said, under her breath.

She exited the air-conditioned casino and headed for the VW. "Come on, Betsy. Do your stuff." Opening the door, she gave a little running push, jumped inside, popped the clutch and started the motor. Betsy bucked a couple of times, then purred out of the parking lot, still headed south, down the two-lane highway. Beer propped between her legs again, she concentrated on putting miles behind her. A northbound truck driver looked down on brown thighs, tooting his loud horn, but Lola, deep in thought, and chewing an unwanted hangnail, was oblivious.

The little green Bug bumped along the roller coaster road as Lola twisted dials on the radio, but found only silence on the airways on this lonely stretch. She tried humming, "Hard Travelin," but her heart wasn't in it.

Blue-gray mountains rimmed the valley of the arid basin she was passing through. The blacktop shimmered and weaved as the noon sun bore down. Lola could see a glistening mirage atop the next rise. Mesquite trees and an occasional Yucca were scattered across the desert. Ocotillo blossoms cascaded brilliant orange along the highway. A roadrunner darted in front of her, crossing at high speed. To her left, jackrabbits raced through scrub brush. Wiping her neck and underarms with a towel, she slowed for the turn-off to Laughlin. A half an hour later, she saw the small gambling mecca that Don Laughlin had built on the Nevada side of the Colorado River. She pulled into the River Queen Hotel and Casino, parked, and grabbed her overnight bag. Entering through large glass doors, she stepped to the front desk.

"May I help you?" A clean-shaven young man smiled down at her.

"Yes. I'd like a room for the night."

"A single?" He asked.

"Yes. How much for a single?"

"A single bed and bath is $60."

"I'll take it." Lola laid three twenties on the counter.

He pushed a register toward her. "Please sign here."

Lola took the pen and wrote L. Raines. She filled out the license number, printing a fictitious address in Boulder City.

The hotel employee handed her a key, and gave directions to the room. She let herself in, and immediately turned off the air-conditioner, which was blasting arctic air over her bare arms and legs. She locked the door, pulled down the blinds, turned back the covers, and climbed fully dressed between the clean sheets. Shivering, she willed herself to be still, at last.

Exhaustion gripped her body and began to close down her mind. Lola always slept when she was in crisis. She inhaled deeply, then released a long sigh. Within seconds, she was sound asleep.

※

*N*ext morning, Lola woke at eight a.m., having slept fifteen hours. She showered, dressed, and grabbed a doughnut and coffee in the cafe downstairs. Leaving Laughlin, she crossed the river at Davis Dam, entering Arizona. Heading south again, she passed through Bullhead City, which consisted of a cluster of bars, restaurants, motels, and a few small grocery, bait and tackle stores. Everything appeared green for a few miles back from the river, then, the earth suddenly turned barren and dry. It was as immediate as night from day. Stucco, brick houses, and mobile homes were spread across the fertile areas; horses and livestock grazing nose-deep in chartreuse fields.

Where would she go? She had no idea or agenda. Trying not to think about Tony and the world she'd just left, was hard. From past experience she knew the best thing for her to do was to get started with a new life as soon as possible. Start over again. Well, she'd done that a few times in her life. That meant she'd have to find some kind of work. Best to stay out of the spotlight for a while, literally.

Forty minutes down the road following the Colorado River, she saw a sign ahead. Sweeney's Tavern and

Motel—Vacancy. She pulled off the road and parked on a knoll. Taking a sweater from her bag, she entered the bar through a red door. Sunlight flashed inside for one second, illuminating the dark, smoky interior, then the room returned to blackness. Lola heard the sound of billiards smacking together. The sweet, yeasty smell of spilled beer assailed her nostrils. Her eyes gradually became adjusted to the dimness, and she made out the outline of the bar. Finding the stool with her hand, she hoisted bare legs over the edge, tucking her feet over the boot rail. She draped her sweater around her shoulders and lit a cigarette.

"Whatcha' have?" the woman behind the bar asked.

"Bud Lite," Lola answered.

A couple of old-timers were at one end of the bar. An extremely large, probably Mohave Indian, since they were known for their size, with straight, black hair in a ponytail, sat at the other end. Two guys in jeans and cowboy boots were playing pool. Lola and the bartender were the only women.

The bartender placed the Bud and a glass in front of Lola. "Passin' through?"

Lola nodded. She poured the beer into the glass and took a long drink, froth settling around her lips.

"Where you headed?" the woman asked.

Lola shrugged. "Not sure. Down the road, somewhere." She drained the glass and poured the remainder of the beer.

One of the pool players stood beside her. "Give us two more, Pat." Pool stick in hand, he looked down at

Lola on the stool. "Care to play a game with us?"

She looked up into blue eyes, blond hair drifting on his collar. "No, thanks."

"Sure? Billy and I'll give you a handicap." He gave her a lopsided grin.

Lola shook her head. "I just want to relax. But, thanks for asking." She gave him her best smile, dimples dancing.

"Okay. By the way, my name's Ronnie. And that's my friend, Billy Jim, over there." He offered his free hand.

Lola shook it and turned around to smile and acknowledge Billy Jim. Across the room she saw a tall, slim-hipped cowboy with long legs. Stetson pushed back on his head like Earl Hollister in the movies. A tuft of sandy brown hair lay across his brow. Billy tipped his hat and smiled back.

Ronnie picked up the beers and headed back to the pool table.

"My name's Pat," the woman behind the bar said. "Pat Sweeney. Don't know if you saw the sign when you came in. We're looking for help. Need a bartender a couple nights a week."

Lola turned around and saw the Help Wanted sign on the inside of the door. She turned back to Pat. "I'm Lola Raines."

"Couldn't help noticin' how you handled that invitation. Nice goin'." The woman on the other side of the bar was in her forties, medium-length brown hair, wearing slacks and a blue tee-shirt with Sweeney's Tavern across the front. "My old man, Paul, and me own this place. It's been real hard keepin' the bar staffed. Ever had any experience tending bar?"

"No." Lola was thinking, why not spend a few weeks here and pick up some extra money. "But I think I could catch on real quick."

Pat nodded. "Not much to serve, usually beer and wine to the customers. Got a place to stay?"

"No."

"Well, we own the motel, too. If you want to rent a room, I'll give you a nice discount." Pat wiped the bar around Lola's glass.

Lola smiled. "Thanks," she said, finishing the last of the beer.

Pat opened another Bud Lite and put it in front of Lola. "This one's on the house. We need someone behind the bar tomorrow night and I'll help you. We're usually real busy and bein' new and all, you might get swamped. Think you could start tomorrow?" She smiled, large teeth protruding from her mouth.

"Sure." Lola leaned her elbows on the bar and listened to the tune on the jukebox; Merle Haggard singing, "Okie from Muskogee."

The two old-timers thanked Pat and slipped off their stools. One of them walked toward Lola.

"Hi, little lady. Marsh's the name." He extended a gnarled, dirty hand. His gray uncombed mane and beard, soiled jeans and shirt reminded Lola of an old desert rat.

"Hi," she said. "I'm Lola." She grasped his hand, feeling the deep creases of life etched across his palm.

"I just heard Pat bring ya on board as our new bartender. Welcome. And don't let none of these young colts rattle ya. Don't mean no harm. " He saluted her and limped to the door. "Be seein' ya," he said over his shoulder.

"Ole Marsh never misses a thing," Pat said. "He heard our conversation clear down the end of the bar. Other times, I tell him he's had enough to drink, he can't hear a word I say." She laid an application in front of Lola. "Here, honey. Just take this with ya and fill it out tomorrow."

Lola's glass was half-full. She stubbed out her cigarette and left five dollars on the bar.

Pat eyed the beer. "One other little thing, honey. I probably don't have to tell ya, but I don't want my bartenders drinkin' on the job. It's against the law, you know, but plenty do it anyway."

"No problem, Pat. I don't drink when I'm working."

"Good girl. You go on over to the motel and Paul, my husband, will show you a room. I'll just give him a call, and tell him yer comin'."

"Thanks. See you later." Lola opened the red door to three o'clock sunlight. The thermometer on the side of the Tavern read 110 degrees. She looked toward the river. On both banks as far as she could see, green fields, dotted with horses and cows. Farms and small houses were scattered along the river. Quite a change from Vegas. Here was time to get her life back to some kind of normal. She could hide here, she thought. At least for a while.

*B*illy Jim Andrews loved his mares. He loved to ride and he loved taking care of his five acres. He spent a lot of time feeding, brushing and riding Sedona, his beautiful sienna quarter horse. Sedona had the company of Apache, a paint, a real nice, easygoing horse. Sedona bossed Apache and Apache didn't seem to mind. Whenever Billy Jim wanted to load Sedona into a trailer, she became the most contrary, obstinate animal ever bred. But, if Apache was already loaded, Sedona would go meek as anything, right up into the trailer, nuzzling the paint's muzzle.

Billy thought of himself as a cowboy, but he worked as an engineer on the Sante Fe Railroad, out of Needles. Besides the horses, he had a peacock and pea hen, a steer he was fattening up for the freezer, and numerous chickens. So, when he was on a work-run, a neighbor boy fed the animals. Billy'd had a wife several years ago. She'd come to town on the train from back east, and got off at Needles to attend her father's funeral. Billy met her at the Red Dog Saloon, courted and married her within six weeks. After two years, she left him, because there were no art galleries or good restaurants, or music concerts any nearer than Phoenix, which was about three hours away. After that, he'd had a series of girlfriends, but none of them lasted very long. Being the girlfriend or wife of a railroader took a particular kind of person. Someone that didn't mind being alone for a couple of days at a time. And, of course, could stay alone, at night.

Billy deadheaded home from Seligman unexpectedly one early morning, and caught his girlfriend in his bed with a fellow railroader. This wasn't too unusual as things went in Mohave Valley. But when Billy shot the railroader, a former friend, in the foot that did cause a bit of trouble. Fortunately, there was an old law that Billy cited which maintained that if an intruder was trespassing on your property, and refused to leave, a show of force was acceptable. Billy said the gun went off accidentally, but he was known for a particularly wicked temper. Especially if he'd been drinking. Also, fortunately, the shot just nicked the flesh and the foot healed quickly, so not much harm was done. But the Valley gossips had fun for weeks repeating Billy's exploit, until another railroader beat his wife almost to death after catching her in a similar position. Then, Billy's deed became old news.

"Hereeeee chickee, chickee, chick, chick, chick." Billy tossed the grain on the ground in front of his silly-looking South American chickens, with the red and green feathers sticking straight up on their heads. When they bobbed for the grain, their topknots jumped and fluttered. But, they laid beautiful pale green eggs that were delicious.

Billy stood with his chickens eating around his feet, thinking of the woman he'd seen at the Tavern yesterday. She was sure good lookin' — some dimples! What was her name? Lola. That was a mighty unusual one. He'd only heard it in a song.

Billy stepped into the cool, damp house. The window unit swamp-cooler caused sweat to roll down his neck. In the bathroom he stripped off his dirty jeans and wet shirt, and entered the white-tiled shower, turning on the faucets. Biceps danced over tanned arms as he soaped up his extraordinary body. He thought of Lola again as he lathered himself up and down. Soon, he responded to his fantasy, and spread his seed on the shower floor.

After shaving, he put on a fresh short-sleeve western shirt, clean jeans and his Tony Lama boots. Grabbing his Stetson, he headed for the corrals, grained the horses and steer and threw down a few chips of hay. Sedona whinnied and tossed her head. She always ate her grain immediately and then asked for more.

"Hey, sweet girl. You just eat your hay and stop tryin' to weasel more grain." Billy stroked her long brown neck and laid his nose on the side of her head. When he turned away and headed for the truck, Sedona decided the alfalfa wasn't so bad, after all.

Billy climbed into his new Ford truck and headed for the Sports Lounge for dinner.

※

Sherry Brown rolled over in the double bed crammed wall-to-wall in the single wide trailer. Greg mumbled and pulled her close. He patted her buttock, half asleep, then coming awake, he slid his hand down between her thighs.

Sherry squirmed in invitation. Soon Greg mounted her and they were pumping hard, rocking their small home like a teeter-totter. Just as Greg came, Sherry heard something on the dish drain fall into the sink.

"Christ, honey," Sherry said. "Can you be a little less athletic? I don't like Bill jokin' about our sex life. Every time he sees our trailer movin', he makes a smart-ass remark." Bill was their next door neighbor.

"Aw, he don't mean nothin'. Just his way," Greg said, rolling off Sherry's damp body.

"Well, I don't appreciate his way."

Greg looked at the clock, and then remembered it was Saturday. "Wanna go for a swim?" Sherry climbed out of bed, and moved a few feet into the tiny bathroom, stepping over piles of clothes and boxes.

"Okay," Sherry said, running a brush through her tangled blond hair. "Hey, let's go down to the Tavern tonight. I hear Russell's playing."

"Weren't you gonna try to get a job there? Maybe you can talk to Pat tonight," Greg said, throwing the sheet back, revealing his limpness as well as brown, hairy legs.

"Yeah, I could do that."

"Listen, babe. You gotta get a job, pretty soon. I can't support us on what I make. Working at the liquor store don't pay shit."

Sherry flushed the toilet and came around the corner. "I'm tryin', honey. Jobs are few and far between around here."

"Well, if we can't make it here, we may have to go back to Phoenix. You had a good job tendin' bar, there."

"We can't go back to Phoenix," Sherry reminded him. "You got those unpaid tickets. We go back, you go to jail." She stepped gracefully into her blue bikini.

"Oh, yeah, right." He'd almost forgotten about the warrant out on him. Greg got out of bed, went to the stool and peed a strong stream into the bowl. He flipped his penis twice and opened his stash box. Skillfully rolling a joint and placing the joint above his ear, he spotted his swim trunks in a pile of clothes on the floor and slipped them on. Hair dangled over the waist band. Greg had hair all over his body. Black hair. Sherry wondered how the sun could tan him so evenly with all that forest to penetrate.

"Last one in's a farthead," Greg said, as he ran out the door and down to the river, twenty yards away.

Sherry strolled past his Harley parked beside the faded-blue trailer. Sometimes Greg was such a child. She put up with it because he was a good fuck. Although lately, he hadn't taken as much time with her as he used to. He just jumped on and off like he wanted to get it over with. Well, she'd damn well slow him down, next time.

≋

*L*ola turned over on her stomach, sliding legs across soft, yellow sand. Someone had gone to a lot of trouble to truck in the sand and spread it along the river banks. Up at the Tavern, Pat waved as she headed for the bar. Lola waved back.

Lola thought of last night. Pat had invited her over for dinner after she'd settled in the motel room. Two of their neighbors tended bar so Pat and Paul could have a night off together. The couple lived behind the office in a one-bedroom apartment. Pat had cooked lasagna and made a salad, and they drank Chianti out of whiskey-sour glasses.

"So, where ya hail from?" Paul asked between mouthfuls of lasagna.

"I was born in California." Lola looked up, meeting pale green eyes.

"Where 'bouts in California?" He persisted.

"Glendale. That's a few miles from Los Angeles."

Paul nodded. "I was in California once. Stationed at Point Hueneme. Sure liked the country but didn't care much for the folks there."

"Paul! That's not very polite." Pat nudged his arm with her elbow, knocking his food off the fork.

"That's fine," Lola said. "Paul's being honest. I like honesty. Actually, I didn't much care for California, either. That's why I left." She smiled at them.

"See, I said she was an honest-lookin' girl, hon, didn't I?" He nudged his wife back with his elbow.

"Well, we're just happy you stopped at our place," Pat said. 'Now, tomorrow night there'll be quite a crowd. Live music always brings 'em in." She poured more wine for herself and Paul. "More wine, honey?"

Lola shook her head. "No thanks."

"If you come into the Tavern 'round six, I'll get ya acquainted with the routine."

Lola nodded, listening.

"We have a real nice little beach down on the river," Pat continued. "In the mornings, it's nice swimmin' before all the boats and jet skis get goin'. By noon, ya take a real risk going in the water. Why, last summer, a jet ski ran right over a man swimmin', and cut off his leg."

Lola tried not to grimace as the red Lasagna sauce slid down her throat. Pat's story brought images of Tony to mind.

"Can't be too careful," Pat said, wiping the marinara from her mouth with red fingers, leaving a smudge of sauce on her nose.

"What decided ya to leave Las Vegas? I hear it's a pretty wild town." Paul said, getting her attention.

Lola shrugged. "It was time to go. Been there long enough." She gave Paul the benefit of her dimples.

He seemed satisfied. "Well, sure glad ya stopped by. Hope yer gonna like it here."

Lola jumped. The raucous sound of a jet ski brought her back to the present. In front of her, a young man did a sliding turn, spraying water on her back. "Thanks a lot, you jerk," she muttered. He never even looked her way; continuing up river at high speed. She remembered Pat's warning and decided against going for a quick swim. It was time to go back to her room, anyway. No use getting too much sun in the middle of the day. Picking up her towel, she wrapped it around her chest. She didn't particularly like the way Paul's eyes slid over her body. He had a head of thick white hair and a basketball belly. But it was his eyes that bothered her. They made her want to run and hide. And Lola didn't hide easily. Pat was a real nice woman, but how she'd settled for Paul was a mystery. Never can tell about people.

Back in her room, she showered and lay down on the bed. Her mind jumped back to the big house in Las Vegas and Tony. She shivered, remembering him and the way he had died.

Being an exotic dancer wasn't as much fun as she had expected. It wasn't the most enjoyable way to make a living. She hated the whistles and catcalls from the audience, but it came easy for her, with all her dance training. She'd made good money and spent it as fast as it came in. Tears welled up in her eyes as she thought of Tony. He had been good to her, in his way.

Lola pushed Tony from her mind, dressed and drove to the Sports Lounge for an early dinner. She backed Betsy onto an uphill grade in the restaurant parking lot. It was time to get a new starter as soon as she made a couple of paychecks.

Her dark hair flowing over bare shoulders, she grabbed a red sweater from the backseat. Black slacks clung to round cheeks and the red tee-shirt hugged her full chest.

The sign by the road read: Sports Lounge— Dinner and Dancing.

Lola entered the dining room and a woman with white hair and a long dress came forward. "Just one for dinner?"

Lola nodded.

"This way please."

She was seated at a small table and the hostess placed a menu in front of her. "Our special tonight is prime rib, mashed potatoes, gravy and green beans."

"Thanks. I'll just have a look at the menu."

"Would you like a cocktail before dinner?"

"I'll have a beer. Bud Lite, please."

The hostess smiled and headed for the bar.

Lola decided on lake bass sautéed in white wine, Idaho baked potato with sour cream and chives, and a dinner salad.

A waitress brought the beer and took her order. Lola noticed the couple next to her consulting a map; obvious travelers. Band instruments were set up in one corner, but it was still too early for music. Across the room, one of the cowboys she'd seen at the Tavern yesterday morning was eating dinner. Lola checked him out. Wide shoulders, dark tan, sunburned nose. Hair the color of sand curled across his neck. Gray Stetson rested on the chair beside him. At that moment he looked up and met her eyes. She smiled, then turned away, drinking her beer. In a few minutes, her eyes wandered back in his direction. He was still looking at her and smiling; a broad grin, showing white, even teeth. He dipped his head. Then he put down his fork, stood up, and headed for her table.

Damn! She had definitely invited him with her smile. Now why had she done that?

"Hi. I'm Billy Jim. I saw you yesterday at the Tavern. Since you're eatin' alone and so am I, would you like to join me for dinner?" His large brown hands rested comfortably on the back of the nearby chair, one booted foot crossed over the other.

Lola hesitated, then said, "Sure. Why not." She picked up her beer and stood up, aware of his body, just a hand away. He reached out to take her glass. When his fingers touched hers gripping the cold, moist beer, they both felt the jolt of static electricity between them.

His eyes widened. "Damn, woman. You got some energy field." Billy Jim laughed good-naturedly.

Lola liked his easy way of talking. "Just making sure you were on your toes."

Billy laughed out loud in deep chuckles. He pulled out the chair and she took a seat across from him. The waitress noticed she had moved and served her dinner at Billy's table.

"Seemed like you said your name was Lola. That right?" Billy resumed eating his 12-ounce steak.

She nodded.

"Lola what?"

"Lola Raines."

"What brings you to the Valley, Lola Raines?"

"Just passing through."

"Well, lucky me, that you did." His penetrating blue eyes held hers as she slid the fish between open lips.

"How come you decided to work at the Tavern?" Billy motioned for the waitress to refill their drinks.

"Seemed like a good idea. I needed some extra money and Pat needed help. And I don't want any more to drink. I got to tend bar tonight."

"Where you stayin'?"

"At the Tavern Motel."

"Not much room." Billy finished eating, lit a cigarette and leaned back in his chair.

"I don't need much. Just a place to lay my head."

"Like to ride?"

"Horses?"

Billy nodded.

"I used to. Haven't done much of it, lately."

"I have two. Like to come ridin' with me, sometime?"

"Sure."

Billy's drink arrived just as Lola finished her meal. "Where you from?" he asked, lighting her cigarette.

"You sure ask a lot of questions, Billy." Dimples flashed in her tanned cheeks.

"I'm interested in you, woman. Everything."

Lola looked away. "I worked in Vegas for a couple of years."

"Doin' what?"

Lola stared at him, eyes never wavering. "I was an exotic dancer."

Billy grinned. "So why'd you leave?"

I wanted some quiet time in my life for a change, so I headed out. Figured I'd stop whenever the urge grabbed me."

"Do you usually act on your urges?" Blue eyes sparkled.

"Usually." Then she added, "I need to get going. I'm meeting Pat at six at the Tavern so she can show me around." Lola signaled the waitress for her check.

"Well, I'll see ya later on. I plan on droppin' in and listening to Russell and the band. He's a friend of mine." The waitress started to put the check in front of Lola, but Billy intercepted it. "I'll get that. Dinner is on me."

Lola started to protest. "No, please..."

"You can dance with me on your break," Billy said, laying cash on the table.

"I'm not sure that's a good precedent. Then I'll have to dance with all the cowboys on my break."

Billy shook his head. "Nope. Just this one."

"Thank you for dinner." She smiled, and stood up, pushing back her chair.

"I'll walk you out." He slipped his arm lightly around her waist. No sparks this time, but she was very aware of the warmth of his fingers spreading down across her hips.

In the parking lot, Lola opened the unlocked door of the VW. "I have to give Betsy a little push."

"What's wrong?"

"She needs a new starter. Just haven't gotten around to it."

"You get in, I'll push."

Lola slid behind the wheel. Just a small shove started Betsy right up. Lola revved the motor. "See ya, Billy," she said, leaning out the window.

"Ya sure will, Lola." He liked the way her name rolled off his tongue. Billy watched her sail down River Highway. Hot Damn! He sure as hell was gonna be first in line.

§§

*L*ola entered the dimly-lit Tavern, looking around for Pat. The bar was empty except for Paul behind the bar filling the ice bin.

"Hi. Where's Pat?"

Paul turned around. "Hi, Lola. She'll be over in a minute. I did the day shift 'cause you and her are workin' tonight." He began wiping down the bar. "Come back here and you can help me do this. Start at the other end."

Lola hesitated. Then, she went through the gate, put her purse on a shelf, and picked up a towel in the hot, soapy water. She noticed his buttocks sticking out as he leaned over the bar. Carefully, so as not to touch him, she started to pass behind, when he backed up, pinning her between his large cheeks and the ice bin. He stood there, pressing himself into her stomach.

"Would you move, Paul?" Lola didn't make any attempt to hide her displeasure. She put both her hands on the small of his back and shoved.

"Oh, sorry. Sure." Shifting his weight, he leaned against the aluminum sink, which allowed enough room for her to pass. "It's kind of tight back here. Hope you don't mind if I bump into you from time to time."

Lola meant to start off exactly right. "I know you like honesty, Paul, so I'll tell you right now, I *do* mind. If you want me to work here, this better not happen again."

Paul turned to look at her, his face bright red in the bar light. He began to sputter. "Well, ah, I... I hope you don't think I did that on purpose."

"Whatever, Paul. You *heard* me." Lola continued to the end of the bar and began wiping down the counter. She returned with a couple of glasses and dumped them in the sink, splashing hot water on Paul's arm. The red door opened, casting a triangular shaft of light across the sawdust floor as Pat entered.

"Hi, Lola. Paul been showin' you around?"

Paul was silent.

Lola did her best to brighten up. "Yes."

Pat walked through the swinging gate. "You can go now, honey. Us girls will take over." She put an affectionate hand on his shoulder.

"Okay. See ya later." Paul didn't look back, making a quick retreat.

※

"*H*ey, babe. Can we have two Coors down here?" A tall skinny man with black hair curling around his neck and abundant hair on his forearms waved at Lola.

She carried the beer and two glasses to the end of the bar, setting them down in front of the man and the lovely blond girl beside him.

"Hi. I'm Sherry," the blond said. "This is my old man, Greg." She poured her beer, foam brimming over the rim.

"I'm Lola, the new bartender. Nice to meet you." She smiled at Sherry and nodded to Greg.

"This your first night?" Sherry asked.

Lola nodded. Several people came in and stepped up to the bar. "Talk to you later. I have to take care of business," Lola said over her shoulder.

"Damn. Pat's already hired someone," Greg complained. "You shoulda got here last week." He showed his disappointment by scowling and gulping down his beer.

Sherry smiled and squirmed on her stool. "Oh, something else will turn up. It always does. Stop worryin'. Let's have a good time; it's Saturday night." She snapped her fingers and did a little body-dance movement on the stool.

"I told you we need some money so I can go to L.A. and get a pound," Greg said under his breath.

"Oh, lighten up. It'll be okay. You'll see. I promise I'll check out the Sports Lounge and the Sundancer tomorrow. Okay?"

Sherry's offer seemed to pacify him, somewhat. "Okay," he grumbled.

Smoke was heavy in the bar. Even though the Tavern had a window air-conditioner and ceiling fans, it didn't quite take care of the heat and cigarette smoke of four dozen bodies. Russell on guitar and Carl on banjo were tuning up. The drummer, Rick, and fiddle player, Joe, completed the band. Someone turned off the jukebox, and Russell opened the set with "Boot Scootin' Boogie." Several of the cowboys at the bar grabbed their girls and hit the dance floor. Lola had to remember who left their drinks with the intention of coming back.

Out of the corner of her eye she noticed Billy Jim and his friend Ronnie come in and take a seat in Pat's section. Billy caught Lola's eye and they exchanged smiles. She didn't have much time to enjoy the music or have any conversations beyond taking orders, the night was so busy. Around ten o'clock, Paul came in and she took a fifteen-minute break. First thing she did was hit the can, then combed her damp hair and rubbed her nose with her palm. When she came out into the hallway, Billy was standing in her path, legs crossed, leaning against the wall.

"I'm here to claim that dance."

Lola started to pass. "You know, Billy, I'd just like to cool off with a coke."

"Okay. Meet ya outside."

Without answering, Lola made for the red door. She stepped outside into the cool river breeze, enjoying its gentle touch on her skin. In a few minutes, Billy joined her. He had a coke in one hand and a beer in the other.

"Nice out here. You shore are workin' your tail off. Did you think it'd be such hard work?" he asked, handing her the coke.

"No, I didn't realize how warm it would be. In Vegas everything is *very* air-conditioned." Lola took a long swig, throat burning from the carbonation.

"Well, I still claim that dance with you. Will you save it for me?"

"I'm not likely to dance with anyone tonight. Some other time." She looked up at the black skies. Directly above them winking stars outlined the Big Dipper. "I'd forgotten how beautiful it can be in the desert at night. In Vegas the stars aren't this visible, because of all the neon lights."

Billy turned his gaze from Lola and looked up. "Yep. Desert nights are mighty powerful." His shoulder brushed hers as they leaned against the Tavern wall. Just at that moment, they both saw the shooting star. "Look." Lola pointed. "It's been ages since I've seen one." Her voice was soft.

"Reckon you'll see a whole lot of them in Mohave country," Billy said. "You city reared?"

"Yes, but, I've always loved the country. I never felt totally at home until I slept under the stars."

Just then, Paul came through the red door. "Pat said to come in and help her," he said, eyeing Billy.

"How ya doin' Paul?" Billy asked.

Paul nodded. "Can't complain."

Lola watched Paul go before she turned to go in. "He's an odd one," she said, quietly.

"That he is," Billy agreed.

Smoke clouds poured out the door when Lola opened it and Billy propped it wide with a large wastebasket.

"Get cooled off?" Pat asked.

Lola nodded.

The high voltage of the band plus the fast pace of the bar made her first night pass quickly. At ten minutes to two, when Pat announced no more drinks would be served amid groans and protests, the Tavern began to slowly empty. The band was packing up and Lola helped Pat clean behind the bar. Billy hung around the jukebox, watching. When Pat said good-night, Lola picked up her purse and pushed through the swinging gate.

"Wanna go for a walk down by the river?" Billy asked, holding the red door for her.

"No thanks, Billy. I'm turnin' in. I'll take a raincheck on that, though." She brushed his forearm with her fingers and smiled, showing her dimples. "Goodnight," she said, and headed for her room across the parking lot.

Billy watched her go. "Night, Lola." Damn, he thought. She was more complicated than he'd figured.

※

Lola worked Saturday and Sunday nights at the Tavern. Everything had gone well. She had even done one song with the band when Russell found out she could sing. He was sitting at the bar early Sunday night when she came to work.

"Hi. I'm Russell Sykes." He was very tall and wound his long legs around the bar stool. "Me and my band play here on the weekends."

Lola set a Coors in front of him. "I know. I enjoyed your music last night. Lola Raines," she said, and offered her hand.

Russell reached across the bar and shook it. "Pat told me she heard you plunkin' on a guitar in your room. You play?"

Lola shook her head. "No, just sort of plunk while I'm singing."

"Pat said you sounded real nice. Care to sit in with us for a song, later?"

Lola hesitated. She had sung with a group in Vegas on her night off at an open-mike club. "Yeah. That sounds like fun."

And it was. On her first break, she sang, "Help Me Make It Through The Night," and got quite a bit of applause. Marsh stomped and shouted from the bar. A large Mohave Indian nearly fell off his stool when he hooted a cry of approval. Then she went back to work and everyone told her what a nice voice she had.

Billy showed up late on Sunday and invited her to go riding the next day. She accepted, deciding she had said no enough times to discourage him. She really didn't want to get involved or send the wrong signals, but riding was harmless.

She slept until noon on Monday, then walked down to the Best Buy and picked up coffee and doughnuts, a few snacks, and the Vegas Sunday paper. Sitting up in bed she scanned the news section. On the third page the headlines shook her up.

Casino boss murdered — Girlfriend still missing.
On Monday Morning of last week, Tony Ricco, Manager of the Calendar Club Theatre and Casino, was found in bed with his throat slashed in his exclusive Las Vegas Golf Course Manor home. The housekeeper discovered the grisly death when she reported for work. Mr. Ricco's girlfriend, Lola Raines,

an exotic dancer at the theater club, is missing. She has not shown up for work since the murder and is wanted for questioning. The police say they have no leads at this time, except that it looked very much like a Mob execution.

Lola dropped the paper on her lap and stared out the window at the clear blue sky. The police were looking for her. She couldn't go to them. Tony had told her how the Mob deals with anyone who betrays them. She tore the article out and placed it in her wallet, wondering if anyone in this remote valley would read it. If so, she'd toss all her stuff into Betsy and hit the road. But until then, she'd hide out right here. She swallowed the lump in her throat and walked to the bathroom; she had a date to get ready for.

She drew a tub of warm water, soaked for a good ten minutes, then washed her hair. After she had tried on five tee-shirts and three pairs of jeans, she finally settled on an old, faded, and very tight pair of Levis. The blue tank top she selected fit like a second skin. Billy had said seven o'clock was a good time to go riding, after the day had cooled down.

She began to feel a little better as she drove down the gravel road that led to Billy's place. It was only a few minutes from the motel. Following his directions, she saw the circular drive with the wooden fence. Between the house and the road was a lovely cactus garden with Ocotillo, Prickly Pear, Saguaro, and many other varieties that Lola was not familiar with, in full bloom. Olive trees adorned the rest of the front yard, giving the little adobe house shade. She parked Betsy beside an olive tree. A large, colorful peacock, splendid with tail spread, let out his warning call. She could see several chickens, ranging freely, as well as two beautiful horses in the corral. A lone steer was grazing in the nearby field. She started up the gravel path, just as Billy appeared in the doorway in short-sleeve blue western shirt and the usual jeans and boots.

"Hi," he said, cigarette hanging out of one side of his mouth.

"Hi, Billy," she said, anchoring sunglasses on top of her head.

He stood aside. "Come on in." She stepped into his house. The main room was small but bright with a big picture window looking out on the corrals. A swamp cooler protruded from the kitchen window, noisily blasting damp, cool air. Hanging on one adobe wall were antique tools once used to till the earth. The fireplace took up another section of the room. A copy of a Georgia O'Keefe painting of a cow's skull hung over the mantle. The living room had an old brown couch, a couple of overstuffed chairs, and an end table. Next to the kitchen was a larger table and four chairs. Billy had collected a few old milk cans and scattered them around the room. Early desert decor, Lola decided.

"Want something to drink? I have sun-tea made this morning." Billy went to the refrigerator. "Sit yerself down."

"I'd like some tea, thanks," Lola said, sitting on the old sofa.

Billy poured two glasses and handed her a tall, cold one. "Sleep well?"

Lola nodded. Last night she had fallen into bed exhausted and slept deeply.

Billy took a chair across from her. "We'll ride down river. It's a real nice trail."

"I thought there were beaches all along this side," Lola said, drinking from the frosty glass.

"There are at first, then the trail starts."

She looked around the cabin, down a short hallway to his bedroom, door open, bed unmade. She returned her attention to Billy. "How long have you lived here in the Valley?"

"About ten years." Billy leaned back and crossed a booted foot on his knee. "I was born in Texas. Moved up here to get on the railroad. Took the training for engineer and got a job right away. I liked the hours. I'm home for 18 to 24, and then I'm gone 'bout the same length of time."

Lola smiled, nodding.

Billy smiled back. Their eyes met and held until Lola broke their gaze.

"Are we about ready?" she asked, setting her empty glass on the table.

"Sure," Billy said, eyeing her tennis shoes. "Your feet might slip out of the stirrups. What size boot you take?"

"Seven. Don't tell me you just happen to have a pair on hand?"

"Yep. I happen to have a pair of size seven and a half. Will that do?"

"Okay." Lola wondered, but didn't ask, as she looked at his size twelves.

Billy went into the bedroom and returned with a pair of boots that had seen better days. "They're not very pretty but they're fine for ridin'."

"Thanks," Lola said as she slipped off her tennis shoes and pulled on the boots.

When they left the house the Arizona sun was low in the sky above the mountains in the West.

Billy introduced her to the horses, Sedona and Apache, and saddled up Apache. He pointed to the steer in the field. "That's Hamburger. I'm getting him ready for the freezer."

"What do you mean?" Lola asked.

"Well, I'm graining him for a few months before he's slaughtered. A friend across river has a place where he'll hang him for a few weeks. Then he'll cut the meat up and wrap it, and I take it into town to my locker."

Lola shivered and smoothed the hide beside Apache's nose. She murmured to the mare in soft tones. You're lucky you're a horse, she thought.

Billy watched her from the corner of his eye as he saddled Sedona. When he'd finished he came over to Lola.

"I'll give you a lift up." He clasped his hands together at knee level and Lola slipped her booted foot into his palm. He hoisted her up with one graceful motion. Billy couldn't help noticing her beautiful ass as she swung into the saddle. When Lola was seated, he adjusted the stirrups, and once, briefly rested his hand on her thigh.

Lola watched but didn't make eye contact.

They mounted up and headed toward the river, Billy in the lead. Immediately Lola felt comfortable with Apache, guiding her as she stroked her neck.

Billy turned around in the saddle. "She likes you. Apache don't ride easy with everybody."

Lola smiled, beginning to feel at ease with this man and his horse.

They crossed the highway next to the Tavern and saw Paul watching them from the front of the motel.

They rode just above the sandy beach along the scrub brush. The river was sparkling diamond ripples in the late-day sun. A few jet skiers were speeding up river, trying to race each other to an unknown spot, then seeing how fast they could turn without spilling. Lola loved the warmth on her shoulders, hair blowing slightly away from her cheeks. Apache seemed to know the trail and needed little direction.

They entered a small grove of trees and Billy dismounted, tying Sedona to a swinging branch of a Mesquite tree. Lola did the same with Apache. The two horses nuzzled and whinnied softly.

She and Billy walked down river to a spot with a group of rocks sheltered by the trees. The sun had just dipped behind the tallest peak, creating a pink, lavender and yellow pallet of colors that Van Gogh would surely envy. Nature's canvas could rival any hanging in the greatest galleries of the world.

Lola could hear the coyotes yapping, and a desert owl hooting his early evening song. Billy sat on a rock and she sat next to him. Shaking two cigarettes from a pack from his shirt pocket, he lit them both. When he handed one to her, their hands touched.

Lola felt her stomach lurch. Oh god! That old familiar jolt! "You're really somethin', lady," he said, his eyes traveling over her skimpy tank top and down to her borrowed boots. He reached over and took her free hand.

Lola looked down at their brown hands, clasped together. His felt rough, used to hard manual work. It was a strong hand, with long fingers and short, clean nails. She could feel his breath on her cheek as she gently pulled her hand away. "Billy, I'm not ready for anything beyond friendship. I don't know how long I'll be around."

"Whoa! Did I ask for something more than right now? Did I miss somethin' here?"

She looked into his eyes and saw the pupils enlarge. "No, I just wanted to let you know I'm not interested in a... roll in the hay."

Billy stood up. "I'll keep that in mind, lady. How 'bout we head back?"

Lola climbed back into the saddle knowing that Billy's feelings were hurt. She hadn't meant to do that. She was still on edge about seeing the article in the Las Vegas paper. Christ! Did she have to cut out all male companionship? Would men always want to have sex with her before they took the time to know her? Maybe she did jump the gun. He only wanted to hold her hand.

On the ride back to Billy's place, as the early evening faded into dusk; no conversation passed between them.

At the corral, she dismounted and Billy unsaddled both the horses and turned them out to pasture. Lola stood around watching him grain and feed the animals. He didn't look at her or speak. She kept shifting her weight from one foot to the other, wishing she could go back and change some words or do something different. When he started to go for the chicken coop, she said, "Guess I'll be on my way. Can I go in and change my shoes?"

"Sure. The door's unlocked," Billy said curtly, his back toward her as he walked away.

She entered the cool interior of the house, the swamp-cooler blasting away like an old propeller airplane taking off. Locating her tennis shoes on the floor, she pulled off the boots. They were brown leather, the heels worn down. On the bottom, small flakes clung to the sole and smelled suspiciously like dried chicken shit.

She laughed to herself, wondering if his last girlfriend had left them behind. She set them beside the couch, just as Billy came in.

"Thanks for the ride, Billy. I'm sorry for our misunderstanding." She stood with her car keys in hand.

He met her eyes. "I feel like something special has entered my life, and I don't want to lose it. Can't blame me for that."

She shook her head. "Of course not. I don't blame you for anything. And I'm not special, Billy. I've got history that I can't share right now. Please try to understand."

She walked toward him and he stepped aside to let her out the door. Just as she started to pass, their eyes locked, he reached out slowly and pulled her to him. She felt warm and secure in his arms. He held her for a moment, then leaned toward her face until his mouth softly covered hers. Lola returned his kiss, her arms clinging to his waist.

When he took his lips away, she gently pulled back and walked outside. She gave Betsy a running start and jumped in, popping the clutch. The wheels spun and gravel sprayed on Billy Jim's cactus garden as well as on Mr P.'s tail. The peacock screeched his disapproval as Lola raced out the gate, barreling down the desert road.

≥≤

*P*aul Sweeney's breath came in short gasps. His skin was clammy with sweat. Below hairy armpits, dark circles bled onto his dirty-white tank top. One flabby arm lay across his fat stomach, gripping the erection climbing out of the fly of his pants. A few pubic hairs swirled around his zipper. His hand moved faster and faster until he finally spurted a white glob across his exposed belly. Paul released a deep sigh, hand now motionless. Gradually his penis slunk downward, headed back into his jeans. He slipped the *Hustler* beside him under the bed. Honey, the carmel-colored Pekinese, crawled over and licked his cheek. He gently patted her head as she curled up beside him.

Paul had substituted Lola for the playgirl in the magazine. The model's legs were spread, as she touched herself, and he imagined Lola's legs spread in just that way. He sure would like to fuck her, but she'd already cautioned him about touching her again. He thought of her every morning when he awoke and every night before he fell asleep. A few nights ago, he'd tried to get it up for Pat, by fantasizing Lola, but it didn't work. He hadn't been able to get it up for his wife in a long time. Damn! He'd have to figure some way of getting that girl alone. Then if she complained, he'd deny it, and convince Pat that she was a troublemaker and should be fired. He wanted to feel her just once beneath him, within his power. Slide his hands over her smooth, tanned skin. Wind his fingers in that long hair, forcing her head down.

He went into the bathroom and wiped himself off, throwing the towel on the floor. Zipping his jeans, he made an attempt to tuck in his shirt, shuffling toward the kitchen. He took a beer from the refrigerator, pulled the tab off, and swigged half the can. The cold liquid bit into his throat, causing him to stop breathing momentarily. He hiccupped, then finally caught his breath and chugged down the rest. The Coors can hit the corner wall, bouncing into the garbage can. He took his straw hat from the nail, locked the door and headed across the parking lot for the Tavern.

⋙⋘

Sherry got the job at the Sundancer on a Tuesday morning. The regular bartender had broken her leg in a car accident on Sunday night, so Judd, the owner, called Sherry at ten and she was behind the bar by five. She called Greg to let him know where she was.

"Bout fuckin' time you got a job," he said over the phone.

Sherry hung up without a response. She was thinking her time with Greg was getting old.

Two Harleys roared into the Sundancer parking lot. Their riders dismounted, entered through the swinging doors, and bellied up to the bar.

"What'll it be, J.J." Sherry said, setting napkins down in front of the two leather-clad bikers.

"A couple of cold Coors, babe," he said. His face was streaked with dirt and he wiped debris out of his long greasy hair. "This a new gig for you?" he asked.

"Yeah. Just started this morning," Sherry replied. "Where you guys been?" She set the bottles on the bar.

"Out Topock way," J.J. said. "Hell of a ride. Where's yer old man?"

"He's workin' at the liquor store in Needles."

The other biker, Benny, rolled his eyes. "Some of us gotta work and some don't." He gave her a mischievous smile.

"We can't all get a settlement from the railroad for being injured on the job," Sherry retorted. Benny had been in a minor train accident and hurt his foot, making it impossible to walk the length of the train as all brakemen had to do.

Sherry saw Marsh beckon from down the bar. "What you want, Marshmallow?" she called. "Another vodka tonic?"

Marsh nodded, pushing his glass toward her, his eyes at half mast. Marsh made the same circuit every day. He'd hit the Red Dog in Needles as soon as it opened at 8 a.m., ordering his first beer. Then he'd drive across river around noon, and stop at the Sundancer, ready for a vodka and tonic. By the time he ended up at the Tavern, he was usually quite drunk, but was served as long as he could keep his butt on the stool. When he passed out, someone always took him home. But he usually managed to drive his old '49 Chevy truck the half mile home every night, often weaving across the gravel road a few times. More than once he ended up in the ditch. Usually the first person on the scene hauled him out, making sure he didn't have any broken bones, or wasn't bleeding too profusely, and took him home. Marsh was one of the few old-timers left around Mohave Valley. He would tell stories about the wooden road that was built in the early twentieth century from Needles to Barstow. Of course, no one believed him, but that didn't matter. What did matter were the colorful tales he would spin by the hour. Marsh was a shriveled, sweet, kind old man that most everyone called Marshmallow.

The swinging door banged and Lola strode into the bar, red shorts brightening the dimness, the back of her tee-shirt dark with perspiration. When her eyes adjusted, she headed for Marsh. "Hi ya, Marshmallow," she said, sliding her rump onto a barstool.

Marsh turned to her, a big smile on his face. "How ya doin', my pretty one? Can I buy ya a drink?"

"No. I'm just having a coke, right now, thanks. Saw your truck out front."

≳≲

Sherry came down the bar. "Hi, Lola. Just want a coke? It's on the house." Sherry half-filled a glass with ice, and poured coke from the fountain spigot.

"Thanks," Lola said. "New job?" She pulled a pack of Marlboros from her purse and Marsh lit her cigarette.

"Just started today," Sherry said.

Lola took a big gulp of coke. "Ummmm.....that tastes so good. Christ, it's hot out there."

"Yup. Gonna hit 120 again today," Marsh said.

One of the bikers motioned to Sherry. He leaned toward her and whispered, "Whose the good lookin' chick? She new in the Valley?"

"She's the new bartender at the Tavern. And she's way out of your league, Benny. Down boy." Sherry smiled to soften her words.

Benny continued to eye Lola. "She's probably just waitin' for me to come into her life." He picked up his beer and strolled down to where Lola and Marsh were sitting.

Lola was aware of him, hair wild and tangled, road

dirt and yesterday's food on his pants, but she didn't turn around.

After a few seconds, Benny said, "Hey, babe. What's yer name?"

Lola did turn then. She gave him a cold look. "Lola," she said and turned back to the bar.

"Well, mine's Benny. Why dontcha come sit with me and we can git acquainted."

Without turning this time, Lola said, "I don't think so. I'm talking to Marsh."

Benny stood there a minute, then put a greasy hand on her shoulder. "You ain't very friendly."

Lola spun off the stool, slapping his hand away. "That's right, I'm not. So go away. And don't ever *touch* me again."

The biker's eyebrows shot up and his eyes widened. "Well hell, babe. No need to get nasty about it. You don't know what yer missin'," he sneered, and went back to his seat.

"Good girl, Lola. Cut 'um off at the knees," Marsh said, draining his glass. "Well, I'm off to the Tavern. See ya later." He slapped the sides of his thighs as he slid off the stool.

"Okay, Marsh. Take care." Lola gave him her best smile.

He patted Lola on her shoulder. When he staggered past Benny, he said, "You leave her alone, boy, else I'll have to take care of you, myself."

"Shut the fuck up, old man." Benny spat out the words.

Sherry slammed a beer can hard on the bar. "Don't you talk to Marsh that way if you ever want to get served in here again."

Marsh ambled out the door, oblivious to the ruckus inside. The girls could hear his truck chug out the parking lot. Scowling, Benny finished his beer, then he and J.J. left, too.

Sherry went back to Lola and leaned across the bar, hand cupping her mouth. "What a creep. He's trouble. One of the big dealers in the Valley."

Lola looked into Sherry's river-blue eyes. "Yeah. I could smell him before I even saw him."

Both girls giggled.

Lola waited until she no longer heard the roar of the Harleys. "Thanks for the coke, Sherry. I gotta go." She left through the swinging doors, striding into the brilliant Arizona sunlight.

※

Ronnie Webb was Billy Jim's best friend. They tried to get the same shifts, whenever possible on the railroad, so they could bunk together on the other end in Seligman. They drank beer together, and slept with some of the same girls (and generally shared most male pursuits.) Ronnie had defended Billy in several jams and Billy had done the same. When Billy shot his friend, Jess Colton, in the foot, Ronnie was there to bail Billy out of jail.

He lived in a double-wide trailer at the end of Billy's

road. A series of short-term girlfriends had lived with him. They stayed for a few weeks or a month, then moved on, usually out of the Valley.

Ronnie rolled over and turned off the alarm that was buzzing through his dream. He didn't want to lose the image of Sherry, the new bartender at the Sundancer, sliding into bed with him. Finally he opened his eyes to his room, a double bed against one wall with a built-in dresser, double-door sliding closet, but no Sherry. He tried to get back the dream, but it slid away. Only the remembered feeling of her tanned skin brushing his. He raised up on one elbow and looked at the clock. Ten a.m. He'd got into town around ten last night, having finished his shift, and went to the Sundancer where Sherry was working. When she closed the bar, he walked her to her car and then headed home. He'd wanted to kiss her, or at the least touch her bare arms, but he hadn't. She was living with Greg, and he had some undefined morality about treading on another man's territory.

The ringing of the phone interrupted his thoughts as he stumbled out of bed. "Yeah," Ronnie mumbled into the receiver.

"Hey, man, what you up to today?" Billy Jim said.

Ronnie rubbed his eyes. "Hadn't thought. Why?"

"Smitty's comin' by to shoe Sedona and Apache. I was hopin' you'd come over and keep us company."

Ronnie didn't hesitate. "Sure."

"Lola and I went ridin' yesterday," Billy said.

"Yeah? What happened?"

"Nothin'. I got a kiss, and she left."

Ronnie was at a loss for words. Women usually fell for Billy immediately.

"But I haven't given up hope." Billy laughed.

"Sounds good." Ronnie couldn't think of anything else to say. "I'll jump in the shower and be over soon."

"Could you stop and get a couple of six-packs? Smitty always drinks at least one while he's here."

"Okay. See ya later," Ronnie said, and hung up. He couldn't remember any woman refusing Billy Jim. Maybe she was on the rag. Ronnie went into the bathroom, stepped out of his shorts and into the shower stall. In the face of Billy's rejection, his dream of Sherry ever becoming a reality in his life dimmed even further.

※

*L*ola drove down Hwy 95, long hair blowing out the window, Willie Nelson's "Help Me Make it Through the Night" blaring from a country radio station, her nails tapping rhythm on the dash. The Colorado River on her right flowed swiftly toward the Gulf. Mohave Valley stretched out in front of her, lush and verdant for two miles on each side of the river. Then, as quickly as turning off a faucet, the earth turned brown and parched, where only scrub brush and sidewinders could find a place to exist.

She turned sharply into the Tavern Motel and backed her VW Bug, Betsy, onto a small rise in the parking lot. (Lola was used to giving the little car a rolling push, hopping behind the wheel and popping the clutch.)

She glanced nervously at the other parked cars for Nevada plates, and a man and woman standing at one end of the parking lot. There were no Nevada plates and the couple didn't seem interested in her.

When she unlocked the door to her room, cold air from the air conditioner blasted her face, arms and legs, sending goose bumps over her damp skin. The back of her tee-shirt and shorts were soaked from the 110 degree weather.

Gazing at the pictures on the wall for the fiftieth time, she still couldn't get over Pat decorating with the same flower picture in two places; red flowers in a blue vase over the bed and the identical picture over the TV. The blue chenille spread on the double bed and blue plaid curtains gave a measure of peace to the room. Blue being one of Lola's favorite colors, and having read that blue soothed the mind as well as the inner spirit, she guessed she could forgive the duplicate pictures.

Tossing her sunglasses and purse on the bed, she stripped off her clothes and stepped into the cool shower.

She thought about Billy Jim. Ever since he'd kissed her, she couldn't get that sweet-talkin', overconfident cowboy off her mind. Possibly because she was so damn horny, but also because there *was* something between them. A spark of communication on a deeper level than words? Yeah. Right. She laughed out loud. Sex had always been her way of communicating with men.

She had told herself she was not falling for anyone until she got her heart back together from the last relationship.

Poor Tony. Witnessing Tony's murder was one of the most traumatic experiences she'd ever had. She hadn't been able to sleep for weeks. It was just lately that she could get through the night without having nightmares. She figured she'd lay low in this small community for a few months until she was sure no one was looking for her. She knew the police were, but if the killers ever figured out she'd seen them, she'd be dead too. She shivered at the thought of the white-haired man cutting Tony's throat. Gradually his death was receding in her memory, but it was a slow process. She had to be damn careful. Leaving town the way she did without even quitting her job caused the police to list her as missing. She couldn't afford to get tied up with a charming cowboy right now. She might have to move on quickly.

Her mother once told her that Sagittarians were very flexible and could adjust to a new situation at a moment's notice. Chameleon. That's what her mother had called her. She accused her of changing her colors to fit the occasion. Well, Damn! It had saved her life in at least one instance. Thank God for things easily shed.

Lola let the water pour over her long hair and down her tanned back. Shutting off the faucets, she toweled dry. She pulled white linen slacks and a white tee shirt from the closet, then blow-dried her dark hair. Just as she finished with her hair there was a knock at the door.

She opened it to Billy Jim, wrench in one hand and a piece of machinery in the other. His muscled shoulders, glistening with sweat, stretched wide beyond his blue tank top. A lock of sandy hair rested on his forehead.

"Hi, lady. I got this starter that's dying to get inside Betsy."

Lola stifled an impulse to laugh. "What did you say?"

"You need a new starter, and I know how to install one. Seemed like a good match," Billy said, grinning.

She followed him out to Betsy, her engine hood already up. He knelt down, jacked up the right side of the VW, and removed the wheel. Then he crawled under the engine to dismantle the old starter.

"Ah… Billy. Are you sure you know how to do this?"

"Sure do. Don't think I'd experiment on Betsy, do ya'?"

"How much was the starter?"

"Not too much."

"Well, I'll pay you whatever it costs. And for your labor too," she added.

Billy started whistling softly, under his breath. "Don't worry about it." From beneath the car he watched her sandaled feet; the little gold chain around one ankle, her red toenails, the big toes longer than the rest.

Lola stood around for a while, not wanting to sit on the steps in her white slacks. Finally she went back in the motel room, leaving the door ajar. The hot afternoon air drifted in, diluting the cool air. She filed her nails, and then sorted her clothes to be washed. She kept going to the window to check on Billy's progress. Christ! Now she would owe him. She'd just insist he take money.

According to her watch, Billy had been at it almost an hour when he finally stuck his head out from the engine. "All done," he called. "Get in and start her up." He wiped the dripping sweat from his brow.

Lola came outside, slid behind the wheel and turned the key. Smooth as oil, the little car purred to a start. She turned off the engine. "Thanks, Billy. How much do I owe you?"

"I told you not to worry about the cost. I'll take it out in dancing."

Lola got out of the car. She put her hand on his arm and felt the familiar tingling. "I do appreciate it, very much. No one's been so nice to me in a long time."

"If you'd just let me, I'd be nice to you all the time." He put his hand over hers.

They stood for a moment, looking at each other. Lola had an irresistible urge to throw her arms around him and drag him inside.

"Can I...ah... buy you a beer at the Tavern? I was on my way over when you arrived."

"You sure can, lady. Can I wash my hands?" He gestured toward her room.

She nodded.

Billy went in the bathroom, leaving the door open. She followed him into her room even though she knew it was a mistake She watched him splash water over his face and scrub his hands with soap. He came out of the bathroom wiping himself on a towel, and looked her full in the face.

She pushed the front door closed and locked it.

He went to her, pulling her into his arms. Their mouths met half-open and wet. He smothered her face with kisses. They fell on the bed and started undressing each other. Billy's fingers twined in her hair as his lips slid over her throat, nuzzling her neck. He slipped her white slacks off in one sweeping motion. Lola unzipped his jeans, wrapping moist fingers around his erection. He cradled her breasts with his big hands, kissing each nipple. When he pulled her knees up and entered her, she moaned. He moved slowly, back and forth, up and down, Lola uttering small gasps and sighs. Billy slowed himself down in spite of his heat. After a while, he pulled out, and Lola climbed on top, rocking back and forth to her own rhythm. When she began moving faster and harder, Billy plunged deeper and they came together. Afterwards, they curled up spoon-fashion, quiet, each with their own thoughts.

Billy knew this was much bigger than he'd imagined.

Lola knew she had one more complication than she needed.

At the Sundancer, Lola finished the beer in front of her and shook her head as Sherry held up another. It was her night off, and the girls had decided to eat dinner at the Sports Lounge after Sherry's shift was finished. Greg was out of town; in fact, Sherry had confided to Lola, he was in L.A. buying some weed to bring back and sell. The two girls had been hanging out together on their days off, going to the river for a swim. Sherry was delighted that she had some free time without Greg, and a new friend to spend it with.

Marsh was beside Lola, still upright, not having made it to the Tavern yet, but he *was* weaving, in serious danger of falling off the stool.

Judd walked in and went behind the bar. He was doing the late shift because his regular bartender, Jeff, had called in sick. More likely drunk, Sherry said.

Sherry hung up her apron, grabbed her purse and joined Lola and Marsh.

"I think we ought to take Marsh home," Lola said quietly to Sherry. "Can you follow me in your car, and I'll drive his truck?"

Sherry had a little MG; just room for two. "Sure can," she said, and put her arm around Marsh. "How'd you like to have two pretty girls take you for a ride, Marshmallow?"

Marsh continued looking straight ahead. "Depends on what they're gonna' do with me."

Laughing, the girls got on either side of him, ready

to bear his weight as they pulled him off the stool.

He turned blurry eyes to Lola. "Anywhere you want to take me, honey, I'm ready and willin'." He slid off his perch, supported by the two women.

"Need some help?" Judd asked.

"We got him," Sherry said confidently. They walked him over to the door, amid shouts from the bar. "Hey, Marsh. How come you get all the pretty women?"

Marsh was beyond answering. His head, lolling over to one side, rested on Lola's shoulder.

They shuffled him out to his truck, just as Ronnie, Billy Jim's friend, was getting out of his. He helped them maneuver Marsh into the front seat. Ronnie's eyes slid over Sherry's bare shoulders as she smiled up at him.

"Need help gettin' him home?" Ronnie offered.

"No, thanks. We got it covered," Lola said. She climbed into the driver's side and saw the keys hanging right where Marsh always left them, in the ignition. Sherry gunned her MG and headed for Marsh's trailer, Lola right behind.

Ronnie watched Sherry handle her little sports car with admiration. He thought she was about the finest-lookin' woman he'd ever seen.

The two vehicles pulled up in front of a dilapidated, old, silver Airstream that stood on an acre of land, dried brush and yellow grasses surrounding it. A couple of scrawny hens were scratching in the parched earth. Together they managed to slide Marsh out of the truck and half-dragged him inside.

"Marsh, wake up. Walk. Make your legs move,"

Sherry kept repeating, loudly.

Marsh only moaned and slobbered down his dirty shirt.

Once inside, they laid him on the couch, not wanting to take him though the narrow hallway to the bed in back. Lola slipped off his boots, put a pillow behind his head and a blanket across his lap and the girls left quietly.

They piled into the MG and roared down the dirt road to the River Highway, kicking up Mohave Valley dust in their wake.

"Geez, I feel so sorry for old Marsh. He doesn't seem to have any family," Sherry said.

"He's got plenty of people who care enough about him to take him home when he can't make it on his own," Lola said. "Sometimes that's better than having family."

Sherry glanced over at her. "Do I hear some bitterness in that sentence?"

"Possibly."

"Want to talk about it?" Sherry offered.

"Maybe another time. Tonight we're having fun. Girls night on the town."

"And believe me, I'm ready," Sherry said. "You know, Greg and I have been on each other's nerves lately. I'm glad we have this break." Her blond locks blew in the wind as she pulled sharply onto the main highway.

"How long you been together?" Lola asked.

"About two years. He has the worst luck with the law. I guess he'll never learn. Still dealing weed and taking chances. He did some time back in Phoenix for stealing cars."

Lola was thinking the less she knew about Greg the better.

Sherry pulled into the Sports Lounge's parking lot, and the two girls entered the club. The country band was playing "Crazy," Patsy Cline style. A few couples were dancing on the floor, but it was still early. The mike screeched in feedback and the band members fiddled with their equipment. Smoke drifted above the dancers, making cloudy patterns against the ceiling.

The girls were seated at a table and ordered margaritas and dinner; Lola had fish and Sherry, chicken. When the drinks came, Sherry raised her glass and toasted: "To new friends."

"Cheers," Lola said, clinking glasses.

※

The girls had just finished dinner when the two guys who had been watching hit them up for a dance.

Sherry looked at Lola. "Guess there ain't no harm in dancin'," she said.

A tall slim cowboy, by the name of Tom waltzed Lola out on the floor and proceeded to do the Arizona two-step. At least that's what he called it. "I haven't seen you in the Valley before. Where you from?" he asked.

"I've only been here a few days," Lola said. "Thanks for the dance." But he wasn't to be put off that easily.

"Like to dance the next one?"

"No, I don't think so. I'll sit this one out."

"Mind if I just sit here with you 'till your friend comes back?"

Lola wished she could think of something else to say instead of, "Guess not." Her thoughts turned to Billy who was out on the railroad tonight; she wished she was dancing with him.

Tom ordered a couple of beers for himself and his friend. Sherry and Chuck came back to the table and sat down.

"You gals want another margarita?" Tom asked.

Lola said "No" at the same time Sherry said, "Sure."

"Wanna' come over to my place later? We could have a party," Tom said.

Before Sherry could answer, Lola fibbed, "No, thanks. I have to get up early for work."

The guys looked like they were settled in. The girls continued to dance with Tom and Chuck, sometimes changing partners. Sherry said she loved to dance, and rarely sat one out. Lola realized that after four margaritas Sherry was pretty high, in fact, too high to drive. Lola had changed to coke, but didn't look forward to driving the MG. And the alternative was not an option. She would not let these guys drive them home. No way.

Around one thirty, the girls went to the restroom. "Let's go," Lola said. "I don't want them following us home." Lola was staying the night at Sherry's; she'd left her car at the Sundancer.

"Oh come on, Lola. Just one more drink and another dance. The band hasn't stopped playin' yet." Sherry's eyes were beginning to drift shut.

"No," Lola said, firmly. "We're going home now. Come on. Let's go out the back. That way we don't have to make our excuses."

"I don't wanna go yet," Sherry whined, salt scattered across her lower lip.

Lola put an arm around her waist and gently pushed her out the back door and toward the MG. She helped Sherry into the passenger seat.

"Where are the keys?" Lola asked.

Sherry's head fell back against the seat and she didn't answer.

Lola went through her bag and found them. She put the key in the ignition and started the MG up. This was her night for taking home the inebriated.

She tried to shift into reverse but the stick wouldn't budge. Sherry had told her this car had 101 idiosyncrasies. Lola tried several times to move the shift, getting more and more frustrated, then, suddenly, it popped into gear.

Just as she drove out of the parking lot, Tom and Chuck hurried out the front door. "Hey. Wait up," they called.

"No fuckin' way," Lola said under her breath, as she sped away from the Sports Lounge down River Highway. She saw the two men run to their truck, back up and start after them.

"Oh Christ!" Lola said. Sherry mumbled something on her side of the car. Lola stepped on the gas but the little MG didn't have much oomph. The turn for Sherry's trailer came up, but Lola passed it by. She could see the truck in the rearview mirror gaining on them. When she approached the Needles Bridge she instantly decided not to go into town. There was a split in the road and in the dark, without thinking, she took the left fork although she had never been on that road before. The wheels squealed as she turned sharply. About a hundred yards later the blacktop stopped and Lola bumped onto a gravel lane. By the time she knew she had made a serious error she saw the end of the road up ahead. The sign read Road End. A small white railing separated the lane from a ditch. Nowhere to go but back. She braked to a stop, throwing Sherry forward in the seat.

"What the hell?" Sherry muttered, opening her eyes. "Wha's happenin'?"

"Nothing. Just relax." Lola tried to sound reassuring, but her heart was pounding wildly and her breath came fast and shallow. She fiddled with the stick, trying to get it into reverse. "Damn! Damn," she swore.

Sherry tried to help. "Just ease it into gear, don't force it," she mumbled. "Oh, Christ, I feel sick to my stomach." She swallowed hard and leaned back against the seat, forgetting Lola's struggle with the gears.

Lola saw the headlights turn into the road even before she heard the engine. Her persistence finally paid off, and she got the MG into reverse. When she pulled around, the truck had stopped abruptly in the middle of the road, about twenty-five feet away, headlights still on. Tom and Chuck got out of the truck and started walking slowly toward them. With the lights behind them, they were black silhouettes. Scary monsters surfaced from Lola's childhood; she remembered black objects flickering across her bedroom walls. She was acutely aware of the hot smell of an engine run hard. The acrid odor of scalded tires burned her nose. A fine mist of gravel and dust, kicked up from the truck's braking stop, blew around her head. She stifled an impulse to cough. Behind her a barn owl hissed his raspy call.

"You girls thought you were gonna ditch us, huh? Not on yer life. Not after we bought you all those margaritas." Tom's voice came from a dark shadow in front of the car.

The night was humid and Lola's hands were clammy gripping the steering wheel. She felt both hot and cold at the same time. Her normal self-confidence deserted her and she began to tremble.

"Stop right there, or I'll run you down," she yelled, trying to sound fierce.

Both of the guys laughed. "Oh yeah? Well you can't hit both of us, and one of us will still be here," Tom hollered.

Sherry came to again. "Wha's all the shouting?"

"Be quiet and don't ask me right now," Lola said.

Sherry obeyed.

The men continued to walk toward the MG. If she waited any longer, it might be too late. She had to chance it. Now! Adrenaline rushed through her body like a hit of speed. She stomped on the gas and the little car spit gravel as it surged forward. She headed right for the two of them, but before the car hit Tom, he jumped aside. She kept her foot on the gas, maneuvering between the truck and the brush along the road. The car slid, but Lola wrestled with the wheel. Just as Chuck reached for the back of the MG, Lola gunned it and gravel hit him in the face. She tore down the lane to the main highway. In the rearview mirror she saw the men jump in the truck and turn around. This time at the fork, she turned left and took the old two-lane bridge over the Colorado River. When she reached the California side she headed for the police station. She pulled up in front and laid on the horn. When Tom and Chuck saw her stopped there, they passed by, speeding down the street. They were gone by the time the deputy came out of the station.

"What the hell's the problem?" the deputy yelled at them. "Don't you know it's 3:00 a.m.?"

Sherry opened her eyes again. "Wha's happenin'?" she asked for the second time.

Lola explained to the deputy.

"Well, come on in and file a report. I'll look into it tomorrow."

Lola decided she didn't want to do that. "Can we just come in and stay for a while so they won't follow us home?"

"Tell ya what. I'll follow ya over the bridge and then I'll close off the traffic 'til time for you girls to get home. Won't be many cars this time of morning, anyway. How's that?"

Lola said that would be fine, and thanked him.

The deputy locked up his office and got into his car, leading them back to the bridge.

By the time Lola pulled up in front of the trailer, Sherry was fast asleep. Lola heaved a great sigh of relief. Lucky Lola again. Tony had nicknamed her that in Vegas, because every time she put a quarter into the slot machines, she hit a jackpot.

Getting Sherry inside was easier than moving Marsh. She pretty much walked under her own power, complaining all the way about their evening being ruined because they'd left too early.

"We did what we said we'd do," Lola insisted. "We had dinner, a few drinks and some dancing." She didn't know if Sherry had expected more out of the evening, but for sure Lola had no other intentions. Sherry didn't seem to remember the wild ride they'd just had.

She helped Sherry undress and crawl into bed. Lola grabbed a pillow and sheet from a shelf and headed for the couch. Before she finished undressing, light snoring came from the back of the tiny trailer. Lola turned out the lights and lay down naked on top of the sheet. The night was warm and her hair felt damp against her neck. She licked her lips and tasted lingering salt from the margaritas. The crickets and katydids were chattering along the river, and far off, she heard the lonesome call of a coyote. She thought of Billy Jim and his arms around her, as she drifted off to sleep.

*N*ext morning Lola cooked breakfast for Sherry, bacon and eggs and white toast, and made a pot of strong, black coffee.

"Geez, my head hurts. What time'd we leave, last night?"

"Around one thirty." Lola poured her another cup of Maxwell House.

"I don't think I can eat anything," Sherry said. "The smell of the bacon makes me sick." She grimaced and held her stomach.

"Eat. You need food before going to work." Lola took a seat across from Sherry in the tiny dinette.

"Lola, I'm sorry I got smashed. Thanks for drivin' home. Please don't mention to Greg about the guys."

"Of course not. I won't tell Greg anything. We girls stick together." Lola smiled across the tiny vinyl tabletop. "Do you remember our wild ride last night?" she asked Sherry.

Sherry shook her head. "Whadaya' mean?"

Lola told her what had happened with Tom and Chuck and the wild ride in the MG.

"Geez… we could'a got raped, or worse…" Sherry's eyes were wide. Then she looked embarrassed. "I'm sorry I wasn't any help. Thanks for getting us out of that jam."

Lola leaned over and squeezed Sherry's arm. "That's what friends are for, but I don't mind tellin' you now, I was scared that we *wouldn't* get out of it."

"Guess it was good I didn't know what was happening. I might 'a panicked," Sherry said.

"Well, I was about to panic myself. If the MG had stalled, we might not be here talkin' about it."

They agreed to keep their adventure between themselves and not mention it to anyone.

Sherry dropped Lola at her car in the Sundancer parking lot when she went in to work.

When Lola pulled into her space at the Tavern Motel, Billy Jim was leaning against his red truck smoking a Marlboro.

Lola climbed out of her Bug. "Hi. When did you get in?"

"About seven this morning. Came by here but you weren't home. So I went out for breakfast. Just drove up a minute ago."

Lola put her key in the lock and opened the door to the cold interior. She had left the air conditioner on all night. She walked to the window unit and turned it to low.

Billy followed her inside, noticing the unused bed. "Where you been all night?"

Lola turned and looked into his uptight face. She didn't like what she saw. "I was at Sherry's. I spent the night there. We went out last night. She got a little tanked, so I drove her home."

"Yeah? And where was Greg?"

"I don't have to explain where Greg was, but, for the record he's in L.A." Lola took a clean tank top and shorts from the chest drawer.

Billy continued. "Where'd you go with Sherry?"

"Billy, I think you'd better go, now. I'm getting pissed off and I don't want to say things I'll be sorry for later." She went to the door, and opened it, one hand on her hip.

Billy stood for a few minutes looking at her. "I thought we had an understanding," he said, his cheeks fire-red.

"I can't imagine what that understanding was, since we haven't talked about it."

He continued staring at her, shifting from one foot to the other, as if undecided what to do. Finally he moved through the door, swore under his breath, and climbed in his truck. He gunned the engine and burned rubber as he left the motel.

Just what she needed. A possessive cowboy. She slammed the door, locked it, and grabbed her clean clothes, heading for the shower.

≷≶

*T*he first thing she heard was soft footsteps on her bedroom floor. He pulled back the covers and slipped in beside her. She felt his hand creep around her buttocks, then move down, between her legs, to the place her mother said was private. For Lola, it had been shared with her father for a very long time. One of her first memories was of him touching her, down there.

This time, he pushed her head down under the covers until she ran into his penis, hard and wet, probing her forehead. He had taught her to rub her tongue in circles around the end. Sometimes he would lay her back and put his tongue into her private place. At first, she was scared, but much later, she began to like it. She knew it was wrong; he had warned her never to tell her mother or anyone. And she hadn't. When she was thirteen, the boys in school began noticing her blossoming chest. It was then she refused him.

"Damn you," he said, his eyes red with fury.

"Damn you," she said, realizing she had the power now. For the first time, she threatened to tell her mother if he ever climbed into her bed again. He never did.

※

Lola unlocked the door of her room, the air-conditioner blasting cold air. She turned it down, and dropped her purse on the bed, slipped off her sandals, jeans, tank top and walked naked to the bathroom. Turning the faucets to cool, she stepped into the shower. The soft water pouring over her body unkinked the tensions of the day. She wasn't sure what to do about Billy. She didn't want this to be the end for them, but she couldn't tolerate his possessiveness. Maybe she should go to his place tomorrow and talk to him.

Her experience with men convinced her that they couldn't reason where women were concerned. But she was attracted to Billy, and yes, did want to see him again. God, would she never learn? She always seemed to pick the wrong type. Tony had been the wrong man for her. She'd never forget the horrible way he died.

A vague memory from her childhood flashed through her brain. The time her father had taken her to a slaughterhouse and she had seen the animals hanging by their legs, blood dripping on the floor. She gagged at the recollection. Even now, Lola felt bile rise in her throat and she leaned toward the basin.

She hadn't been deeply in love with Tony. She knew instinctively that it was not a long-term relationship. But she had cared for him, and she mourned him. She felt some guilt for his death, but realistically she knew there was nothing she could have done. And here she was, ready to get involved with another man, completely wrong for her.

≶≶

Lola drew draft beer from the fountain and served the two railroaders at the bar. One of them, Kenny Landers, had been coming in pretty regularly on his day off.

"Thought you might like to go up to Laughlin. Take in a little gambling some evening," Kenny said, drinking half of his beer in one gulp.

"Thanks, but I don't think so," Lola said. "I'm not much into gambling."

"That's okay. We could have dinner and see the show," he persisted.

"Not interested," she said, coldly. She went to the other end of the bar to wait on Marsh. "The usual, Marsh?"

He nodded.

She poured a vodka and tonic and put it in front of him.

"Leave her alone. She's Billy Jim's girl." Marsh directed his words at the other end of the bar.

"Now Marsh, that's not so. Billy and I are friends. I'm not his girl."

"Why not?" Marsh asked.

"Well, because I'm not," Lola said.

Paul came in the back door, making a wide berth around Lola. He went to the cash register and took out all the twenties.

"Aren't you gonna put a slip in the drawer?" Lola asked, watching him. She didn't want to come up short on her shift.

"I'll tell Pat when I go in," he said.

"Paul." Lola walked over to him. "Please count the money here. I don't know how much you're taking. What if I need twenties for change?"

He stared at her over his horn-rimmed glasses. "If you need change, just call the office. I told you, Pat will count it." He turned abruptly, a fistful of bills in his hand, and went out the back door.

Lola felt irritation and at the same time a crawling in the pit of her stomach. She had no way of knowing how much money she had taken in tonight. Pat usually came in at two a.m. and they counted the till together.

"What's wrong, buttercup?" Marsh asked.

"Nothing," Lola said as she wiped down the bar.

"Come on. I know something's wrong. What'd Paul do?"

"He took all the twenties and didn't leave an IOU." Lola spoke softly so only Marsh heard.

"Well, don't worry. I saw it." He patted her hand as she lifted his glass and napkin to wipe under them.

Dear Marsh. He would be lucky to remember where he passed out tonight, let alone their conversation. But Lola gave him her best smile and moved on down the bar.

"Say, since you're not Billy Jim's girl, how 'bout going with me to the Elks dance on Saturday night?" Kenny winked at the railroader next to him.

"No. And don't ask me again."

His friend laughed and slapped Kenny on the back. "You owe me a fiver."

Kenny shrugged off his hand, scowling. He finished his beer and the two left the Tavern.

At 1:55 a.m., Lola looked at her watch. Marsh was asleep in the booth near the door. Pat came in the back, cloth satchel in hand that she would stash the day's take in, until she went to the bank.

"Hi, Lola. Not too busy tonight, eh?" No one was left in the bar except the snoring Marsh.

"Not very." Pat had asked her to take on the extra night shift, Thursday, and it was usually slow.

Lola had already washed all the glasses and cleaned up behind the bar, ready for Friday morning.

Pat went to the front door and locked it from the inside. She came back behind the bar and opened the register, and began counting the money. When she finished, she frowned. "Is this all the money for today?"

"Yes, except for the twenties that Paul took," Lola swallowed nervously. "I asked him to put a slip in the drawer, but he said he was taking it to you."

Pat counted the take a second time. "Sixty dollars, here. How much did he take?"

Lola shook her head. "I don't know. It looked like a handful. I was making a drink for a customer. I asked him to count it here, but he refused." A lump was forming in Lola's throat.

"I see." Pat rolled the money double and put a rubber band around it, then stowed it in the satchel.

"I told him I didn't want to come up short during my shift," Lola said.

Pat looked at Lola and patted her shoulder. "Don't you worry, honey. I'm not. Are you gonna take Marsh home?"

"Yeah. I thought I would and then hike back to the motel."

"Come on. I'll help you get him in the truck. I'll follow you to his house and give you a lift home."

They got Marsh home and onto his couch, then the women headed back down the gravel road.

"Paul didn't happen to tell you where he was goin', did he?" Pat asked.

"He said he was goin' inside and give the money to you."

"Well, I haven't seen hide nor hair of him for several hours."

"Pat." Lola's voice was quiet. "You do believe me?"

Pat turned and noticed Lola's eyes shining in the moon's reflection. "Course I do, honey." She reached over and squeezed Lola's hand.

She dropped Lola off at her room, and they both noticed that the space for Paul's jeep was still empty.

Lola peeled her clothes from her damp body and slipped between cool sheets. Thank God, Pat believed her. She didn't need any attention from law enforcement right now.

≳≲

Sherry at the wheel of her MG was heading down the winding road from Oatman, an old mining town on Route 66. She slid around S-turns, and hills made of rock, great for climbing or hunting rattlesnakes, but treacherous for driving. The MG convertible maneuvered the curves easily, hugging the side of the mountain. The other side had a thousand-foot drop, with no railing or barrier. The land was high desert-mountains with cactus and Yucca trees scattered across the terrain. Occasionally, they would glimpse a view of the Valley below as they drove around a sharp curve.

"Slow down, Sherry," Lola complained with a giggle. "Every time I get the stuff in the paper, you take a curve and it falls back in the bag." Rolling a joint in a moving vehicle on a twisting mountain road called for more skill than Lola possessed. They had just picked up a pound of grass from a friend of Sherry's, and were on their way back to the Valley. Of course, they had to sample it before buying, and were both quite stoned.

Lola finally managed to make a half-assed joint, lit it and inhaled deeply. Sherry's blond and Lola's dark hair entwined in the wind as Lola passed it over.

They were down off the mountain now and approaching the intersection of Highway 95. Lola put the extra weed back in the large bag at her feet.

Seeing a truck in the distance, Sherry pulled onto the highway and picked up speed again. About a mile down the road, she saw the truck coming up fast, making no attempt to brake. By the time the driver realized he was going to hit the MG he braked a few times, but realizing he couldn't stop, tried passing her on the two-lane highway. His right front tire bumped Sherry's MG and the car sailed up in the air like a kite taking off, then fell to the ground, landing on all four wheels in the ditch at the side of the road. The truck flew by, his horn blaring.

Lola came to in the rumble seat, her legs resting between the two bucket seats. She had no memory of how she got there. The last thing she remembered was a hard jolt and the sensation of flying as the wind whistled in her ears. Dazed, she called to Sherry. "Are you okay?"

Sherry mumbled. "Not sure. I'm bleeding from somewhere. Blood on my hand."

Suddenly Lola's mind went on alert. Christ! They had a pound of weed in the car! The cops would throw the key away on their jail cell! She tried moving. First she extended her legs. They seemed okay, then her arms. They worked too. When she sat up, her neck hurt, but now was no time to worry about that. Carefully, so she wouldn't incur any more injury, she climbed into the front seat. Sherry was slumped over the wheel, her cheek bleeding; the bag of weed miraculously still lay on the floor.

"Sherry. We got to get out of the car." Visions of gas tanks exploding flooded her mind. Lola opened the car door and stepped out, paper bag in hand. The field right next to them was full of artichokes, their large leaves spreading shade like small trees. Lola stuffed the bag under the nearest artichoke plant. She looked up to the road and saw a telephone pole with a red stripe around it. That was the only landmark she had time to see before she heard the siren. Stumbling around to the other side, she opened Sherry's door.

"Come on, girl. Get out." She took her arm and tried pulling her out, but Sherry was deadweight.

"I can't. My leg won't move." Sherry's voice was flat; her eyes glazed and unresponsive, like she'd had too much booze.

Lola pushed Sherry gently off the steering wheel, back against the seat. She reached across and pulled out the roach-filled ashtray, dumping it in the weeds beside the ditch. Pulling a tissue from the pocket of her jeans she pressed it against the jagged cut on Sherry's cheek.

"Damn, that hurts," Sherry cried out.

"Sorry, honey. I just want to stop the bleeding."

She picked up Sherry's hand and pressed it against the tissue. "Hold it," Lola ordered.

Just as the sheriff's car pulled up alongside, the truck driver arrived, having walked back from where he'd stopped his truck down the road.

Lola sat on the ground next to Sherry. Her neck ached, now. And her back was beginning to hurt, too.

Del Long, the Mohave County sheriff, climbed down the bank. "You girls okay?"

Lola had met him a few nights ago when he came into the Tavern. "We're alive, but hurting. Sherry cut her cheek and her legs won't move."

"What happened here?" Del asked.

The truck driver stood on the side of the road above them. Lola glared up at him. "He damn near killed us, that's what happened. He was goin' so fast he couldn't slow down."

The man swung his arms nervously at his sides. "They pulled out in front of me. I didn't have time to slow down."

Lola shook her head. "That's not true. We turned onto the highway back there at the intersection to Oatman."

Del looked back down the road, noticing the intersection was at least a mile away. Then he looked up at the truck driver standing on the gravel.

"I've called for an ambulance. It should be here soon." He reached down and patted Sherry on the head. "You two were damn lucky. Could of been thrown out. You hold on there, Sherry. We'll get you to the hospital in a jiffy." Del climbed back up the bank. "I'm gonna' cite you for a moving violation. May I see your driver's license, please?"

The driver began arguing with the sheriff as he reached for his wallet. Del wrote him a citation and took his insurance information. The man strode angrily back to his truck.

Lola stared down at the ground beside her leg. In plain sight lay the remainder of the joint that Sherry had been toking on when the accident occurred. Del was on his way back down the slope. Lola scooped it up and put it in her mouth, swallowing it whole. She coughed once and choked, but created enough saliva to get it down. Sherry saw her and started laughing. The two of them were convulsed in giggles by the time the sheriff stood beside them.

"Guess you two hit your heads. What the hell's so funny?"

Sherry immediately started crying.

Lola put her arm around her shoulders. "Don't cry, honey. We're gonna be all right."

She turned to Del. "Don't you know shock when you see it? I think we're both in shock." Lola started concentrating on her painful neck. She could hear the ambulance siren down the road.

"Yeah. Sorry, girls," Del said.

The ambulance pulled up and two attendants rushed down the bank with a stretcher. They checked Sherry out, put her on a stretcher and carried her up the bank. Lola walked behind. They scolded her for not waiting for a stretcher and then put a neck brace on her right away.

With her last view of the accident scene, Lola tried memorizing the site of the artichoke plant. She could see for the first time that the little MG was pretty bashed up.

"Greg will kill me when he finds out I crashed the MG." Sherry began crying again.

"Shushhhhhhhh," Lola tried to comfort her. "It'll be okay. I won't let him kill you."

Sherry went from tears to giggles. "I didn't mean that he actually would," she managed, through her laughter.

"Whatcha girls been smokin'?" the young male attendant said, wearing a big grin.

"Is it that obvious? Sherry asked.

"Try not to laugh at the hospital. That's a dead giveaway."

They attempted holding their faces straight, but once again broke into laughter.

"We'll plead hysteria," Lola gasped.

"Ohhhh... My cheek *is* beginning to hurt. Is it pretty bad?" Sherry asked the attendant.

"I can't tell for sure," he said. "But I think it will require stitches."

Suddenly Sherry remembered the weed. "Oh, shit. You know what we left back in the car?"

Lola touched her arm. "We left our purses. Del will probably bring them to us. Don't worry." She lifted her eyebrows a few times in a Groucho Marx gesture, then leaned down and whispered in her ear. "I took care of the cargo. Don't say another word."

Lola woke to sun streaming in her motel room. Patterns of light flashed across her blue bedspread in a kaleidoscopic light show. It had been dinner time when she was released from the hospital yesterday. Returning to the motel hungry, she ate one of the spongy apples on her dresser, fell into bed dead tired, and slept through the night. She looked at the clock. 8:00 a.m. Slowly, she extended her arms above her head.

"Owwwww!" She moaned aloud. She sat up carefully; every bone aching. Christ! She needed to soak in a hot bath.

She limped into the bathroom and turned on the hot water. When the tub was full, she climbed in, slipping down into the steamy warmth.

Concentrating on getting her shoulders underwater, she wondered how Sherry was feeling. She had a bruised leg, and they had put stitches in her cheek. There was a 90 degree angle cut on Sherry's face just below the eye on the cheekbone. Lola had wanted the Needles hospital to contact a plastic surgeon in Phoenix, but with no insurance, Sherry decided to let the local doctor do the repair work.

After they'd ex-rayed Lola's neck and back, and found no damage, the girls were released and one of the nurses going off duty drove them back over the river, dropping Sherry off at her trailer and Lola at the motel. The doctor told her to wear the neck brace at least a month at all times. Sure. She was going to show up behind the bar with a straightjacket on her neck. But she would wear it for a while until the soreness was gone. She'd have to talk to Pat and make some arrangement to take off from work for a week or so. Fortunately, her last week's salary was still in her drawer. Now it would be needed to pay the room rent.

Damn! Things seemed to be going okay for her and then, this. She hadn't seen her cowboy since the morning he'd stormed out of her room. She missed his warm hands and hard body. She'd meant to go by his ranch and visit, try to make up, but just hadn't done it. Making up always felt like admitting blame and in this case she had done nothing.

Stepping from the tub she thought she heard a knock. With the noise of the air-conditioner it was hard to tell. Throwing on her bathrobe, and twisting a towel around her long hair, she hobbled to the door. Another knock.

She knew it was him even before her hand touched the knob. Billy Jim stood on the cement step, looking to the left. The first thing she saw was his deeply tanned profile, long lashes outlined against the blue Arizona morning. Her heart added a beat even though she tried to still it. In his right hand he carried a McDonald's box with two coffees. In the other, a white paper bag of Duffy's doughnuts.

"Hey, babe. I heard about the accident when I got off the railroad. I was worried." He transferred his weight to the other booted foot.

Lola stepped back, silently inviting him in.

Billy came in and closed the door. They stood looking into each other's eyes for a moment, then he set the food down, and gently pulled her into his arms.

"Be careful, Billy. I ache in every muscle. Handle with care."

"Of course, honey. No other way."

They held each other for a moment, then Lola pulled away. "Let me sit down. I'm still achy." She walked to the bed, Billy's arm around her waist, climbed under the blanket and leaned back against the pillows.

He pulled a chair up beside her. "What happened?"

Lola told him everything, including hiding the pot under the artichoke plant in the field.

"Is it still there?" he asked, laughing.

"I sure hope so. Would you take me down there before anyone finds it?"

"Of course, babe. I'll go get it, if you want."

"You'd never find it without me. I'm not sure I can find it."

Billy brought the coffee and doughnuts to the bed. "Figured you hadn't had breakfast yet."

They ate the sugarcoated lumps of dough and drank coffee and talked about Sherry's injuries, the loss of the MG, and the asshole that hit them.

"Are you and Sherry gonna sue the truck driver?"

"I don't know about Sherry. I'm certainly not. I wasn't really hurt."

"Of course you were hurt. Look at you."

"Well, we'll see. I'd only want enough to pay hospital and ambulance costs. But I'm not going to *sue* for it."

"Why not?"

She stopped chewing and looked at him. "Because, I don't want to attract any attention."

Billy was silent for a moment. "Are you runnin' from somethin'?"

Lola looked away. "Maybe."

"You can tell me."

She hesitated. "I witnessed a murder in Vegas and the police are looking for me for questioning."

"What murder? Why don't you go to the police?"

She turned toward him. "I can't, Billy. It was the Mob that killed my boyfriend." She told him what she had seen. "Do you know what they'd do to me if I told the police anything?"

Billy looked at her. "Honey, I'll protect you."

He took her coffee and set it on the bedside table, leaned down and kissed her on the lips, then murmured in her ear, "I don't care who's lookin' for you. I'll take care of you if you'll let me." He found her lips again and his body moved onto the bed. She remained on her back as he crouched over her, holding his weight up with strong arms.

She could feel his erection against her thigh. "I don't think I can lift my legs," she whispered.

Billy sat up, removed his boots and slipped off his jeans and shorts. "We'll manage honey. Just leave it to me."

It was early afternoon and the Arizona sun was at its peak. Jet skiers were competing to see how much of the Colorado River they could splash on the banks. Beside the trailer, the Harley stood in the driveway, still hot from the long stretch of desert between Barstow and Needles. A saddlebag gaped open, unpacked. Inside the aluminum-roofed trailer, the temperature was almost unbearable.

Greg brought his fist up and smacked Sherry across her left cheek. "You dumb bitch! You crashed the only car we have. Now what we gonna do?" His eyes bugged nearly out of his head. Sweat trickled down his neck, bleeding into his dirty tee-shirt.

The wound opened and she cried out in a pitiful wail. Tears streamed from her eyes.

Greg put his hands behind his back, then sat down and hung his head between his knees, forearms wrapped around his head. He had just returned from L.A. with a pound of weed, which at that moment sat in a brown grocery bag on the tattered green couch beside the other bag that Lola and Billy had retrieved from the artichoke field.

"Jesus, Sher. I didn't mean to hit ya. I just can't think what ta do."

Sherry blotted her face with a towel, saw the blood, and walked to the mirror in the tiny bathroom. "I think I'd better go back to the doctor, Greg." She began to whimper.

He stood up, his fists clenched again. "Damn it, Sherry. It's always about you, ain't it? Whatever happens, ole Sher gets the limelight. Well, *fuck you!*"

Sherry cowered against the sink, arms across her face, her head inched into her shoulders like a turtle.

For one instant he turned toward her, then strode to the trailer door, slamming it against the wall. Taking the three wooden steps in one leap, he jumped on his Harley.

"Where you goin'?" Sherry called after him.

"None of yer fuckin' business," he yelled. Kick-starting the cycle, he roared out the driveway.

Sherry pressed the towel to her cheek and cried. After a while she picked up the phone and called Lola.

"Hello," Lola answered.

"It's Sherry. Could you come over and take me to the doctor?"

"What happened?"

There was silence on Sherry's end, then, she said, "Greg hit me."

Lola could hear her sobbing. "Where'd he hit you?"

"On my cheek," Sherry garbled through her sobs.

"That bastard! I'll be right there."

Lola laid aside *Portnoy's Complaint*, took off the neck brace, and slipped into her sandals. She grabbed her car keys and purse and locked the motel door. Carefully getting into the VW Bug, as she was still sore, she steered Betsy down the river highway.

She pulled up in front of the trailer and went in

the open door. Sherry was sitting on the green couch, towel to her cheek, eyes swollen.

"Let me see," Lola said, gently taking the towel away. The flesh lay open in irregular edges, like a torn page from a magazine. "Let's go," she said.

The two of them got into the VW. Lola put the little bug in reverse and skidded away. "Tell me," she demanded as she headed for the Needles Hospital.

"As soon as he came in the door, he asked me where the MG was," Sherry said in a subdued tone. "I told him about the accident and that it wasn't my fault." He didn't even ask about my face. I told him I had the car towed to Perkins Garage. Bill Perkins said it would cost a thousand dollars to fix the damage, and us with no insurance. That's when he lost it."

"You need to get away from that bastard," Lola said.

Sherry nodded, but was silent.

※

*L*ola came out of a deep sleep slowly, still in that soft, foggy place between wakefulness and dreamland. A noise awakened her. She half-listened, then went back into the delicious dream of Billy holding her in his arms. Suddenly the bed jiggled and a black wall hovered over her menacingly. The nightmare she'd had since she was a little girl brought her father back into her room. Her eyes flew open. Paul was crouched above her, the flesh around his pale eyes and fat cheeks sagging. Her body immediately stiffened and she threw out her arms, striking him in the chest.

He grabbed her shoulders. "Don't make a fuckin' sound, girl." Paul lifted his body just enough to pull back the covers and expose Lola's legs. But he made a grave error in not pinning down her arms, because in that instant Lola reached back beneath her pillow and felt the handle of her open buck knife. Her right hand grasped the hilt and brought it down beside her hip.

Paul began forcing her legs apart. His breath came in shallow gasps. "You thought you could tease me, and get away with it? Well, no way, honey. Yer gonna put out for ole Paul."

Lola brought her hand up with the knife clutched in her palm and drove it into the soft, flabby flesh under his armpit.

"Jesus!" Paul screamed, toppling off Lola and falling to his knees on the floor. "You fuckin' bitch," he cried. "You stabbed me!"

Lola sprung out the other side of the bed and stood with the knife poised in front of her breasts. Her trembling hand nearly dropped the knife. "You get your ass out of here, right now," she snarled at him. "If you ever touch me again, I'll kill you. Do you understand?" Cheeks flushed, her heart pounded in her ears. Her eyes flashing red sparks, she resembled a demented woman.

Paul lifted his arm and looked at the wound dripping blood down his side. He struggled to his feet. "You bitch! I'm bleeding."

"Get out!" Lola ran to the door and opened it.

Paul zipped up his fly and limped to the door still

holding his side. "You ain't gettin' away with this," he threatened, but he left quickly, avoiding her furious stare.

She watched him shuffle to the back door of his apartment behind the motel office. She locked her door, this time putting a chair under the knob. Still clutching the knife, she looked down at her shaking hand, then rubbed her neck. She still hurt from the accident.

In the bathroom, blood dripped from the five-inch blade into the white sink. The bright red against the stark white porcelain made her think of a Pollack painting. She remembered reading somewhere that he started his paintings with one color and dripped layer upon layer. Bet he never used real blood, she mused, realizing in the same instant, what a gruesome thought. Her anger dissipated, her mind was suddenly in a strange, emotionless limbo. She turned on the faucet and rinsed the blood down the drain, then looked up and caught her reflection in the mirror. Her summer tan gone, like the last blush of fall, the red-rimmed eyes of a stranger looked back. She saw blood smeared on her blue cotton nightgown. Drying the knife she laid it on the back of the commode and slipped out of the garment. She drew a basin of cold water, putting it in to soak. Then she went back to the bed, turned on the light and checked the sheets and rug. There were drops on the top sheet. She carried it into the bathroom, filled the tub and tucked the stained part of the sheet in the water. She poured cold water on the blood drips on the rug and blotted it with a towel. The stains didn't come out completely, but she hoped when they dried they would blend into the earth-colored carpet. Turning out the lights, and placing the knife beneath her pillow again, she climbed back into bed, naked, wishing with all her heart that she had a safe haven.

She thought of Billy Jim and his strong and comforting arms. He had murmured words of love their last time together. She didn't know what to make of it. She couldn't bring herself to return those words. Please God, don't let any more trouble come my way. Lord, she'd nearly killed a man! She didn't even care that Paul was hurt. No, wait a minute. Paul deserved everything he got and worse. How dare he try to invade her body. She realized she had done to Paul exactly what she had fantasized doing to her father all these years. The memory of those nights would never go away. Finally she allowed her feelings to seep back into her heart. With the swiftness of a desert storm she started sobbing. She cried for the nights she spent in fear. She cried for all the unfulfilled relationships. She cried for the lack of closure with her mother, and for Tony. Gradually the sobs subsided and Lola wiped her swollen eyes and drifted into sleep. Tossing fitfully, she awakened several times thinking she heard a key in the door. Finally, toward morning, her body relaxed into a quiet slumber.

≳≲

Willie Nelson's sweet rendition of "Crazy" played softly from the country radio station. Early morning light streaming through un-shuttered windows fell across Lola's clothes, flung on the floor where she'd hastily shed them. The smell of freshly percolating coffee drifted in from the kitchen. She and Billy lay in his double bed in each other's arms.

This morning when she awakened and saw the sheriff's car in front of the Tavern she'd dressed quickly and driven to Billy's. She'd told him about last night when Paul had tried to rape her.

Now he was kissing her behind the ears, nibbling down the side of her neck, across her cheek to her lips, then up to her eyelids, and down to her breasts. He continued to plant kisses on her ribcage, fluttering his lips across her stomach, finally arriving at the place between her thighs.

"Oh, yes, baby," Lola murmured, as Billy concentrated on her pleasure dome. When she climaxed, he entered her, and within seconds came too, rearing his chest back, groaning. They lay for a while clasped together as one body.

"I love you, Lola."

Lola said nothing.

"I know you feel it, too, you just can't say it."

"Yes."

"Yes what, baby?" Billy prodded.

She hesitated. "I feel love for you."

He rolled off and cuddled her head on his shoulder, her long hair brushing his cheek.

"I think you should move in with me. Get away from the motel. I'd love to have you here, and so would Sedona and Apache."

Lola adored Billy Jim's horses and sometimes fed them when he was out on the railroad. But she felt this was a big step, perhaps too big for her, right now. "I don't know. I'm not sure I can live up to your expectations," she said.

"Look, I wanna protect you and have you for my woman. I don't have any expectations beyond that." He leaned down and kissed her mouth.

The fresh aroma of lime aftershave lingered on her lips. Tucking her arms around his brown neck she kissed him back. She did feel love for him, but she had some fears about his possessiveness. However, he had promised that he wouldn't do that to her again. Lola leaned her head back and looked into Billy's eyes. Choosing her words carefully, she said, "Billy, I don't know if I'm ready to settle down here. If anyone comes asking about me, I'll have to move on. You'd be taking a gamble."

"Okay. I'm willing to take that gamble. No one's gonna hurt you livin' with me. I'm bettin' I can keep you here… and happy. Whadaya say?"

Lola felt suddenly giddy. Tears sprang to her eyes. She would be safe here. She made a snap decision. "I say…yes." She smiled up at him, pushing any doubts to the back of her mind.

"Hot damn!" He said, rocking her in his arms.

"We're gonna have ourselves a time, baby. I'm gonna do everything in my power to make you wanna stay." He gave her several short, quick kisses. "Boy, oh boy! When ole Paul hears that you're livin' with me, he won't dare mess with you." Billy sat up. "I wonder if you cut him badly. Think he needed a doctor?"

"I think he did. I'm kind of worried that he involved me."

"Well, don't worry, honey. You was here with me last night. It's our word against his. No one needs to know what really happened. Besides, if he ever touches you again…I'll take care of him."

Lola didn't tell Billy *her* threat to Paul.

"In a little while, we'll go over to the motel and pack your things. When you go to work tonight, you tell Pat that you've moved in with me. Okay?"

Lola nodded.

"But right now, baby I got other plans for you." His mouth covered hers as he stroked her breast.

Billy was already taking charge, and she was letting him.

≥≤

*P*at poured the rest of Lola's Bud into a glass. "Billy Jim's known for his fast work," she said, teasing Lola about moving over to Billy's.

"Yeah, so I've heard," Lola said, as she took a swig of beer.

"Course that don't mean he ain't crazy 'bout you.

Just want ya to know, he's not too reliable." Pat said this quietly so the other customers couldn't hear. "He shot his best friend in the foot when he caught him in bed with his girl, so I'd be mighty careful, honey." Pat delivered this warning with a smile. "It don't hurt to know certain things."

From the other end of the bar, Marsh shouted, "Billy wouldn't do nothin' like that agin, Pat. You oughta know that by now."

"I swear that Marsh has ears on the end of his fingers. Never hears "last call" at 1:45 in the morning, though." She giggled at this quirk in his nature.

"Yeah, Marsh is something else," Lola laughed too. "I hear you, Pat. "Thanks for telling me. I didn't know about him shooting his friend, but I do care for him and I'm really a one-man-at-a-time woman. I'm not likely to be slipping around." She still felt a tiny bit uneasy around Pat because of the incident with Paul. That had been two days ago. Paul was recuperating in his apartment. Pat said a guy had pulled a knife on her husband up in Laughlin, taken his money and then stabbed him. Lola hadn't seen Paul since that night. In fact, she had contemplated packing Betsy up and leaving while Billy was out on the railroad. Just head down the road and keep on going until the next place beckoned. That would probably be the wisest thing to do. Not having the inertia to make that decision, she'd stayed.

"Think you could help me out tomorrow and work the afternoon shift?" Pat asked. "I got Sherry coming in today. It's her day off from the Sundancer."

"Sure," Lola said, "No problem."

"I need some extra help 'til Paul's on his feet again. Damn fool! Gettin' hisself stabbed! Bet he was flashin' his money in the casino. Sheriff Del don't have no leads. Prob'ly some drifter passin' through."

"Probably," Lola agreed, looking down at her beer.

Marsh slid off his stool and hobbled down to Lola. "Billy Jim can be a fine fella. He just needs a good woman, and it looks like he's got one, now." He patted Lola on the shoulder and headed toward the men's room.

"Marsh, you be sure and hit the stool, now. Don't be makin' extra work for me," Pat called after him.

"Now Pat, when have I ever missed the stool?" Marsh shouted as he went down the hallway. The entire place broke into laughter.

Pat started to put another Bud in front of Lola but Lola held up her hand.

"No thanks. I'm headed home to put some dinner on for Billy. He'll probably be in around suppertime."

"Okay, honey. See ya' tomorrow at one." Pat waved as she dropped the empty glass into the dishwater.

A couple of railroaders sitting at the bar watched Lola leave. "Damn lucky man, that Billy Jim," one of them said.

"Sure the hell is," the other one agreed.

Lola had just finished an eight-hour afternoon shift at the Tavern. When she pulled into Billy's, she saw Sherry sitting on the front step with a suitcase. Lola parked and got out. "Sherry. What's wrong?"

"I just packed a few things and left. I got a ride here with Old Dewey. Think you could let me sleep on the couch tonight?" Sherry's eyes were puffy.

Lola hesitated, as this wasn't her house. She didn't know how Billy would react to having a house guest, but she figured he'd be okay with a night or two, until Sherry decided where to go. "Sure. Come on in." She opened the unlocked front door and they entered the cool interior

"What did Greg say?" Lola asked.

"He's at work. I just left a note saying I was leavin and goin to your house."

"Jesus, Sherry. He's going to be mad when he finds you gone. You know he'll be over here tonight."

"I'm afraid of him, Lola. I had to get away." Sherry started to cry, her cheek reddening around the new stitches.

Lola tried to think what to do. Billy would be home sometime tonight. But Greg might visit them before Billy got home.

"Okay, honey," Lola said. "It may get sticky if he comes around. I need to know if you want me to call the cops."

Sherry wiped her eyes. "No, please don't do that.

There's the pound of grass he brought back from L.A. in the trailer. He'd be busted if they search the place. And he has some outstanding warrants in Phoenix."

"Okay. Don't you worry. We'll be fine." Lola didn't want to call the Sheriff either. She opened the refrigerator and placed a pot of vegetable soup on the stove. Then she cut two slices of homemade bread and took two bowls from the cupboard. "We'll have some dinner. You try and relax."

Sherry started to cry again.

"Now, honey, stop that," Lola said. "I'm not going to let him hurt you. Trust me." Lola walked to the fireplace and picked up Billy's .22, which had been leaning beside the rock wall. She checked to see that it was loaded, and brought it back to the kitchen, placing it beside her chair. Then she went to the front door and put the chain on and turned the lock. When the soup was hot she filled the bowls and they sat down to eat.

Just as they were finishing supper they heard the squeal of brakes in the driveway. A car door slammed and she heard boots kicking up gravel. Lola stood and picked up the .22. She put her finger to her lips, noticing Sherry's pale face.

"Lola...Sherry." Greg pounded his fist on the front door. "Open this damn door." He rattled the knob violently and found it locked.

Lola and Sherry remained quiet.

"If you don't open this door, I'll break the son-of-a bitch down," he growled.

Lola stepped closer to the door and raised the gun,

gut-level. She spoke slowly. "If you touch that door, I'll blow a hole in you. Now get out of here."

Greg stopped pounding. "I just want to talk to Sherry. I know she's in there. Just let me see her."

Lola continued to aim the gun. "Leave, Greg. You can talk to her later. Now is not the time."

There was silence outside, then the sound of one last frustrating smash of a boot against the door. "Damn you. I'll be back. I want Sherry."

They heard him shuffle back to the car, start it up and spin the tires as he raced out onto the gravel road.

Sherry rushed to the window. "I wonder whose car he borrowed?"

Lola stood behind her, watching the dust cloud move away.

Sherry turned to Lola, her eyes full of admiration. "You called his bluff. He wasn't sure but what you'd shoot him." She smiled at her friend. "But you wouldn't have, would you?"

"I never threaten anything I'm not prepared to carry out," Lola said, as she put the gun back beside the fireplace.

"God, Lola. Do you even know how to shoot a gun?"

Lola looked at Sherry's face, still damp from crying. In spite of the life Sherry had led, skirting the edges of the law, she had an innocence about her. Lola went to the sink and began washing up the bowls. "I can shoot a gun if I need to," was all she said.

Later, the two of them watched a little TV and smoked a joint. Around eleven, Lola made up the couch for Sherry. She took the chain off the door and picked up the .22.

"Don't open the door for anyone," she said. "When Billy comes home, he'll use his key. Be sure to let him know you're here."

"Will he be mad?" Sherry asked.

Lola didn't know, but she said, "No, of course not. He wouldn't want Greg to hurt you anymore than I do. Just try to sleep."

Lola double-checked the back door, and the windows, making sure they were all locked. She undressed and put on a nightgown in case she had to get up unexpectedly. Climbing beneath the clean, sun-dried sheets of Billy's bed, she wondered why trouble always seemed to find her no matter where she went.

※

*P*aul eased himself off the bed and limped toward the kitchen. Sweat oozed from his armpits. A dirty undershirt bunched around his waist. He threw the beer can toward the open garbage pail, missing it by a foot as it hit the back wall. A large section of the paint about the size of a butter plate had been chipped away. Flies scattered as the missile whizzed by their domain. As soon as the container landed on the floor they returned to feed on the dribbles, then taking flight, they made lopsided circles in the air.

He was sick of lying around the apartment. Pat wouldn't let him even go to the store. Stepping into the bathroom, he opened his fly and lifted the lid. The liquid leaving his flaccid penis was very yellow and smelled astringent, almost like horse's urine. He guessed it was the antibiotics he was taking to prevent infection. He flipped his member, wrinkling his nose at the offensive odor. God, he hated her! He'd figure something out to pay her back for what she'd done to him. The wound in his side didn't hurt nearly as bad as the discovery that the magazines wouldn't work anymore. He couldn't even get a hard-on. She'd done that to him. He'd always relied on the pictures of naked women. Now he was fucked. Well, not really. He hadn't fucked Pat or anyone in so long, he didn't remember the last time.

He stumbled back to the rumpled bed and gently lay down. Honey, reclining on the other pillow, licked her nose and crawled up beside Paul. He reached up, petting her silky coat. Her tongue cleaned his cheek and she snuggled next to him. "Honey, sweet baby. You love ole Paul, don'tcha?" He planted several juicy kisses on her nose. The dog licked Paul's lips and nestled in the curve between his neck and shoulder.

Attempting to blame Lola for money gone in the till hadn't worked. Marsh had told Pat that he saw Paul take some of the cash. So he would have to think up another plan. Too bad she'd moved out of the motel and into Billy Jim's place. He should have gone through her things before she left. Maybe he could've found something out. One of the railroaders was talkin' the other afternoon in the bar about Lola. He thought she was mighty closed-mouthed. Maybe she had something to hide. Now there was an idea. He could start a rumor. What could he make up about her? Of course, Billy Jim was a wildcard. Being careful not to rile him was important. But he'd start the talk like he'd heard it from someone else. What could he say about that bitch? An intriguing thought took shape. He'd say he'd heard from an unnamed source that Lola was a hooker on the run from Vegas. Mixed up with the Mafia. Sounded possible, since she was from Vegas, and everyone knew the Mafia ran things there. Who should he tell first? Someone that would protect his identity. Ah hah...he knew just the man. Old Dewey. He was so hard of hearin' he got everything mixed up, anyway. He'd probably add his own twist to the rumor. He was just the one to tell. A smirk settled on Paul's face. Maybe the police would even get involved. Check her out in Vegas. Where the hell did she work? She'd written some casino down on her application.

He carefully stood up, wincing at the pain in his side, and went into the front office. Opening a drawer he reached for the work files. Lola's was on top. He scanned it until he came to the section where she had previously worked. The Calendar Club Casino and Theater — Las Vegas Blvd. at Sahara. Bosses — Tony Ricco and Ritchie Aparte. Maybe he'd give them a call when he felt better and see what they would tell him. He dropped the file back in the drawer smiling, his large teeth opening from his thin lips like a Venus Flytrap waiting for its next insect.

Part 2
Down Hill Slide

Billy drove into the circular drive, parked his truck, and pulled his grip from the back. He walked to the front door and turned the knob, but the door was locked. Finding his keys, he opened it and stepped inside.

"Billy?" A strange female voice spoke from out of the darkness.

"Yeah. Who's there?" Billy demanded.

"It's Sherry. Lola said I could bunk on the couch tonight." She reached up and turned on the light beside her.

Billy saw the blond that Lola had been hangin' around with, on the sofa. One tanned foot peeked out from under the blanket. "Okay. Go on back to sleep." He walked into the bedroom and shut the door just as Lola pulled the chain on the bedside lamp.

"What the hell's goin'on? I come home to not one, but two women in my house." He took off his cowboy hat, tossing it on a chair, and sat down on the bed.

"Some men wouldn't complain," Lola said with a grin.

He didn't respond. "Why is she here?"

Lola told him what happened with Greg. When she told him she'd picked up the rifle, it was Billy's turn to grin.

"Jesus, I got myself a wild woman. Do you know how to shoot my gun?"

Lola nodded.

He ran his fingers through thick, sandy hair. "Guess you held down the fort while I was gone. But why do you have to be Sherry's protector?"

"Because she came to me for help."

Billy sighed deeply. "Well, I'll talk to Greg, although you probably scared the crap out of him. I don't want him thinkin' he can come back here when I'm gone."

"Okay," Lola said neutrally.

Billy pulled off his boots and undressed. He crawled in beside Lola as she turned off the light. "I hope you ain't gonna bring home all the stray animals you come across," he said, cuddling up to her buttocks. He spoke lightly, squeezing her breast, but she knew he was half-serious.

※

*P*aul was on the afternoon shift at the Tavern. A 300-pound Mohave Indian named Oscar was at one end of the bar and Old Dewey at the other. Paul leaned over the bar stiffly, as he still had a bandaged side. He whispered in old Dewey's ear. "I heard that Lola's on the run from Vegas. Call girl for the Mob. Apparently she rubbed a big boss the wrong way. But keep it quiet."

Old Dewey looked up from his beer. "Where'd you hear that?"

"An old friend from Vegas told me."

Dewey looked thoughtful. "She's a mighty purty girl. Can't see her as a call girl, though. Maybe your friend's mistaken."

"No, he's not mistaken. He said her name was Lola Raines," Paul said with irritation. "And he saw her here the other day on his way to Phoenix."

Dewey continued to stare down in his beer.

"Well, Whadaya think, Dewey?"

"I said what I think. I don't believe it," the old desert rat said.

Paul turned away in frustration. "Shit, Dewey. I try to tell you some juicy news and you doubt my word."

"Ain't doubtin' you. Doubtin' yer friend." Dewey pulled a container of chewing tobacco from his pocket and stuck a pinch behind his lip.

Paul moved down to the sink and began washing beer glasses. Damned ol' fart. He always loved gossip. And he usually got it all screwed up when he passed it on. What the hell was happening? Had Lola captivated Old Dewey as well as Marsh and Billy Jim? By God, when he got off work, he'd call that casino where she used to work. Then if he found anything interesting, he'd call the sheriff, anonymously, of course. He owed her, and he was gonna pay her back for the grief she'd caused him.

Pat entered through the red door, sunlight flashing across the sawdust floor. She went behind the bar to relieve Paul. "You gonna stay home tonight?" she asked, looking carefully at her husband.

"Yeah. Where would I go?" he said, indignantly.

"Just askin'. Don't get riled. Do you think you could fix the door on number 12? It's not lockin' properly."

"Yeah," Paul mumbled. He planned on calling Vegas first.

He left the Tavern and entered the back of the apartment, making his way to the front office. Opening the drawer he picked up Lola's application on top. He dialed the number beside her last place of employment.

"Calendar Club Casino and Theater," a feminine voice answered. Paul could hear the familiar sounds of slot machines in the background.

"Hello. My name is Harry Smith and I run a bar in Mohave Valley, Arizona. I'm checking on a new employee's application. Her last place of employment was your casino theater. Could I speak with one of her bosses, Tony Ricco or Ritchie Aparte?"

≷≶

*T*here was silence on the other end. Then, the female voice said, "Mr. Ricco is deceased and Mr. Aparte is out of town. Who is the person you're inquiring about?"

That took Paul by surprise. "Uh....Lola Raines."

Another silence. "Lola Raines is a missing person as far as we know. You say she is applying for a position at your bar?"

"Yeah." Paul's breath was heavy.

"What position is she applying for?"

"Bartender."

"Well, she'd probably be a good one."

"Can you tell me anything else about her?"

The woman hesitated. Then she said, "No. I'd give her a good recommendation, though."

"Who am I speaking to?" Paul asked.

"This is Caroline Pines. I'm a bartender here."

"Could I speak with your boss or manager?" Paul pressed.

"I'm sorry; no one is in right now. Would you like to leave your number?"

Paul didn't think that was a good idea. "No. Thanks for the info." He hung up. So the bitch *was* on the run. But why? Was she mixed up in her boss's death? Maybe he'd make a call to the Vegas police and see what they had to say. He'd find out about her, by God, if it was the last thing he did.

Caroline Pines hung up the receiver and waited on a customer at the bar. So, Lola was in Arizona. When Tony's body was discovered, there was speculation that perhaps she'd been killed, too. Lola had never returned to work and most of the casino employees and strippers hoped she was all right. She'd be careful who she told about this, but she had to tell the girls over at the theatre. They'd all wish Lola the very best.

※

*R*onnie stepped down from his truck and walked up to Billy's open door. Billy stood leaning against the doorjamb.

"Come on in, man," Billy said. "We're just about to eat dinner. Wanna stay?"

"Oh, probably not. Thanks. I just stopped by on my way home."

Billy raised his eyebrows. "Not because you'd heard about our new houseguest?" He smiled.

Ronnie flushed. "Well, maybe," he said quietly. He looked around Billy and saw Sherry and Lola in the kitchen.

Billy put his arm around his friend's shoulder. "Come in, Ronnie. The girls are fixin' spaghetti and meatballs. Stay and help us eat it." The two men walked inside and into the dining area.

"We have lots of food, Ronnie. Do stay," Lola said.

Sherry looked at him and smiled, her nose wrinkling.

That did it. Her smile could convince him of anything. "Well, guess I am a little hungry. Haven't eaten since we left Seligman. We got hung up on a side track for two hours." Ronnie took off his Stetson and hung it on the hat rack.

"What happened?" Billy asked.

"Something wrong with the front-end connection. They finally got it fixed. When you due to go out?"

"Around two or three this morning. I plan on getting a few hours' shut-eye before I get called."

The girls set the table and dished up the spaghetti. "Soup's on," Sherry said.

They sat down, Billy and Ronnie at each end and the girls on the sides. Ronnie noticed Sherry had on her usual tight tank top with no bra. She had the most beautiful breasts. Firm and round. He looked up quickly into her eyes when he felt her staring at him. She was grinning. Uh, oh. He'd been busted. He flushed again. Damn! What to do with such a fine-lookin woman sittin' across from him? He felt all tingly and happy inside. Billy Jim passed him a beer across the table and winked.

※

The Tavern was packed on another Saturday night. Lola and Pat were swamped with customers three-deep at the bar, with Paul covering the tables. Russell and his band were high on the music, sliding into their rendition of Willy Nelson's "Rainy Day Blues." Ronnie, Sherry and Billy sat together on bar stools.

Ronnie offered his arm to Sherry and they skipped out on the crowded dance floor. Billy leaned on his elbows, watching Lola. He caught her eye and she smiled at him.

Lola came down to his end of the bar. "Want another beer?"

"Sure, babe. I always want another beer. When's your break?"

"As soon as the bar clears a little, I'll ask Pat. I can't leave now."

"Wanna dance or go outside?"

"I'd like some fresh air, I'm sick of the smoke." Haze wafted across the large room, making Russell and the band members appear in a fog. The ventilation system wasn't working well, because Paul hadn't found time to fix it yet.

Earlier, Shorty, the fiddle player, had asked Lola if she wanted to do a song with the band on her break. She'd declined.

When Paul relieved Lola behind the bar, she and Billy picked up their drinks and walked through the swinging doors into the warm Arizona night. As soon as they reached the corner of the Tavern, Billy pulled her close with his free arm and kissed her.

"Did you notice Sherry and Ronnie?" he whispered. "I think they're fallin' in love." He nibbled her ear as he spoke.

"Yeah, I noticed."

"Well, I don't know Sherry, but Ronnie's the best. He's a great friend. Always been there for me."

Lola pulled away and took a drink of her coke. "Thanks, Billy, for letting Sherry stay at the house. It's really sweet of you."

"You know ole Billy. Always there to give Cupid a hand. Especially after the girl of his dreams was delivered to him."

Lola smiled. "I think maybe you're an incurable romantic."

"Yep. You could say that." Billy changed to a more serious note. "How's Paul been around you?"

"He's been avoiding me, thank God."

"It's a cryin' shame that a nice woman like Pat is hooked up with that worm." Billy chugged the rest of his Bud.

"You never know about people," Lola said. "Pat chose him. She told me he was her next door neighbor when her parents died. She was only sixteen then. He helped her through the funeral and her grieving period, and eventually they got married."

"Well, something turned him into an asshole."

"Yeah. He's sick." Lola spoke quietly. "He needs help, but my guess is he'll never get it."

They heard the Tavern doors swing shut as someone came outside. Billy pulled Lola back into the shadows. Ronnie and Sherry walked toward his truck. He opened the door for her, then bent down and gave her a long kiss. Sherry reached up, twining her arms around his neck, and they stood there for a moment in the moonlight. Then she stepped up into the truck and slid into the seat. Ronnie walked around to his side and climbed behind the wheel. He backed out and headed down River Highway.

"Bet they're headed for his place," Billy said. "Whatcha think?"

Lola gazed after the retreating taillights. "Maybe. I hope Sherry doesn't get hurt." She wondered if Sherry was moving too fast. Her clothes were still in Greg's trailer. Lola had promised to go with her tomorrow to pick up all her things. She hadn't said anything to Billy because she knew he wouldn't like it. Lola figured Sherry was the type of girl that moved on quickly. On second thought, if anyone got hurt, it would probably be Ronnie.

※

Ronnie pulled into the driveway and turned off the engine. "If I act a little nervous, it's 'cause I am." He gave a small laugh.

"That's okay. I'm nervous too," Sherry said, touching his hot arm with her cool palm.

He pulled her across the seat in one swift motion and kissed her, stroking her lips with his tongue. When he released her he said, "Let's go in where we can be more comfortable."

Sherry giggled and jumped out of the truck. When they stepped inside his double-wide trailer, she saw an old leather couch against one wall, a green chair with an ottoman in one corner, a coffee table, literally on its last legs, and an end table with a green lamp. A small table and two chairs were in the dining room. The rug was green shag with long tuffs. The kitchen was small but neat, and the place looked surprisingly clean for a bachelor pad. She figured it wouldn't take much to fix it up into something a little homier.

"Want a beer?" he asked, opening the refrigerator.

Sherry sat down on the hard leather couch. "Sure." She watched him move around his territory. He put two Buds on the coffee table and sat down next to her.

"I've admired you for a long time. I used to daydream about you here in my place." He looked into her blue eyes. "Now, you're here." He leaned over and kissed her gently. She kissed him back, hard and wet. When they came up for air, she slowly pulled her tank top over her head and watched Ronnie's eyes.

He couldn't take them off her breasts. He took one pink nipple into his mouth, sucking gently.

"Ohhhh...." Sherry murmured.

Then Ronnie licked the other nipple and placed his lips around it.

Another moan came from Sherry. Suddenly she stood up, unzipped her jeans and stepped out of them in one graceful motion. Ronnie was surprised when he saw she had no underpants on. She pushed her pelvis close to his face. When she staggered under the heat of their passion, he laid her back on the couch, stepped out of his jeans and shorts and plunged inside. Ronnie was so excited that he came immediately, his groans smothered in her hair. Then he slid down between her thighs and brought her to orgasm.

"Oh, Ronnie," Sherry cried out.

Afterwards, Ronnie held her in his arms, vowing to himself to keep her with him always.

≋

Lola and Sherry had passed by the trailer once and noticed the Harley gone. They turned around and pulled into the driveway. The two of them entered the trailer and saw clothes were scattered everywhere. The small table was stacked with dirty dishes and rotten food, and the sink overflowed with pans. When Lola pulled up the window shade, roaches scrambled for cover over days-old bacon rind. The place smelled like dirty socks and decaying meat. "Lord, it smells bad," Lola said, holding her nose.

Sherry went to a cupboard above the bed and started pulling down clothes.

"Guess Greg doesn't do dishes," Lola observed, trying not to breathe deeply.

"He's always been a slob," Sherry said, continuing to hunt for her things.

"What do you want down here?" Lola called from the other end of the trailer.

"Grab the books off the end table and the blue dishes in the cupboard."

Lola used the newspapers on the floor to wrap the dishes. She shook them first, making sure there weren't any roaches hidden between the pages. Then she packed the dishes in a small box with the books.

"It's none of my business, Sherry, but I think you should tell Greg that you're really finished. It's only fair. Especially before you start out with Ronnie."

"I'm just too afraid to face him," Sherry said, biting her lip.

The girls carried the bags and boxes out to Lola's VW. Betsy's backseat was nearly filled when the Harley chugged up the drive. Sherry stood beside Lola, their shoulders touching. "Oh God," she whispered, clutching Lola's arm.

"Don't worry. Just get in the car."

Sherry ran around the front of the VW and jumped in the passenger side. Lola got in behind the wheel, and started the engine.

Greg pulled his bike right behind Lola's bumper and got off, leaving the cycle idling.

"Whatcha' bitches up to?" he said, as he came around to Sherry's open window.

"I'm movin' out. I'm through, Greg." Sherry's voice quavered. "Please leave me alone."

He leaned down and rested his forearms on the window edge. "Well, now, maybe I ain't through with you, yet."

"I don't want any trouble." She wouldn't meet his eyes.

Lola gunned the engine. "You'd better move that piece of junk back there or I'm gonna run over it."

Greg straightened up and backed away from the car. "You wouldn't dare," he snarled, glaring at Lola.

"I'm giving you one chance. Move it or lose it." Lola gunned the engine again and waited.

Greg stood motionless, trying to make up his mind.

Lola began backing up very slowly, then pulled forward to the steps of the trailer. She threw Betsy into reverse and stepped on the gas pedal, revving the engine with her left foot still on the brake.

Greg ran for his Harley and quickly moved it to the side.

Lola roared out the driveway. When she pulled away, Greg swore at them. He gave them the finger and yelled, "I ain't finished with you."

※

Jonathan Marsh, better known as Marshmallow, had lived in Mohave Valley for eighty years. He knew about everybody and everything that went on. He'd seen men and women come and go, marry, give birth, die, go to prison, cheat on their spouses and get drunk every night of the week. That's what *he* did best.

Marsh opened his eyes slowly and looked up at the rounded ceiling of his ancient Airstream. He moved his head gently from side to side. A splitting pain ran across the frontal lobe of his brain. He guessed the damn tumor was getting bigger every day.

He reached out and put his hand down on the floor, gently pushing himself up into a sitting position.

"Damn," he swore. "Wonder who brought me home last night. Think they'd get me to bed once in a while," he said, out loud. 'Course, if it was that sweet gal, Lola, she could leave him on the couch anytime.

Marsh stood up slowly, supporting himself by holding on to the arm of the sofa. He limped into the kitchen and filled the coffeepot with water, then pulled a can of Maxwell House from the cupboard, and poured a small amount into the paper filter. Next, he found a can of beans on the shelf, opened it with a rusty can-opener, grabbed a spoon, and started eating the contents, cold. Marsh loved baked beans. He'd eaten them from the can for forty years. He could eat them morning, noon and night. Of course, a lot of times, especially lately, he didn't eat lunch or dinner. He preferred to drink his meals at the Red Dog.

He hadn't always been a drunk. He remembered back to the time when he and Bill Baxter had owned that gold mine. They'd been prospecting out near Essex, when they'd stumbled on it, just like that. They saw a mine entrance, went inside and found gold nuggets scattered all over the ground. One day Bill said they needed to register it at the County Assayer's office so they would be the legal owners. Bill went into town and did just that, and for years Marsh thought he owned half the mine.

Maybe seven years later, after they'd taken enough gold to keep them in food, shelter, and a few luxuries, they hit a main lobe. Marsh was so excited he got drunk that night, bragging that he was half-owner of the mine. The County Assayer happened to be in the Red Dog at the time. He put Marsh straight right then. "Bill Baxter registered that mine to hisself nearly seven years ago," he said. Even though Marsh had a buzz on, his heart nearly stopped beating. In that quiet moment he knew it was true. Bill had cheated him out of his share. He never even confronted Bill, and Marsh never went back to the mine. He just continued to drink, and moved from bar to bar in his ancient truck, relying on handouts for years, then living on his meager social security when it started coming, and never really touching anyone's life, least of all, his own.

Once he'd met a drifter and in a moment of weakness spoke of his long-ago loss. The drifter looked him straight in the eye and said, "Want me to off your ex-partner? I'll do it for train fare to Chicago."

It took Marsh a minute to think about it, then he said, "Nope. He'll get his, one of these days."

And Bill did. Not long after the drifter left town, Bill was in a fatal car accident out Topock way. His car was totaled and they had to use the Jaws of Life to get him out. But it was too late. He died on the way to Needles Hospital. Marsh could have gone to the County Assayer's office then, and tried to claim the mine, but he didn't. By this time, he was used to his days as a drunk and his nights being carried home by some good samaritan.

Marsh poured himself a cup of coffee. Damn! Still rememberin' all that history. He threw the empty tin in the garbage, and hobbled back to the couch with his coffee. He noticed a plate of brownies on the end table. He tore off a piece and stuffed it in his mouth, savoring the rich chocolate chunks, washing each bite down with his coffee. Lola knew he loved brownies and she was always leaving them in his trailer.

He rummaged around on the floor for his dirty socks that someone had been nice enough to remove with his shoes. That musta been Lola too. She always took off his shoes. Finishing his coffee, he limped out to the old Ford truck. If he hurried, he'd get to the Red Dog by nine o'clock, in time for his first vodka tonic. And before the pain became too intense.

≶≷

*P*at was working the Tuesday evening shift. Paul was helping out Clyde and Leila at the Red Dog, in Needles, as they were short handed.

The usual crowd was sitting at the bar with the old timers, Dewey and Marsh. A few railroaders were relaxing in the booths, but it was a pretty quiet night, as Tuesdays normally were.

A tall stranger came through the red door and walked over to the bar, climbing on a stool.

"I'll have a Whiskey Sour," the man said.

Pat figured him to be from the big city because of his order. No one around here ever drank whiskey any way but up or neat. "Comin' right up." She finished it off with a maraschino cherry and set it in front of the man. She noticed his white hair worn in a crew cut, kind of like a military man. He seemed too old for the service. Maybe an ex-marine.

He stirred his drink with the cherry and popped it immediately in his mouth. In five minutes he'd drained the glass and ordered another.

"Whiskey's a nice thirst quencher, huh?" Pat said as she set his refilled glass down.

The man nodded and took a long swallow.

He looked Pat square in the eyes. "I'm looking for a young woman that might be working here. Lola Raines?"

Pat was surprised but hid it well. "Oh yeah? What's ya lookin' for her for?"

"She left her last place of employment in Las Vegas rather suddenly without picking up her final check."

Pat stared right back at the man, her gaze never flinching. How the hell did he know Lola worked here? Pat felt her suspicious instincts turn on. "Well, she was here, briefly, left last week." Pat turned and wiped the counter next to the stranger.

The man looked down at his drink and spoke softly. "Would you know where she might have gone?"

"Well, she did say something about Phoenix. But I don't know if she went there."

The man slid a hundred-dollar bill beside his drink. "I'd be real grateful if you could give me any information about her. Did she hang out with anyone while she was here?"

Pat put her hand on the bill, covering it. Then she slid it back toward the stranger. "Sorry, don't know nothing more. She was a loner. Only worked a few weeks. Say, how'd you know she'd been here?"

The man hesitated. "The proprietor of Sweeney's Tavern called her last place of employment for a recommendation."

"Well, that must have been my husband. He's real good about checking up on employees."

"Is your husband around?" The white-haired man drained his glass.

"Nope. He's off fishin'. Up in the White Mountains, near Pine Top. Won't be home for a couple of weeks."

The man took a card from his wallet and handed it to Pat. "Would you mind giving this to your husband when he returns and ask him to call me? I'd like to talk to him."

Pat took the card. It read, Martin Fellino, Private Investigator.

"Sure, Mr. Fellino."

"To whom have I been speaking?" he asked.

"I'm Pat Sweeney. My husband and I own Sweeney's' Tavern." She tucked the card in her pocket.

Mr. Fellino stepped down from the stool. "Thank you, Mrs. Sweeney."

His hard blue eyes tried to look friendly, but Pat wasn't fooled for a minute. She watched him walk carefully over the sawdust floor and open the red door. He stopped at the entrance and stamped his feet, removing the sawdust from his shoes. Some of the warm evening air flowed into the dark bar before the door swung shut.

Marsh came down from his end of the bar and leaned over toward Pat. "Why's he lookin' fer our Lola?"

"I don't know, but keep this under your hat, Marshmallow. I gotta tell Lola right away."

She went to the phone and dialed Billy Jim's number. She didn't trust that guy as far as she could throw him. What in the hell kind of trouble was Lola in?

※※

*L*ola put down the phone. Tony's killer was here… looking for her. Pat had said he had white spiky hair. There was no doubt in Lola's mind. That was him. Oh God! What should she do? He would kill her without even asking any questions. She fell into the chair beside the phone. Her hands shook. She tried to swallow the lump that had formed in her throat. She needed to run. But she would tell Billy. He deserved that.

She looked out the window and saw Billy cleaning out Sedona's corral. When her hands stopped trembling she picked up her sunglasses and sun visor and left the cool interior of the house. Walking outside was like opening an oven door at 450 degrees. It was still very hot at five in the afternoon.

"Billy. I need to talk to you."

Billy was busy scooping up Sedona's manure into a wheelbarrow. He didn't answer.

"Billy. Please. This is important."

He stopped and looked up. "What's up?"

"Could you stop a minute?"

Billy straightened up and leaned the shovel against the water tub. He walked over to her and lit a cigarette.

"I just got a call from Pat. A strange man came into the Tavern asking for me."

"Whatdayamean? Asking for you?"

"He asked if Lola Raines worked at the Tavern."

"Who was the guy?"

"Pat says he was from Vegas. She described him. It's him…the killer." Lola was taking deep breaths to stay calm.

Billy put his arm around her shoulders. "It's okay, honey. We'll handle it. Don't panic."

She told Billy Pat's conversation with the man.

"So he thinks you've moved on to Phoenix?"
Lola nodded.

"Well, see? There's no problem." Billy ground his cigarette into the dirt.

"Pat thinks I should stay home for the next two weeks. In case he comes back."

"Sounds like a good idea, honey. You can ride Apache and make some pies and enjoy stayin' home."

Billy kissed her and gave her a hug. But Lola had a sick feeling in the pit of her stomach.

≷≶

Martin climbed into his blue four-year old Cadillac and lit a cigarette. He tossed the match out the window, started the motor and backed out of the Tavern parking lot. The horsy-faced woman behind the bar seemed to think Lola had moved on. She could have given him the straight scoop, or…she coulda' been lying. The woman's body language seemed to be tellin' the truth. No nervous tics or quick movements. He'd drive into Needles and ask around — see what some other people had to say. Before he drove to Phoenix, he'd make damn sure Lola had left this area. He had some old contacts in Phoenix. He could call them to help look for the girl. If he didn't have to do the four-hour drive, he'd be happier. If he found her here, he'd take care of business and get back to Vegas in time for the big meeting next week. The bosses had been real upset that Lola mighta' been there at Tony's that night. And the fact that she'd disappeared had made them suspicious. He'd been told to find her and make sure there were no loose ends. His job was on the line here. And a bit more too — like his life. But he hated to hurt women. It went against his upbringing. His mother had always taught him to be gentle with the opposite sex. But a man had to do what he had to do.

He thought back to his first job and how he came into this line of work. His father had been a bookie in Brooklyn and he'd owed quite a bit to the Mob. In lieu of getting his legs broken he'd promised his son would work free for two years as a pick-up man.

Martin had no choice then either. He couldn't let his father get hurt, he was the bread winner. Martin had only been sixteen, but he was built big and strong and had powerful arms and shoulders. He soon learned how to rough up anyone that didn't pay on time. When his indentured time was finished, the boss in his neighborhood asked him to stay on and get paid. He agreed. He had been nineteen when the boss told him to kill one of the local shopkeepers because he was in cahoots with the cops. He was given a new, shiny forty-five, and he did what he was told. After that, he started getting more assignments, sometimes working with another hit man. He never got any on-the-job training other than going to a firing range and practicing shooting his firearm, but he took to his work well. His reputation grew in the East and when his father died, he was sent to Vegas to work for one of the bosses out there. He sent money regularly to his mother, called her on Mother's Day and her birthday. He'd never married, as he never seemed to have time for relationships with women. It was easier to just take advantage of the many call girls in Vegas. He had no close relationships with men either. He respected the man that did Tony with him, but they never saw each other after work hours. He knew if he didn't find Lola, his partner would be the one to take care of *him*.

※

Russell's front yard opened onto the Colorado River. The warm Arizona night blew a soft breeze onto shore, and along the banks the katydids and bullfrogs were in full symphony. A few of Russell's guests were sitting on the dock with their feet in the water; others necked in the shadows.

On the porch, Lola's clear soprano voice harmonized with Russell's alto as they swung into his version of "Take the Ribbons From Her Hair." Shorty played back-up on mandolin.

It was a Tuesday night and Russell had decided to have a party. Chicken and ribs were cooked earlier on the barbecue, and the refrigerator was stocked with beer. Several of Billy and Ronnie's fellow railroaders were there with their wives and girlfriends.

Billy wandered into the kitchen and pulled a Bud from the refrigerator. An attractive blond was standing by the sink in tank top and jeans.

"Hi, Billy. Got a light?" She held a cigarette between her red lips.

"Sure, Rhoda." He pulled his lighter out and struck a flame to her cigarette.

She sucked deeply. "Haven't seen you in a while. Whatcha' been up to?"

"Well, not much. You know the usual." He'd had a brief affair with her several months ago. It hadn't gone anywhere and he'd forgotten all about her.

Rhoda moved over next to Billy, touching his hip with her own. "Kind of missed you. I was hopin' you'd call sometime."

Billy was uncomfortable. He sidled his hip away a few inches. "Yeah, well I just got busy and… you know…"

She took a long swallow from a bottle of beer and licked the neck with her tongue. "Well, whatcha doin' now?"

Jesus, Billy thought. Why don't she get the hint? "Well, I'm sort of attached now. You know, to Lola, the gal singin' out there."

Rhoda stepped around facing him. "Oh. I didn't know. Well, too bad. I'm disappointed, Billy." She winked at him. "I was hopin' for a return engagement."

Billy rubbed the back of his neck with his free hand. "Sorry. I'm pretty much taken, these days." He smiled sheepishly.

"See ya 'round." She blew him a kiss as she moved into the living room.

Ronnie banged the screen door as he entered the kitchen. "Uh oh. I saw that blond. What'd she want?"

Billy told him.

"Lucky you ain't with her anymore. I heard she's been treated by Doc Holly for the worst case of the clap the Valley's ever seen. At least a dozen guys had to go to the Doc. You been checked lately?"

Billy looked worried. "Jesus, that the truth? Maybe I'd better get a checkup. I haven't noticed anything, though. Lord, can you imagine my havin' to tell Lola? And what if I passed it on to her? Oh Christ," Billy moaned.

Out on the porch, Lola, Russell and Shorty took a break. Everyone headed for the kitchen and cold beer. All six-foot six inches of Russell unwound as he stood up and set his guitar in the corner. His long black hair was tied back in a ponytail and he wore a bandanna around his forehead like his hero, Willie Nelson. His dark, kindly eyes looked down on Lola. "You sure sing purty, lady. How come you don't sing with a group?"

"Well, I just sing for fun. Not interested in all the work that goes into making it perfect for a performance."

"Yeah, I know what you mean," he said. "Me'n Shorty and the band rehearse two or three times a week just for the weekend gigs." He put his arm loosely around her shoulders and they walked into the kitchen.

"I sure appreciate you letting me sing along with you at the bar," Lola said.

"Anytime, honey. You got a place in this band, if you want. Come rehearse with us sometime. You may find it ain't so much work, after all."

Lola smiled up at him. "Thanks," was all she said.

Billy's eyes narrowed as he watched them from his perch on the kitchen counter.

Lola opened the refrigerator and took out two beers, handing one to Russell. Billy jumped off the counter and moved over to her. "Hey, babe. 'Bout ready to call it a night?" He threw his empty can in the trash so hard it knocked out a couple of cans and didn't bother to pick them up.

"Aw, what's yer hurry, Billy?" Russell said. "We're just gettin' warmed up."

"Well, I can see that. I figure she'll be all hot when we get home, won'tcha honey?" Billy turned toward Lola.

"Now, Billy. That ain't..." Russell started to explain.

Lola recognized what was happening immediately. Her smile vanished. "Okay, Billy. Let's go." She nodded to Russell. "Good-night."

She walked away from Billy and on her way to the bedroom, passed Sherry. "Billy's getting weird. We're leaving." She picked up her purse from the bed.

"What's the problem?" Sherry asked.

"Nothing, that's just it."

"Sorry, honey." Sherry squeezed her arm.

"Say goodnight to Ronnie for me," Lola said. Sherry had moved in with Ronnie two days ago.

Lola headed for the front door where Billy was waiting. As they walked to the truck, he grabbed her arm.

"Billy. You're hurting my arm. Don't do that." She tried to shake off his hand.

"Don't mean to hurt you, honey. I'm just in a hurry." He spun her around to face him. "I wanna get you home before you cool off. Looks like Russell did all the work for me."

Lola pulled away from him. "You're being an ass! Russell did nothing. You embarrassed me in there in front of those people." She rubbed the place on her arm where his fingers had pinched her flesh.

Billy looked at her in silence. He opened the truck door for her and waited, one hand on his hip.

She didn't move for a moment, as if making up her mind. Then she climbed in. He slammed the door and went around and got in behind the wheel. The tires squealed and kicked up gravel as Billy stormed down the road to his place.

≥≤

It had been two weeks since the stranger had come into the Tavern looking for Lola. It was a Friday night and Billy suggested they go down and hear Russell and the band. No one had heard from or seen Martin Fellino during that time so Lola figured she could venture out, but she was somewhat nervous. Billy assured her that with all the railroaders around them at the Tavern she would be perfectly safe.

The bartender from the Red Dog was helping Pat out. Lola and Billy were on the dance floor kicking up the sawdust. The jukebox was playing a mambo.

Billy stood facing her. "Now just step forward as I

step back, then bring your feet together and then you step back and do the same again. The rhythm is, one, two, three, four, pause." He was showing her how to dance to the mambo tempo. "Now place your left foot behind the right and do a little ball-change dance step."

Lola followed Billy's body and feet successfully. She knew how to mambo but she thought letting Billy teach her was a good idea.

"Now, we're gonna open up so's we face the same direction, placing our feet in the exact pattern as before." He let go of one of her hands, still holding the other. They danced together in a line.

"Now slide in front of me and we do the same steps together." He put his hands on her hips. "One, two, three, four, pause. Twirl around to face me and do the steps again. Good, honey. You got it! That's the Mohave Mambo." Billy laughed and pulled her to him, swinging her around and starting over again. "It's just a little variation on the Cuban version."

"Well, I never knew how to do the original mambo," she lied, "so this is all new to me."

"You're a quick learner, babe. I like that about you. The way you sing with the band, without any rehearsals is really somethin'."

"If I continue to sing with them, Billy, I might need to rehearse a little." She was carefully testing his reaction.

"You're doin' fine the way things are. You don't need rehearsals."

Billy had apologized for the other night at Russell's place and they had agreed she could sing a song with the band, now and then. But Lola knew she was skirting a touchy subject.

The record came to an end and they went back to the booth where Sherry and Ronnie were sitting. Lola kept looking at the red door every time it opened. Her stomach would do a flip flop until she recognized who came in.

"Hey, you two were great out there," Sherry said.

"Mighty fine dancin'," Ronnie agreed.

Billy shrugged good-naturedly and lit two cigarettes, handing one to Lola.

Pat came over and brought four beers. "I see Billy's taught you the Mohave Mambo. You've been accepted into the inner circle. Only the old-timers and some young ones, like Billy, know how to do that shuffle anymore."

"Why's that, Pat?" Lola asked.

"Billy'll tell ya." She collected the money and went back to the bar, carrying the empty cans.

Lola looked at Billy. "So?"

"Seems there was this Latin dancer from Cuba back in the Forties, whose car broke down in Needles. So while it was bein' fixed, he romanced the local ladies. 'Course the garage had to send to Los Angeles for parts, and that ran into several weeks. One of the things he taught the women was the mambo, but it got changed a little as the lady's memories faded, and he was long gone. They would teach it to their men and so on, until it evolved into what it is today. Not too different really, from the original." Billy took a swig of beer.

Lola was fascinated. Billy had the attention of Sherry and Ronnie, too. "I'll bet Marshmallow remembers him. Did he ever mention the Latin dancer?" Lola asked.

"Can't say as I ever heard him talk about it, but he is full of stories, so you could ask him."

"But why don't more of the locals know the dance?" Lola asked.

"Country music's mostly played here, anymore. It don't lend itself to the mambo too well."

The jukebox started playing a Patsy Cline song and the four of them got up to dance.

Ronnie and Sherry danced close, her head on his shoulder.

Billy gave Lola a quick kiss and swung her around and around in a twirl.

"You're a good dancer, Billy. I didn't realize how good until tonight." She smiled up at him.

"I'm good at other things, too."

"Yes, you are."

They continued to swing around the dance floor, the old-timers at the bar watching. Lola suddenly felt dizzy. Billy's face continued to swirl even after they stopped. His eyes floated in circles across her vision and his smile looked lopsided. She gripped his arm to steady herself as they moved back to the booth.

"You okay, babe?" he asked.

"Yeah, just a little dizzy, from all the twirling, I guess." She sat down slowly and her vision cleared.

When Ronnie and Sherry came back to the table, she took one look at Lola. "What's wrong?"

Lola shook her head, slowly. "Nothing much. Guess the spinning got to me."

"Well, you look strange. Yer white as a sheet. Sure you're okay?" Sherry persisted.

The more Sherry fussed, the worse Lola felt. Now, her stomach began to feel queasy.

"Actually, I'd like to go home, Billy, if you don't mind. I am feeling a little nauseous." She laid a hand on her belly.

Billy jumped up. "Sure babe. I'm ready. Hey, see ya later." He waved to Ronnie and Sherry as he and Lola got up to leave.

In the truck he said, "What's goin' on? You think it's somethin' you ate?"

"I really don't know. I just know I want to get home and lie down as soon as possible."

"Want me to call in and stay home?" Billy was expecting to be called to go out on the railroad in the middle of the night.

"No. You go ahead. I can be sick alone as well as with you there."

"Well, if you're gonna be sick, I'll stay home and take care of you."

Lola shook her head. She didn't like to be fussed over when she was sick. "I'll probably be fine in the morning."

⋛⋚

*B*ut in the morning she wasn't fine. Billy left on a three a.m. train for Seligman, and Lola woke up at six with a fever of 102 degrees. She took three aspirins, climbed into a tub of cold water, and finally managed to get back in bed. She slept all that day, barely aware of the sweat-drenched sheets. She'd remembered to put a pitcher of water beside her bed before she became so weak, and that had kept her from becoming dehydrated. The phone rang several times, but she didn't hear it.

Finally, around five o'clock, Sherry drove up and knocked on the front door, but found it locked. She walked around to the sliding glass door to the bedroom and opened it. Lola was shivering in a wet bed.

"My god, you're burning up with fever," she said, feeling Lola's forehead. Sherry went to the kitchen and fixed some ice cubes in a towel. She put it on Lola's forehead, holding it in place. Picking up the thermometer on the bedside table, she took Lola's temperature; 102 degrees. She brought a pan of cold water from the bathroom, stripped Lola's nightgown from her clammy body and began sponging her down. When she had finished, she put a fresh gown on her and changed the sheets. Sherry had worked as a nurse's aid at one time, and knew how to change a bed with someone in it. When she had finished cleaning Lola up, she took her temperature again. This time it was down to 100 degrees. She lifted Lola's head and placed a cup of water to her lips.

"Take a sip. Come on, Lola, drink." Lola's lips gradually moved and she swallowed. Sherry repeated this several times until Lola had finished a full cup. When Sherry became aware of the darkness moving in, she turned on the soft lamp by the dresser, went into the living room and turned on the lights in there. She found a chicken in the freezer, defrosted it in the microwave and began the long process of making chicken soup. Once the soup was on she went back to Lola and continued bathing her face and chest with cold water to bring her fever down. A few hours later, she brought a bowl of soup to the bed. Stacking the pillows behind Lola's back, Sherry pulled her into a half-sitting position.

"I want you to eat this," Sherry said, bringing a spoonful to Lola's lips.

Lola shook her head.

"Come on, honey. I made you some good soup."

Lola opened her eyes, puffy from sleep and fever. "I don't want anything," she mumbled.

"That's too bad. Cause you're eatin' this." Sherry pushed the spoon into her mouth.

She hand-fed Lola most of the bowl. By the time Lola had finished, she was actually feeling like she would live, after all.

"Thanks," Lola said, not realizing that Sherry had fed her soup with chicken in it.

Sherry smiled. "Yer welcome, sweetie. Isn't that what friends are for?"

Lola made a half-hearted attempt to smile. She did feel better.

Sherry pulled the pillows from behind her. "Now, you go back to sleep and I'll be here in the living room. Ronnie's out too, so I won't be missed."

Lola fell into a deep restful sleep for the first time in twenty four hours. She dreamed of Billy's kisses as they danced in circles under a yellow umbrella.

Billy came home at midnight to find Sherry asleep on the couch. He went into the bedroom, turned on the lamp and gently shook Lola's shoulder.

"Owwww..." Lola mumbled, as she opened her eyes. She saw Billy standing above her, still wearing his Stetson. "What?" she said.

"That's what I wanna know. Why's Sherry here again? She and Ronnie have a fight?"

Lola shook her head to try and clear it. "No. I think Ronnie's out. She came over to take care of me."

"Whadaya mean?"

"You knew I wasn't feeling well when we came home from the Tavern. After you left, I had a fever and I just stayed in bed. I can't remember too much. Next thing I knew Sherry was here, forcing soup down my throat."

"Why the hell didn't you call me in Seligman? I'm the one should of been here. I coulda dead-headed home." Billy's voice was rising.

"Shhhhh. Don't wake Sherry. I was delirious. I didn't have it together enough to call you. I barely made it to the bathroom."

Billy took off his hat and threw it on a chair. "Damn. You shoulda called me."

"Well, you're here now. Why don't you come to bed

and keep me warm. I'm cold."

"It's a little late now for me to do anything for you, ain't it?" He stomped off to the bathroom and slammed the door.

Lola could hear him running water. She began to sob, burying her face in the sheet so she wouldn't disturb Sherry. How could he be so concerned and so unfeeling at the same time? Were all men so damn insensitive, or just the ones she fell for? Her head ached and her sinuses began to drain. She reached for the tissues beside the bed and blew her nose. But the tears wouldn't stop.

Billy turned out the bathroom light and came into the bedroom in jockey shorts. He looked down at Lola sobbing into the bedcovers.

"Now why the fuck are you cryin'?" He sat on the side of the bed and put his hand on her shoulder. "Don't cry, honey, please." This time his voice was plaintive.

She turned her head and looked into his face shining in the moonlight. "Billy, I hate it when you're mad at me."

"I'm sorry I got riled so easily. I'm sorry for making you cry. I love you, Lola." He leaned down and kissed her.

Lola curled her arms around his neck and pulled him closer. "Come to bed," she said.

In the living room, Sherry heard it all and wagered that Lola would get tired of Billy's temper before he got tired of apologizing.

Three weeks had passed since the stranger had asked about Lola at the Tavern. She had told Sherry and anyone who asked why she wasn't working that she was recuperating from her bout with the flu. Lola began to relax a little, almost believing that the killer was gone. She and Sherry were headed into Needles to pick up Ronnie's truck in the Sante Fe railroad parking lot. They were approaching the intersection where their accident had occurred.

"You know, Lola. We were pretty lucky that we weren't badly hurt in that accident," Sherry said as she lit a joint and passed it to Lola.

"As I remember, I was passing you a joint when the truck hit us." Lola took a hit and handed it back.

"No, you'd handed it to me before he hit us. I was smoking it when I lost control of the MG."

"Well, whatever," Lola said. "We were damn lucky that we didn't end up in jail with that pound of weed in the car."

Lola glanced in her mirror and saw a pick-up coming up fast behind them. "Jesus. Speaking of accidents, some guy's hugging my tail."

Sherry turned around and saw the truck right behind them. The man at the wheel had a long black mane, and the arm hanging out the window was equally hairy.

"My god, that's Greg. What's he doin'?" she said.

At that moment, Greg bumped Lola's little VW, thrusting it forward. Lola instinctively stepped on the gas and pulled away from him.

"Damn! I don't think Betsy's got enough power to outrun him." Lola kept her eyes glued to the rearview mirror. The pick-up came up fast behind them and bumped Betsy again. The girls pitched forward in their seats.

"Son of a bitch!" Sherry swore. "He's tryin' to run us off the road."

"Well, he won't do it easily," Lola said. She floored the gas pedal and Betsy once again moved away from Greg's pick-up. Lola saw the Sports Lounge coming up on the right. She made a split-second decision. Slowing slightly, she veered to the right, kicking up dust as she bumped and slid into the gravel parking lot. She held the wheel and kept Betsy from turning over as they spun around in a half circle, coming to an abrupt stop.

Sherry let out her breath. "Jesus, Lola, warn me next time you're gonna do that."

Greg's pick-up flew by, not expecting Lola's maneuver. Down the road he braked, made a U-turn and headed back toward the girls.

"Looks like we can't avoid a face-to-face," Lola said. She jumped out of the car as Greg pulled up beside them, brakes squealing. Sherry came out of the VW like a shot and stormed around to Lola's side, standing beside her, arms folded across her chest. Living with Ronnie seemed to have given her the courage she'd lacked before.

Greg stepped out of the truck and trotted over to the two women.

"Guess you bitches realized you couldn't outrun me," he sneered.

"You know what you did back there was illegal," Lola said. "You can't run people off the road."

"Yeah? Guess I can do what I please. No one here but us three." He took a threatening step forward.

"If you lay a hand on either of us," Lola threatened, "I'll have you arrested and you'll land in jail, I guarantee it. I'm sure if the cops search your trailer they'd find something interesting."

"Fuck you. You don't scare me, girl."

Sherry cleared her throat and spoke for the first time. "What do you want?" she said strongly.

"I wanna give some payback, baby. You walked out on me and left me with nothin'." He squinted at her in the midday sun.

"I left you with nothin', cause we had nothin'. I only took my things."

"I didn't say you could take a whole bag of dope," Greg said.

"I stopped askin' your permission about the time I left. I bought that dope up at Oatman, with money I earned."

"Well, I want it back. I need to sell it and make some money." He stepped toward her and started to grab her arm.

Lola moved quickly between them just as Greg raised his arm.

Greg's arm stopped in midair. "You're crazy, woman. You can't stop me."

Sherry let out a piercing scream.

Immediately three men came out of the bar of the Sports Lounge and saw the two women.

One of them yelled, "Hey!" and they started to run. Greg took one look over his shoulder, jumped in his truck and peeled out of the lot just as the men arrived on the scene.

"What's going on?" one of them said.

"Nothing, now." Lola recognized one of them as a railroad friend of Billy's.

"Was he threatening you?" Billy's friend, Richard, asked.

"Not me," Lola said. "He was harassing Sherry."

"Well, guess we didn't have to rescue two damsels in distress, after all," Richard said.

"Thanks, anyway, for showing up when you did," Lola said. "I think you scared him off." Lola walked to the back of Betsy to inspect for damage.

"Yeah. Thanks, guys," Sherry chimed in.

"No damage here. It's a miracle," Lola said.

"You ladies care for a drink?" Richard asked.

Sherry started to nod, but Lola pushed her toward Betsy. "No thanks. We're on our way into Needles."

The three men smiled and Richard tipped his cowboy hat as they turned to go back into the bar.

"By the way, Richard," Lola said. "When you tell Billy, be sure to mention that it was Sherry's ex-boyfriend who was harassing her."

Richard turned around. "Sure thing, Lola."

*L*ola finally went back to work at the Tavern. Pat had her do the early shift, 7 a.m. to 3 p.m. Billy was still snoozing, his sandy hair tousled on the pillow. Lola got up and got ready quietly and met Pat at 6:45 to open the bar. It was amazing how the locals would come in that early for a drink. But there were always a few.

Lola put on her bar apron and began stocking the ice chest.

"Now don't be nervous, honey. He's long gone from here. But if he should show up, you just call and I'll be over here in a minute with my .38."

Lola had to laugh at Pat's protectiveness. Like a mother hen. But Pat's support gave her the necessary impetus to come back to work at the Tavern.

Lola had told Pat the whole story, about Tony's murder and Pat's heart went out to her. But Pat had not told Paul. And she never gave him the card from Mr. Fellino, the investigator. She had torn it into tiny pieces. Killer, Lola had called him. That had convinced her to help Lola anyway she could.

Lola kept busy with the morning chores for opening the bar. But every time the door opened she strained to see through the dim light. When she recognized the customer, she relaxed, trying to be her cordial self.

Midmorning, Billy came in, took a seat at the bar and had a beer.

"When you going out?" Lola asked.

"Not till late tonight. Want a go to the Sports

Lounge for dinner?" He gave her his charming smile.

"Sure. That would be fun."

≳≲

Lola and Billy raised their glasses and toasted their six month anniversary since they'd shared their first dinner here.

"Did you think we'd be together when I invited you to join me for dinner?"

"I didn't know. I knew you were one cocky railroader," Lola said, grinning.

"I knew what I wanted, and I wasn't about to take no for an answer." He leaned over and bussed Lola on the cheek.

Lola ordered baked fish with a baked potato and Billy had steak and fried potatoes. They had an after dinner drink, Spanish Port, and they danced to the rhythms of a local band.

Around ten o'clock Lola was about to ask Billy if they could go home. They were on the floor slow-dancing. She looked over Billy's shoulder and saw a man come into the club from the front entrance, and head toward the bar. His hair was white and close cropped. Lola's heart almost stopped.

She squeezed Billy's shoulder. "Billy. He's here." She hid her head under Billy's chin and hugged his body.

"Who's here?"

"The white haired man — the man that killed Tony!"

Billy did a half turn with Lola's back to the bar so he could see. He saw the only white-haired man with a crew cut at the bar. He was seated facing the bartender.

"He'll be asking the bartender about me. Let's get out of here."

For once Billy didn't disagree. He shielded Lola as they went back to the booth for her purse. Billy led her away to the far side of the dance floor to get to the main entrance. They hurried out to the truck. Billy got behind the wheel and sat with his keys in his hand.

"What's the matter, Billy?"

"I think I should leave you here and go inside and talk to him. I'll tell him you're not here anymore."

"No, please, Billy. He's too dangerous. Besides he'd wonder how you knew who he was. Please, Billy. Let's just go home."

Billy sat another minute. "I think I'll go in and talk to Bill, the bartender. I'll make sure he doesn't give out any information about you. I'll be right back."

"No, Billy. Don't go." She was pulling at his shirt sleeve.

Billy put his arm around her. "Lola. Trust me. I will make sure that no one here tells him anything. Just be calm and stay here." He jumped out of the truck. "Keep the doors locked."

Lola watched him disappear back into the club. She sent a silent prayer upstairs and chewed a thumbnail until it bled. She put her sweater around her shoulders and slouched down in the seat. She tried to imagine how Billy would handle the situation. Ten minutes later, Billy unlocked the door and climbed inside. He started up the engine and headed down Highway 95.

"What happened?"

Billy lit a cigarette. "I just pulled Bill aside and asked him not to tell anyone asking that you lived here. He said the guy at the bar showed a picture of you and had already asked and Bill told the man he didn't know you."

Lola let out a sigh of relief.

"See? People here in the Valley protect their own. When outsiders start asking questions, we clam up. Don't tell them nothin'."

"Billy, I have to leave. He's bound to find me if he keeps asking."

"Not so. No one's gonna tell him nothin'." He pulled Lola's finger from her mouth. "Stop chewin' on that."

"I don't know what to do. If I stay here, I'll always be lookin' over my shoulder."

Billy was silent. Finally he said, "I'll put the word out that he's a killer. No one will give him the time of day."

"But what if he comes into the Tavern when I'm working? Or runs into me at the market?"

"We're gonna make sure this guy leaves Mohave Valley thinkin' you've moved on. He's already heard that from Pat. I'll get Clyde and Leila at the Red Dog in Needles to say the same. And I'll talk to Judd at the Sundancer. He'll soon give up."

Lola wasn't completely convinced. She felt exposed, vulnerable, like when she was a child, and she was at the disposal of her father. She'd have to think about this. Whether she should keep on running — decide what was the right thing to do.

※

The white-haired man had left town. Two of Billy's friends saw him fill up at the Shell Station in Needles and head out for Las Vegas. After he hadn't been seen around the Valley in a week, Lola felt less nervous and started leaving Billy's place again.

The sun was just setting as Lola dipped the scoop into the grain barrel and carried it over to Hamburger. She opened the gate and offered it to the steer. He came up to her immediately and began eating out of the scoop. She stroked his head and rubbed his horns. The thought of this sweet docile animal being raised for Billy's meat made her shudder. Billy had said not to get attached to him as he would end up in the freezer, but of course she had. The animal was very gentle and affectionate, and started licking Lola's fingers. She couldn't be sure if it was from the molasses in the grain on her hand, or he just liked her taste. She didn't want to think about down the road, for the steer; just now. When Hamburger had finished all the grain he started nuzzling her shoulder with his nose.

"You want some more, eh?" Lola said to the steer. "Well, okay. You deserve another scoop."

She went back to the barrel and got more grain, leaving the gate open. When she turned around, the steer was right behind her. She led him back inside the gate and gave him the grain. He chomped and drooled, rolling his eyes.

Sedona whinnied as Sherry appeared in the driveway, riding Dobbin, Ronnie's swift-footed paint. She waved as she headed for the field and Lola.

"Hi. Thought I'd drop by. See if you want to go out for a bite tonight since the guys are out." She dismounted and tied Dobbin to a fence post.

"That sounds good. I have to finish feeding and get washed up." Lola gave Hamburger a final pat and locked the gate to the field.

"Want me to give you a hand?" Sherry asked, as she put Dobbin in the empty corral.

Sedona threw her head back and snorted. She knew and liked Dobbin. They stuck their heads over the railing and touched noses.

"Sure. Why don't you go to the chicken coop and collect the eggs and feed the hens. I'll feed the horses and meet you there."

"Okay." Sherry headed for the chicken pen in back. She'd done the feeding before so she knew where everything was kept. Soon Lola joined her and they finished up the chores. Lola usually wore old flip-flops for feeding and left them on the porch. Sherry had walked in some manure in the chicken pen and scraped her sandals off on the edge of the step.

"Bring them in," Lola said. "You can wash them off in the laundry sink."

Fifteen minutes later, Lola in blue jeans and clean tank top, and Sherry in shorts and tee-shirt, climbed into Betsy and headed for the highway.

Lola and Sherry had eaten at Denny's in Needles and on the way home stopped at the Tavern for a beer. Pat was behind the bar.

"Well, hi girls. Yer other halves let you out alone tonight?" Pat said.

"They're both out. Billy went to Seligman and Ronnie to Barstow," Lola said. "Since we didn't have to cook, we let Denny's do it for us."

"Hi, you two lovely ladies," Marsh said from the end of the bar.

"Hi, Marshmallow," Lola said, giving him a hug. She and Sherry sat on either side of him and Pat put two Buds on the counter.

"You want a refill, Marsh?" she said.

"Course. Have I ever said no to you, my love?" He stroked Pat's wrinkled hand.

"Not since as long as I can remember." She was thinking of all the times Paul said no to her the last few months. She went back to the bar and fixed another vodka and tonic and brought it to Marsh.

Sherry played pool with a couple of railroaders, and Lola sat next to Marsh and had another Bud. One of the guys asked Lola to play, too, but she declined. Around ten o'clock they said goodnight to Marsh and Pat and left the Tavern.

"Not a very exciting evening, Lola. We act like old married women." Sherry lit a joint and handed it to Lola.

"Well, in a way we are old married women," Lola mused.

"I don't like to think of myself like that," Sherry said. "I'm not married to Ronnie. Just living in sin." She giggled.

"When I commit to a man, I feel married, even if I'm not," Lola said, taking a drag off the joint.

"Think you and Billy will get married?" Sherry suddenly asked.

Lola thought about it for a minute. "I don't know. I don't like what it does to people. I saw what marriage did to my parents. But I do want to find a man that I can marry, someday. Just haven't decided if Billy's the one yet." She gave Sherry a soft smile.

"Do you love him, Lola?"

"I think so. Not sure about that yet either." Lola stared off in the distance. "Life has a way of taking away happiness for me. I'm almost afraid to love him."

"Yeah," Sherry said, thoughtfully. "I know what you mean."

"What about you? Would you marry Ronnie?"

"I'm not sure, either. I think I love him. But I don't know about marriage. Seems like the end of something."

"Lola pulled into Ronnie's driveway. "I'll feed Dobbin in the morning. You can come over and get him tomorrow."

"Okay."

They sat in the car finishing the joint, each with their own thoughts. The stars were bright in the black Arizona night. In the distance they could hear the call of a lone peacock. It was probably Mr. P. Then the howl of a coyote cut the soft, smooth air, as the peacock became suddenly silent.

"I never thanked you for your tender care when I was sick. Thanks for being such a good friend." Lola reached over and squeezed Sherry's hand.

"Don't give it a thought. I just did what you'd do for me. Right?"

"Right," Lola agreed, feeling very close to Sherry this night. Sherry got out and Lola waved as she backed out the drive.

≷≷

Billy and Ronnie lowered the pig wrapped in basil, cabbage leaves and aluminum foil down into the four-foot hole, placing it on a pile of glowing coals. An old car hood was lowered to cover the pig, and then they started shoveling in the dirt. It took about ten minutes to completely fill in the pit.

Ronnie stood up and rubbed the small of his back. "I'm getting too old for this sort of thing, " he complained to Billy.

"I think your suffering from too much fuckin'," Billy said, grinning. They heard the screen door bang and saw Sherry and Lola coming out of the house.

Ronnie's face reddened. "Never too much. That woman could kill me with sex and I'd be in heaven."

The girls brought four bottles of beer and a joint with them. "How long does it take for the pig to get done?" Sherry asked, handing them two bottles.

"It'll cook all night and we'll take it out tomorrow around ten. Should be just right for the party," Billy answered.

Lola sat down on a log beside the pit, handing the joint to Billy. He toked on it and passed it to Ronnie.

"Should we set up the tables tonight?" she asked.

"Naw. We can do that in the morning," Billy said. "Mr. P. would just shit all over them in the night."

Sherry giggled. "Why would he do that?"

"He loves to shit on anything new to his territory."

The four of them had a good laugh as they smoked the rest of the joint.

Billy and Lola were planning a Labor-Day party for all their friends. Chili relleno casserole, coleslaw, homemade baked bread, potato salad, rice and baked beans were some of the dishes Sherry and Lola had been cooking all day in preparation. Everyone would bring a dish and there would be more food than could be eaten. Billy and Ronnie took time off so they wouldn't be called to go out on the railroad, but many of their guests would have to go to work during the day-long party, as someone had to run the trains.

The evening had cooled off from the 110-degree day. Now the temperature beside the corrals read 90 degrees. Sedona and Apache whinnied softly and Mr. P. screeched his evening serenade as the sun sank behind the mountains.

They finished their beer and the joint, and Ronnie and Sherry climbed into the truck and went home.

The next day more than a hundred people dropped in at different times. Thirty cases of beer, seven bottles of bourbon, five bottles of vodka and gin, plus several cases of soft drinks were consumed. Fortunately, Billy had large olive trees in his front yard and the tables and chairs were set up under them. This provided the only shade. The sprinklers were turned on and splashed the brown bodies cavorting through the cool water. The hose was turned on a bevy of females in shorts molding halter tops over taut breasts.

The men dug up the pig and retrieved it from the pit by slipping a thick rope under each end. The dangerously hot car hood was raised first and carefully stored in the tack room so none of the small children would fall on it.

The aroma of cooked pork mingled with the smells of spicy Mexican food and the tartness of potato salad made with a non-mayonnaise dressing. Nothing was prepared with mayonnaise as it would sit in the hot afternoon sun for several hours. Children chased the chickens and Mr. P., and crawled into the corrals, petting Sedona and Apache. Billy saw to it that some of the small fry got to ride Apache around the corral. Russell and his band set up on the porch and played country music.

He moved over to Lola on the steps, guitar across his chest. "Come sing a song with us, lady."

Lola saw Billy pouring himself a straight shot of

whiskey. "Not right now, thanks." She smiled up at Russell.

The phone rang constantly and someone was always near it as it was the only way the railroaders would know when they were called to work.

Marsh leaned his chair against an olive tree, drinking his vodka, and was waited on by Lola and Sherry. They brought him a huge plate of food and, surprisingly, it disappeared in a short period of time. He let the little ones climb on his lap and pull his wild beard.

Pat dropped in and had a beer. "No wonder the Tavern's dead," she said, "everyone's here."

By seven in the evening, the party had thinned down to twenty or so. Lola sang a couple of numbers with the band and Billy was on his best behavior.

"Did I ever tell you what a beautiful voice you have?" he murmured in her ear.

"No, you never have."

"I love to hear you sing." They were sitting on the edge of the porch and he nuzzled her hair with his nose.

"I always thought you didn't much like me to sing."

"Oh, I guess I'm just scared that you might wanta go off to L.A. and get a singin' career."

"Well I can guarantee you that I won't do that, Billy. I'm just not interested in that kind of thing."

"Lucky for me," he said, bringing her hand to his lips.

At midnight, someone took Marsh home, who had passed out in his chair, and Sherry and Ronnie helped with the clean up. Actually, about all that really got accomplished was wrapping the food and storing it away, as Ronnie and Billy were too drunk to do much more. The tables and chairs remained under the trees all night long so Mr. P. could do his thing.

※

One night at the Tavern, Billy Jim, Ronnie, and their pals decided that Mohave Valley, Arizona, should have a rodeo. There hadn't been one for five years and the locals were getting itchy to show off their riding skills. Of course, they were all pretty well smashed by the time the details were worked out.

"Me and Glenn can drive down to Phoenix and pick up a bull," Jack Holmes said, taking a long swig of beer.

Glenn Draper, the butcher from Needles, nodded. "I'll donate a couple of calves for the calf-ropin' event," he said.

"The money we collect at the gate can cover the cost of rentin' the bull," Ronnie suggested. "Anything we have left over can go in the fund for next year."

"We're gonna have ourselves a rodeo," Billy Jim declared, tossing back his fifth can of Budweiser.

The day of the rodeo was perfect weather. Not too hot, not a whisper of a wind. The rodeo grounds were located a few miles south of Bullhead City, on the river. Around the perimeter was a quarter-mile racetrack.

Bleachers were located on one side only, as the unincorporated Valley had never managed to raise funds to build seats on the other side.

Russell had volunteered to be the announcer since he had the PA equipment. Judd, the owner of the Sundancer, once a bit actor in L.A., offered to be the clown. He'd never clowned, but thought he could get the hang of it. His job would be to distract the bull while the rider raced for safety. It could be slightly dangerous, but what the hell, he liked a little excitement in his life, now and then.

People came from Needles, Bullhead City, Laughlin, even Kingman. They brought their children, ice chests, campers, barbeques, musical instruments and dogs and made a weekend of it. Charred hot dogs and hamburgers on the grill mixed with the sweet-sour smells of spilled beer and wine. Baby diapers, two outdoor toilets, and suntan lotion vied with each other as to which was the more powerful scent.

Lola and Sherry adorned the bleachers in tank tops, shorts, sunglasses and sandals, with cowboy hats jauntily tilted over long hair. Billy Jim entered Sedona in the opening event, the quarter-mile race. Sedona was a quarter horse, so she was genetically bred for this race. However, she'd never raced before, except in a few practice runs. Ronnie entered his horse, Dobbin, smaller than Sedona, but as swift as her ancestors who had carried Geronimo and his band to many victories.

There were four other entries, all of them owned and ridden by cowboy friends of Billy Jim's. One of the high school kids from Needles played six notes on his trumpet to start the rodeo. Dut-dut-dut-dut-da-daa. There was the sound of four hands clapping; probably the kid's parents.

Russell's voice came over the microphone loud and clear. "We welcome everyone to the second annual rodeo of Mohave Valley of 1979. The first event will be the quarter-mile horse race. We have six entries." Russell read the names of the horses and their owners. "The horses are taking their positions on the track... uh oh... Sedona seems to be antsy. Billy Jim is having a little trouble getting her to face the right direction. There now, I think he's got her settled down, folks. Whoops! My Life is running back toward the stables. Easy does it. She's turned back toward the gate." Russell and the timekeeper, Old Dewey, conferred for a moment, their heads together. Then Russell's voice boomed over the mike, again. "When Dewey fires the pistol, the race is on!"

Dewey pointed the gun down between his feet and fired under the platform. Fortunately no one was beneath the bleachers. The horses bolted from the gate and headed down the track, encouraged by their riders.

"Dobbin takes the lead, folks, My Life is second, Santa Fe is in third place, Miss Daisy and Fleetfoot are kind of bunched together, and Sedona's last."

Lola and Sherry were in the third row of the bleachers on their feet, yelling and waving at Billy Jim and Ronnie.

Billy Jim leaned over Sedona but didn't seem to be pushing her.

"Coming 'round the first turn, Dobbin's still in the lead, Fleetfoot coming up on the outside into second place, and Sedona's still last," Russell reported.

Lola watched as Billy suddenly dug his heels into Sedona's sides and she sprinted forward in a great burst of energy. "Around the third turn and here comes Sedona, she's passing Miss Daisy, My Life, Santa Fe, Fleetfoot, and she's nose to nose with Dobbin. My God, looks like an upset! Yep, here she comes, folks… Sedona wins by a head!"

The crowd broke into a roar and Russell banged on the mike, his enthusiasm apparent. Billy Jim slowed Sedona down and trotted her back to the bleachers. The girls climbed down to the track and Lola reached up and hugged Billy, petting Sedona's wet neck.

"That was a fine race, honey. You did good," she said to Billy. She nuzzled Sedona's ear. "And you are as fine a horse as I've ever seen." Sedona reared her head up and down as if she were nodding. The three of them laughed.

Ronnie joined them on Dobbin. "Congratulations, Billy." He reached across the saddle and offered his hand.

Billy shook it. "Thanks pal. Couldn't a done it, if we hadn't practiced it that way."

"You mean you guys planned for Sedona to win?" Sherry asked.

"Yup," Ronnie answered. "We let Dobbin lead every time we practiced a run, and then when Billy encouraged Sedona into catchin' up, I'd hold Dobbin back and Sedona would pass him."

"Well, it sure was good strategy," Lola said. "Was it fair?"

"Course it was," Billy said, a little indignant. "Anything's fair in a horse race."

The next event was calf roping and Billy and Ronnie chose not to enter it. They said their roping needed some work.

The barrel racing followed the roping and a few young girls below the age of seventeen entered, and a cute sixteen-year-old from Needles took the best time.

There was an intermission before the big event so the bull could be unloaded and placed in the stall beside the arena. His name was Tornado and he had cost $100 to rent for the weekend. He had a ferocious reputation, having gored a rider just a few weeks ago in Phoenix.

Tornado snorted and twisted as four men coaxed him down the horse trailer ramp. When he was in the stall, they slammed the gate shut. He threw himself against the wooden sides with the rage of a captured animal, but with no room to maneuver, soon quieted down. One of the guys slipped a rope around the bull's neck and held on tight while two others slid a leather strap under his belly and secured it. When Tornado realized something was encircling his middle, he kicked the sides of the stall and tossed his head, rolling tiny, red-rimmed eyes.

Billy had a beer to get himself ready.

"Do you think that's a good idea?" Lola said,

watching him pop the can.

"Lay off," Billy snapped.

Ronnie and Sherry looked the other way, suddenly engrossed in the activity on the platform.

Russell stepped up to the mike. "Well, folks, we're just about ready to start the bull-ridin' contest. I hear we got us a pretty mean bull to ride today. We have five entries. Chuck Landon, Phil Hopkins, Jack Holmes and Billy Jim Andrews. And we got a newcomer. A cowpoke says he hails from Flagstaff. Mike Perez. Good luck to all you guys. Our first rider is Chuck Landon. He's gotta stay on the bull eight seconds. If more'n one rider accomplishes this feat, they'll each be judged on the ride. Dewey, our timekeeper, has volunteered to judge, if necessary, just as he did in the ropin' and barrel racin'. When Chuck's ready he'll signal for the gate to be opened. How's it goin' back there, boys?" Russell looked over at the bull stall and got a nod. "Okay, folks, our first rider… Chuck Landon and… Tornado!" Russell's voice bellowed over the PA system.

The gate slid open and the bull bolted from the stall, smashing against the wooden structure, trying to brush off the rider, then immediately began spinning and kicking. Chuck fell to the ground within a few yards of the gate. Judd jumped down from the fence where he was perched and rushed at the bull, enticing him with a red flag. The bull turned and charged Judd. The bar owner ran backwards into the stall, scrambling up the enclosure just as the bull swooped in, smashing his horns into the wooden slats, barely missing Judd's feet.

"Jesus Christ! Why did I ever volunteer for this job?" Judd muttered.

The second and third bull riders barely made five seconds. They both fell near the entrance to the stall. By this time the bull wasn't coaxed back so easily. Judd had to work extra hard after the bull dumped Jack Holmes. The crowd screamed and gasped and little children cried in the excitement.

Now it was Billy Jim's turn. "Be careful and good luck," Lola whispered in his ear.

He grabbed her in a bear hug and gave her a long kiss. The crowd yelled, "Go Billy!"

He climbed atop the bull stall and waited.

"Our next rider is… Billy Jim Andrews!" Russell shouted.

Billy lowered himself gently onto the bull's sweaty back, grabbing the belt with his right hand. Raising his left, he gave the signal to slide back the gate. As soon as the gate opened, Tornado stormed out of the stall, kicking and snorting as Billy dug his spurs into the animal's sides. Then the bull stopped dead on a dime, nearly loosening Billy from his seat. But Billy held on as the bull began to spin and buck. Then Tornado stopped dead again, only to reverse his spin. The animal became so enraged he lost his balance and pitched to the left, on his side. Billy saw it coming and lifted his leg, raising his butt up slightly, in the process. Too late he realized it threw him to the right too far for him to stay seated, and just before he let go, the whistle blew, signaling the end of eight seconds. Billy landed on his hip in the dirt, but jumped up quickly, raising his arms to the cheers of the crowd. Judd was right there in front of the bull, but Tornado took great offense at Billy's eight-second tenure on his back. Clumsily he got up on all fours and as Billy walked nonchalantly back to the bleachers, Tornado, head down, horns pointed straight at Billy's backside, charged. Billy had sneaked a peek over his shoulder, and broke into a run, making the fence just in time. The bull crashed into the structure where Billy's legs had been a second before. He climbed to the highest rung, bowed to the crowd, and then to the wild-eyed Tornado, who was pawing the ground, foam rolling from his nostrils.

Russell's voice came over the loudspeaker, sounding apologetic. "It looked like Billy made the eight seconds but, our judge Dewey says he raised his rear from the bull's back before the whistle, so Billy's time is seven and fifty-eight tenths seconds. Sorry Billy. Good show, though."

Billy sat down beside Ronnie. "Fuck! I don't believe it," he snarled.

Lola put her hand on his arm, but he threw it off. He leaned down and pulled another beer from the ice chest at his feet, handing one to Ronnie and opening one for himself.

Finally Judd managed to get the bull into the stall again. Tornado was definitely slowing down. He trotted into the enclosure as Judd scurried to safety.

"Our next and last rider is Mike Perez from Flagstaff. Are ya' ready, Mike?" Russell looked toward the cowboy. The rider raised his hand and the gate opened. Tornado bucked, and spun and snorted and did his stop-on-a-dime trick, but he was noticeably slower. The newcomer rode the bull as smoothly as a sidewinder traverses the desert floor. Tornado's obvious fatigue helped the cowboy, but his grace and skill kept him seated for the entire eight seconds.

The crowd rewarded the man from Flagstaff with a cool showing of applause as Russell announced, "The winner of the bull-riding contest is… Mike Perez!" He shouted the name across the arena to the stands. "Congratulations Mike. You can pick up your ten free tickets to the Needles Theater at the front gate."

Billy swore and Ronnie was silent. So were Lola and Sherry.

"Fuckin' bull! I had him," Billy said, under his breath.

※

That evening Billy, Lola, Sherry and Ronnie ended up at the Tavern. They hadn't eaten dinner and Billy and Ronnie had already put away a lot of beer. It was a Saturday night, but Lola had taken it off to go to the rodeo. Pat and Paul were both working the bar. Lola was feeling nervous as Billy's mood had gone downhill since the bull ride.

Russell and the band were in full swing. He'd asked her to sing, but she declined, knowing instinctively that it wouldn't set well with Billy. Around ten o'clock, when Lola was hoping they could call it a night, Billy insisted they dance the Mohave Mambo to a country tune the band was playing.

"Billy, I can't follow you with this rhythm. The Mambo doesn't go with country music. You said so yourself."

"Sure it does, babe." Billy was shouting over the music. "Just follow my body. I'll show ya."

He was quite drunk. Lola couldn't understand how he stayed on his feet. Just as he whirled her around the dance floor to Willie Nelson's "Crazy," a tall stranger spoke at their elbow.

"May I cut in?" he said to Lola. It was the newcomer, Mike Perez. The man who had won the bull-riding contest.

Lola was at a loss for words. "I… ah…"

"No. She's dancin' with me," Billy said gruffly, bumping the stranger's shoulder as they swung away.

When the music stopped, Lola and Billy went back to the table they shared with Sherry and Ronnie, Glenn, Jack, and several other railroaders.

"Can you believe that shit?" Billy said to the group. "That son-of-a-bitch tried to dance with my girl."

Lola was trying to figure out a way of gracefully getting Billy to go home. She sensed he was itching for a fight.

"It ain't enough that he stole the god-damn bull-ridin' contest. If Dewey's eyesight weren't so damn bad, he'd a seen that I sat the bull all the way to the whistle." Billy ordered another round of drinks, changing his to whiskey.

"Can we go soon, Billy?" Lola said, crowded at the table between him and Ronnie.

Ignoring Lola, Billy turned to Ronnie. "You saw I stuck on Tornado's back, didn't ya?"

Ronnie looked down at his beer and nodded.

The band started up with a fast tune and Mike Perez suddenly appeared at the table.

"Could I have the next dance, Miss?" he said, looking straight at Lola and ignoring the others.

Billy stood up and stepped directly in the cowboy's face. "I said before, no, and that's what I meant." So fast that no one saw it coming, Billy raised his right arm and plunged his fist into the stranger's face, punching him between the eyes with a short, quick jab. The cowboy crumpled. Jack and Glenn jumped up and caught Mike Perez by the elbows. They half-walked, half-dragged him through the throng of dancers out the red door of the Tavern. It all happened so quickly that no one else noticed. Not even Pat, whose sharp eagle-eyes never missed a thing. Her vision was obstructed by the crowd at the bar.

"Pity he didn't hear Billy the first time," Glenn said, laying the unconscious cowboy on the ground.

"Yeah," Jack agreed. "Don't wanna mess with Billy when he's drinkin'."

Inside the bar, Lola was deeply upset. She desperately wanted to get Billy home. "Can we go now?" she asked.

"What's your hurry, babe? The evening's still young. We got lots more dancin' to do."

They closed the Tavern that night at 2 a.m. Lola drove home because Billy was passed out beside her. She couldn't get him out of the truck, so she left him there. Sometime in the early hours of the morning, she heard him stagger into the house and fall into bed, fully clothed.

※

*L*ola studied the map while Billy maneuvered the twisting mountain road. They were deep in the White Mountains, pulling Billy's trailer behind his pick-up. Six inches of snow had fallen the night before, so the tall pines along the road were encrusted with several inches of fluffy drifts. Up ahead, above the trees, a lone eagle soared on icy currents, then landed on the highest treetop. The branches swayed with his weight, knocking snowballs to the forest floor. Lola loved snow, but had little experience with it. Billy had traveled up here many times to Pine Top and knew the territory.

"Ya don't have to look on the map, babe. I know where we're goin'." He looked over at her and grinned.

"I know you do. I just love to look at maps. Always have," she said. "Guess it's the wanderlust in my soul."

"Hey, aren't you the poetic one?" he joked.

"Would it surprise you to know I used to write poetry? Well, actually I tried putting words to music."

"I'm not surprised at anything you've done, honey."

They had entered the town of Pine Top and Billy pulled into a gas station in the center of town to fill up the truck.

Lola got out and went to the restroom. She was excited about their trip up here to the mountains. She loved to camp, even though she hadn't done much since she was a kid, and never in the snow. The warmth of the small trailer and a place to cook and sleep made her feel comfortable about the trip. The coldness was a relief from the 110-degree weather down in Mohave Valley. Billy seemed to unwind and relax during the drive. They were having fun together, after weeks of heavy drinking by Billy and a constant feeling of uneasiness in Lola. Billy had taken a week of his two weeks vacation from the railroad to come up here, and she had arranged with Pat to be gone from the Tavern.

When she climbed back into the truck, she pulled her fleece-lined jacket tightly around her. Billy lit two cigarettes and passed one over. They headed for a campground about ten miles beyond Pine Top on the Apache Indian Reservation. The Mescalero-Apaches owned and operated the campground and this was where Billy had camped for years. When they entered the gate, a tall, lean Indian took their twenty-dollar entrance fee for the week and gave them a sticker for their vehicle, nodding to Billy as if in recognition. He also gave them a map and showed them where the restrooms were and the garbage cans and some literature on how to treat the bear. The gatekeeper explained that in April the bear in the White Mountains came out of hibernation. This year, however there had been a freak snow storm in July which nipped the blackberries on the vine. He reminded them to be sure to keep all their food in the trailer, as an occasional bear wandered in and loved to steal the camper's food.

"Bear? You didn't tell me there were bear up here?" Lola said, alarmed.

"They won't hurt you as long as you don't have any food on you," Billy said.

"But Billy, I thought I'd cook outside on the Coleman stove instead of in the trailer."

"You can. When you see a bear just run like hell for the door and lock it." He couldn't keep a straight face any longer and broke into a big grin.

"You think you're scaring me? Well, you are."

"Seriously, babe. If you should see a bear, take cover or make a lot of noise. They'll usually run away unless you have food in your hand. Then you'd better drop the food and run. They can be dangerous."

"Thanks for warning me before we got here. Maybe I would have opted for Sante Fe for a vacation." She threw him an exasperated look.

There were few campers at the campground. Billy found a site away from the main gate and parked, unhitched the trailer, and leveled it with a block of wood. He unpacked the tarp for the doorway and set it up.

Lola went inside, folded up the table and moved the cushions into a bed, putting clean sheets down and a heavy comforter. She stepped into her new deerskin boots with the fur trim. Then she took a cold bottle of champagne from the cooler and two plastic glasses from the cupboard. Finding a chunk of cheese and crackers in a shopping bag, she carried everything outside, where Billy had set up the lawn chairs and a small table. The snow crunched beneath her heels like a mouthful of granola. Billy popped the cork and poured the champagne.

"Here's to us," she toasted, raising the glass to her chilled lips.

Billy winked. "And to many *more* vacations," he said, kissing her.

They sat in the chairs as the light faded to a medium gray. Toward the west above one of the ridges, a muted pink brushstroke bled into the sky like a Charles Reid watercolor. The forest was still, except for the cawing of a few crows overhead. The smell of woods and campfires and pine needles lulled Lola into sleepy contentment. A peacefulness enveloped them, like lovers after coupling. Billy held her hand as they sat quietly at the edge of the great pines.

※

*L*ola heard the bear before she saw it. A low, guttural rumble came from the other side of the bush where she was picking blackberries. Her hand froze in midair as her brain registered the sound. Oh God! Slowing retracting her arm, she started to back up. She glanced behind her to see if she had a clear space. When she turned back, a large black bear standing on his haunches to his full stature faced her on the other side of the bush. His growl became louder and deeper. Lola dumped the berries from the tin pan she was holding and banged on it with her open palm. The rings on her fingers clanged against the tin bottom. The noise was sharp, unexpected, and loud. The bear ceased his growling, turned tail and ran back into the forest. Shaking so hard she had trouble moving her legs, she ran the other way toward camp, a few hundred yards away. When she was within sight of the trailer, she could see Billy sitting beside the campfire, smoking a cigarette.

He looked up and saw her coming in for the finish. "Pretty fair race you just won. Who you competin' against?"

Lola stopped and caught her breath. "The bear! I saw a huge bear back there by the blackberry bushes."

"Were you tryin' to pick the berries?" Billy asked.

Lola nodded, still breathing hard.

"I forgot to tell you, they love blackberries. Best not to pick their dessert."

She looked down at him, annoyance on her face. "You know, Billy, you have a way of not telling me things until after the fact. You could have let me know before I went out for a walk."

He smiled, flicking his cigarette into the fire. "You didn't say where you were goin'. You tend to go your own way and don't ask my advice, much."

"Okay. You've made your point. I'll try letting you know where I'm going next time." She sat down and lit a cigarette, her hands shaking, her face clammy hot in spite of the cold.

"How'd the bear react when he saw you?" Billy asked.

"Well, how do you expect? He growled and looked

like he wanted to eat me up."

Billy laughed. "Not likely. Just me likes to eat you up, little girl." He patted her thigh. "Bears are vegetarians. They don't eat meat. He wouldn't like the taste of you."

"Well, you could have fooled me." Lola managed a smile. "I scared the hell out of him by banging on the bottom of the tin pan."

"Good girl. Did just what I told ya'. Wanna' go for a walk?"

"Walk? I nearly got bear-hugged on my last walk."

"You'll have me this time. I'll protect ya baby." Billy slid his arm around her waist.

"What did you have in mind?" Lola asked.

"Oh, I'll show you some other wildlife down by the river. Maybe we'll see a buck or a mountain lion."

"You know, Billy, this campground has more pitfalls than New York City." She giggled in spite of her recent scare.

"Naw. You'll have your buck knife and me by your side. You'll be safe, I promise."

Lola stood up. "Okay, big boy. Lead the way."

Billy put the food and glasses in the trailer and they walked arm and arm down to the river.

※

*P*aul lifted Honey, the Pekinese, off his chest and threw another beer can across the room into the kitchen, hitting the wall before it dropped into the garbage. Damn! He hadn't had any luck finding out a thing about Lola. He'd called the Vegas police and they said she was a missing person but wouldn't give out any more information on the phone. Said he'd have to come in and talk to a detective. He didn't tell the police that Lola was working at the Tavern. Figured it would complicate things since they thought she was missing. He didn't much like police and decided it wouldn't be a good idea to go to Vegas to talk to them. Her last place of employment knew nothing either; or wouldn't talk about her. His attempt to smear her reputation had failed. Stupid Dewey wouldn't carry the gossip he'd fed him. What could he do to get back at that bitch?

He knew she and Billy Jim were vacationing in Pine Top and they had left Sherry and Ronnie in charge of feeding the animals. He'd driven by their place yesterday and everything looked quiet. Lola's VW was sitting in the driveway. Something in Paul's brain began to connect. That's it! Her car! He'd set fire to her car. Then she'd really be pissed off when she got home. He'd heard her refer to the VW as Betsy. Like her car was a fuckin' woman. Well, he'd have the last laugh.

He climbed into his soiled pants and shirt, put on his shoes and went to the bathroom, giving his hair a quick comb-through. Pat was working the evening shift. He didn't have to relieve her until ten o'clock. So he could sneak over to Billy Jim's place, set the fire and be back in time to go behind the bar.

Stopping by the shed in back, he picked up a can of gasoline and some rags. Then he backed his jeep out of the side driveway so he wouldn't run into any Tavern customers. It only took a minute to get to Billy's place. He decided to park down the road and walk up to the property. If anyone noticed his jeep there afterwards he'd say he ran out of gas. He carried the gas can and put the rags in his back pocket. When he got to Billy's one of the horses reared its head and whinnied. The other horse snorted and pranced around the corral. A loud chatter of clucking came from the henhouse, even though they were all bedded down for the night. From somewhere behind the house a piercing cry from a peacock shattered the stillness, making Paul jump. He poured a splash of gas onto the rags, then walked to the VW and tried the doors. Both of them were locked. Guess he'd have to break a window. He left the gas-soaked rags beside the car and went to the haystack looking for a tool. He found a hay hook, carried it back to Lola's car and swung it against the side window. The glass broke, and a piece fell on his arm.

"Goddamn it," he muttered, as he picked glass from his skin. Just then, an old pickup came barreling down the gravel road, a spotlight wavering all over the place. Paul ducked behind Lola's car. The truck stopped and trained its light over toward the VW. Then Marsh opened the truck door and staggered over to the fence. He hummed a little bit of a tune as he directed his stream along the fence post. "Dum, dum de-dum," he sang, off key. Marsh shook himself, stuffed his ancient manhood back in his pants, and zipped his fly. He looked at Lola's car, sitting in the shadows just beyond the spotlight. Crouched behind the car, Paul shifted his weight slightly, as he felt a leg cramp coming on. Against the bright moon, Marsh saw a shadow by the VW move, then he noticed the gas can on the ground. He shook his head to be sure he wasn't seeing things. Sure enough. The can was still there.

"Who's there?" he shouted across the fence into Billy's yard.

Paul stayed low and swore to himself.

"Well, by God you'd better answer else I'll have to call the sheriff. Ya' got no business here with Billy and Lola gone."

Paul kept his silence.

"Okay. You was warned." Marsh stumbled back to his truck, climbed in and took off down the road.

Shit! Paul thought. What was that old geezer doin' goin' home this early? He never left the Tavern before closin' time. Just as he was gonna get that bitch, his plan failed again. He'd better not stick around in case Marsh really did call the sheriff. He jogged back to his jeep, puffing all the way, jumped in and drove back to the Tavern. Only when he got inside his apartment did he remember he had left the gas-soaked rags and gas can beside Lola's car. Christ! He was getting careless. He didn't think the gas can could be traced back to him, but he wasn't sure. Paul felt tension begin to form in his gut. His palms were sweaty and he was short of breath. Better be more careful from now on. He'd get that bitch yet! Trying to calm himself down, he walked over to the Tavern to relieve Pat.

*P*at left the Tavern after Paul came in. She entered their apartment and hung her sweater in the closet. Glancing at an old cardboard box on the top shelf, her attention was drawn to a maroon album sticking out. Pulling the box from the shelf, she dropped it to the floor, poking through the contents. She found two old books of her mother's — and a dried rose packed in a plastic container. A yellow tie that Paul had worn to her senior prom was tucked neatly next to the books. By the time of her prom, she and Paul were engaged and her parent's estate had been settled. It had been hard for her to finish high school after the death of her parents in the car accident, but Paul, who lived next door, had been so supportive, and later affectionate, and then introduced her into the magic of making love. Those days had been very nice. How had it gone so wrong — Paul addicted to smut magazines, and herself ignoring the entire situation?

She pulled the album out of the box and went to the couch, flopping down into the deep cushions. The first page showed a black and white snapshot of Paul with her the night of the prom. Her uncle had taken it and it was slightly out of focus. But it was clear enough for her to see the sweet glow of a sixteen-year-old, and the big smile on Paul's face. They had made love that afternoon on his double bed. She had taken a while to really get into it, and that was the first time he had brought her to orgasm. She remembered she suddenly really liked having sex. After that Paul had said, "Just relax, baby, and I'll do all the work." She hadn't been sure what he did down there in those days, she was so naive, but he had certainly known what to do.

At the dance, she had felt like a fairy princess, in her pink organza dress that her mother had made for her months in advance (in preparation for the prom.) And her friends had been envious that her date and fiancé was a mature man, all of twenty-six years old.

Her eyes dropped to the photo at the bottom of the page. The morning of her wedding she and Paul had elected to elope to Denver, the nearest large town. The justice of the peace had performed the ceremony and she recalled Paul asking the justice's wife to take their picture. This was a much better shot. Very clear, with the mountains surrounding Denver in the background. Pat had on a white linen suit with one red rose pinned to her lapel, and Paul was attired in his beige suit and the same yellow tie he had worn to the prom. It went well with his blond hair; brought out all the highlights. She looked closely at him. He appeared happy. Not a hint of his later strange personality and disgusting habits. The opposite page held more wedding photos that Pat had asked one of the witnesses to take. Each one mirrored a happy couple.

She turned the page. Paul had joined the Navy and had been stationed briefly at Point Hueneme in California. Both sides of the pages held photos of their life there. They had lived on base and Pat had worked as a secretary. They had been happy then, too. Then Paul had been sent to Germany and for some reason she didn't go with him. It was the late forties and the U.S. was rebuilding that country after the second world war, and Paul hadn't been too eager for her to join him. So she stayed in California, and after two years, he returned home and didn't re-up. That was the point when she first realized Paul had changed toward her, but it was understandable since they had been separated for so long. They had some good years and some bad years. Paul had sold insurance for a living. The loss of her pregnancy in the seventh month had taken its toll. She had grieved deeply and when Paul had said to her, "It was probably for the best that the baby died," she was horrified and took a long time to forgive him. She wouldn't let him touch her for months, and that was when he started going out at night without her. Still, they seemed to get along okay after she got over the loss of the baby, falling into a safe and humdrum existence. There had never been any more pregnancies. Then five years ago they were vacationing in Arizona and saw the Tavern for sale, and Paul thought it would be a good investment. She remembered one of her favorite TV programs of years back. This Is Your Life. Her entire adult life was contained in this photo album. She fanned the pages, getting glimpses of her and Paul's life. Not much for thirty-four years of marriage. These last four years she'd just barely hung on. The smut magazines, his distance toward her, the secretiveness, his pathetic attempts at sex. Damn him! He ruined the promise of their marriage!

 She closed the album and looked down at it in her

lap. Her brown and weathered hand, full of age spots, rested on the cover. She suddenly visualized her hand on her wedding day, soft, white, and without a wrinkle. She'd never had an inkling then that her life would feel as sad to her as it did at this moment.

≳≲

Sherry and Ronnie were sitting at the kitchen table smoking a joint. The dinner dishes were stacked to one side and Sherry had placed a dish of ice cream in front of Ronnie.

"Thanks, honey." Ronnie alternated between the joint and the dessert.

There was a loud knock at the front door. Ronnie put out the joint, waved a newspaper through the smoke, and got up to see who it was. He opened the door and saw Marsh standing under the porch light.

"Jeez, sure glad you're home, Ronnie. I just saw someone down at Billy's place, sneakin' round."

"Who was it?" Ronnie asked, holding the door open for Marsh.

"Well, I didn't see who, but there was a shadow by Lola's car and a gas can on the ground." Marsh came in puffing heavily, and took off his old canvas hat. "Hi, Sherry."

"Hi, Marsh. Sit down."

Marsh sat down at the kitchen table.

"Guess I'd better run down there and see what's going on." Ronnie grabbed his keys. "Give Marsh some ice cream, honey. I'll be back in a jiffy." He went out to the truck and took off.

"How come you're travelin' this time of night, Marsh?" Sherry asked. "You're usually still at the Tavern." She dished up some ice cream and set it in front of him.

"Yeah. I wasn't feelin' so good, so I decided to head home." He picked up the spoon and halfheartedly stirred the ice cream.

Sherry watched. "What's wrong, Marsh. You sick?" She knew for a fact that Marsh loved ice cream.

"Well, kind of." Marsh looked up at her from under his thick brows. "Actually, I've been feelin' poorly, lately."

"Have you been to the doctor?" Sherry asked.

Marsh nodded and looked down at the dish again.

"Well, what did he say?" Sherry wasn't letting him off the hook.

Marsh looked up and met her eyes. "He did some tests and said I had a brain tumor."

Sherry tried not to look shocked. "Well, what treatment is he gonna give ya'?"

"Ain't nothin' he can do about it. Too far along." Marsh tried to eat a spoonful of the ice cream. The coldness in his mouth made his head throb like a toothache.

"Oh, Marsh." Sherry placed her hand over his.

He had put down the spoon, giving up on the dessert. "It's okay. I've had a good trip. Time to go, now."

Tears appeared in Sherry's eyes.

"Don't you be feelin' bad. And keep this to yerself. Can't stand anymore fawnin' over me. Makes me even sicker."

"Lola would want to know," Sherry said, wiping her eyes.

"She's got enough to deal with, Billy Jim and all. Don't want her worryin' 'bout me."

They heard Ronnie's truck come in the driveway. When he walked in the house he had a gas can in his hand. "I found this beside Lola's car," he said. "Also found some rags soaked with gasoline. I left them out on the porch." He walked back through the door and placed the gas can beside the rags. "Her side window was broken. Looks like someone tried to set her car on fire. I'm callin' the sheriff." He went to the phone and dialed, explained to the deputy and hung up. When he turned back to Marsh and Sherry he looked at her carefully, and then at the melted ice cream in front of Marsh.

"What else is wrong?" he asked, softly.

Sherry looked at Marsh.

"Well, hells, bells. I didn't wanna tell nobody, but I just spilled the beans to Sherry." He turned around and looked at Ronnie. "Got me a brain tumor. Looks like I'll be checkin' out soon. I don't want anyone else to know, Ronnie. Sherry caught me in a moment of weakness." He struggled to his feet. "Guess I'll go on home and lay down. If'n the sheriff wants to talk to me, he can come on up to my place."

Sherry jumped up. "Now, Marsh. You come in on

the couch. You can lie down here, just as well. I'll fix you some hot soup. I made a pot today."

Ronnie's face betrayed his feelings. "Sorry, Marshmallow. I mean about the tumor. But, yes, stay here until the sheriff comes. Then I'll take you home."

Marsh let himself be led to the couch by Sherry. He suddenly didn't have the energy to get back in his truck. Sherry put a pillow behind his head, and then she went to the stove to heat up the soup.

Ronnie lifted Marsh's legs up on the couch with his shoes on. He'd known Marsh since he'd been a small boy. Marsh had been a colorful fixture in his life for as long as Ronnie could remember. He couldn't imagine what it would be like without Marshmallow around.

※

Billy and Lola had just returned from their mountain vacation. Lola stood in the center of Billy's living room with the sheriff.

"Can you think of anyone that might have a grudge against you?" Sheriff Del asked. "Enough to want to set your car on fire?"

Christ, she thought. That asshole Paul doesn't give up. "Not really," Lola said. "I don't think I've made any enemies in the Valley. At least, not that I'm aware of." She smiled at him with all the charm she could muster, her dimples flashing.

"Well, it shore looks like someone was targetin'

your car, and not Billy's place. Anyone in Vegas got it in for you?"

He mustn't check her out in Vegas. "No. Can't think of anyone there either." She tried to speak convincingly.

"Any old boyfriends or angry ex-husbands?" Del persisted.

"Never been married. I always try to leave them laughing," she joked, managing a little giggle.

Del laughed, too. "Well, you let me know if anything else strange happens around here. Okay, Lola?"

Lola nodded. "Sure will. And I'll tell Billy when he gets in off the railroad."

"That was my next question, where Billy was. You take care now."

Del went out the screen door and climbed into his sheriff's car. He backed out and headed toward the River Highway.

She'd just about gotten over being nervous every time a stranger entered the Tavern. Now she had a new worry. Of course, it could have been Greg trying to pay her back for his latest humiliation at the Sports Lounge. But, no, her gut feeling said it was Paul. Damn! She thought she was finished with him.

※

*T*he wind was hot. It was not yet noon and the sun was already scorching the dry earth. Billy, Ronnie, and Glenn, the butcher who lived across river, had been drinking Bud Lite all morning. They were hanging out by the horse corrals, getting up steam for the job ahead. Billy was sitting on a bale of hay, finishing the second six-pack, and Ronnie and Glenn were getting the horse trailer ready. They intended to load Hamburger, the steer, into the trailer and transport him over to Glenn's place, where the butcher would slaughter him and hang him for a couple of weeks in his cold shed, before cutting him up and packaging the meat. Billy threw the beer can on the ground and strode to the field, opening the gate. He offered Hamburger a scoop of grain, and the steer came trotting up. While the animal was eating, Ronnie slipped a rope around Hamburger's neck and started pulling him out of the gate toward the trailer. Billy kept the scoop of grain just beyond the steer's nose so that he followed obediently. When they arrived at the trailer, Glenn had laid a ramp down so Hamburger could be led up easily. But the steer took one look at the set-up and balked. Billy tried coaxing him with more grain, but no luck, so they began pulling and pushing him, twisting his tail to make him load.

Lola watched from the big bay window. She was glad they were taking Hamburger to Glenn's place. She didn't want to witness the steer's end. She saw the color come into Billy's face and his mouth curl. She saw all the signs of his rising anger, but she wasn't prepared for what happened next.

Before Ronnie or Glenn could stop him, Billy, frustrated at the stubbornness of the animal, jumped in his truck and backed it up to the trailer. He took the rope around

Hamburger's neck and tied it to the bumper, then jumped back in the truck and started it up with a jolt. He took the curve of the circular driveway in a skid. Hamburger stayed on his feet at first, but soon fell on his side and was dragged around and around the driveway. He snorted and moaned, and finally when Billy stopped and got out, all three men helped the steer to his feet. He staggered and stumbled and then fell again to the ground. The hide was completely torn from his left side, exposing pink, bleeding flesh. The steer laid his head down on his forelegs quietly, a small dust cloud settling over him. Sedona and Apache were excited and paced back and forth in their corrals, Sedona whinnying in a high-pitched scream.

"You shoulda let me get my prodder," Ronnie said, taken aback at what Billy had done. The three men stood together, deep in consultation.

Lola felt sick. She couldn't believe what she had just seen. Coming out of her shock, she bolted out the front door.

"You asshole," she screamed. "Look what you've done to Hamburger."

She ran to the steer and knelt down, touching his face. His eyes were open, bugged and frightened, the blood vessels broken, his eyes filling with blood. Lola stood, her hands balled into fists at her sides. Sweat gathered on her forehead, her face contorted. She was shaking. "You bastard! I hate you. How could you do that?"

Glenn stood back, shocked at her outburst. Ronnie felt awful at what had just happened. But he couldn't quite bring himself to put the blame on Billy. Billy faced Lola, his mouth a thin line, his eyes hard.

Lola turned and ran into the house, slamming the door. She threw herself on the couch, sobbing, rocking back and forth, holding her sides. But she couldn't stay away from the bay window.

After more discussion the three men half-carried and dragged Hamburger by the rope to the edge of the field. Glenn said the steer's flesh would be tough if they didn't slaughter him immediately. They tied his back feet to a hoist that the butcher had loaned Billy several months ago, and lifted him into the air so that his head was just off the ground. The steer swung back and forth, continuing to moan, his legs wildly kicking in the hot Arizona morning.

Then Glenn took a knife from his truck and slit Hamburger's throat. At first, the blood poured like a waterfall from the severed artery onto the ground covered with hay. Then gradually it slowed to an even drip as the life force seeped from the steer's body.

From the window Lola saw it all, sobbing hysterically. She lay down on the couch, holding her shirt across her eyes. She thought she could smell the blood even in the house. It was all she could do to keep from gagging and losing her breakfast.

Glenn backed his truck up to the hanging steer and the three of them loaded the carcass into the truck and Glenn drove away. Ronnie thought it best to leave, too.

Billy came inside, slipping off his bloody boots at

the door, leaving them on the porch.

Lola was balled up in a fetal position on the couch. He came over to her and looked down at her red, stricken face. "What went on out there was farm business." His voice was soft. "Sometimes you have to deal with animals that way. I'm sorry it upset you." He seemed unsure, hesitant, then lowered his hand to her shoulder and touched it. She jumped as if he had struck her. "Don't you touch me, you...bastard!" She looked up at him with swollen eyes.

"I wasn't being cruel, Lola. That was the only language that steer understood." He stooped down on his haunches to be even with her face.

She raised up and slapped him across the shoulder, knocking him off balance, so that he sat down hard on the rug.

"All right. Have your fuckin' tantrum. Hamburger's on his way to gettin' cut up. In a few weeks he'll be in our freezer. So you better wake up to the reality of the fuckin' world, girl." Billy stood up and went to the refrigerator, took out a Bud and flipped the cap. He stomped off to the bathroom and Lola could hear the shower running.

Her sobs became hiccups. She mourned Hamburger, her friend. Of course, she'd known Billy had always intended him for meat in his freezer. Becoming attached to an animal could have its down side. But torturing it was unforgivable. She felt her love for Billy slowly drain from her heart.

⋛⋚

*B*illy rolled over, and opened his eyes, squinting at the morning sunlight filtering through the bedroom blinds. Somewhere within his brain he could hear a roaring sound, much like the engine of a train when it pulls out of the station. He could smell coffee coming from the kitchen. Then he remembered he was in Seligman. Billy had been called just as Ronnie got into Needles. So who the hell was making coffee? He froze as he heard a female voice humming. He knew it wasn't Lola. She never drove up here. Besides, this was a rich alto, chanting in a sing-song rhythm. Oh Christ! What had he done?

Neva, the Yavapi Indian girl poked her head around the doorway with a cup of steaming coffee in her hand. "Hi, sleepyhead. Thought you'd never wake up. Boy, you tied one on last night. How you feel this morning?" She giggled as she put the cup on the table beside him.

The headache came full force upon him then, like a locomotive smashing through a plate glass window, pounding his frontal lobe, as pistons attacked the inside of his skull. "Oh God!" he moaned, sitting up slowly and reaching for the coffee. How could he have been so drunk that he'd brought her home? He'd done this before, many times, but not since Lola lived with him. Jesus! Better lighten up on the booze from now on. He couldn't remember a thing about last night.

"Did you stay all night?" he asked, tentatively, as

he sipped the coffee.

"Course, silly, what you think?" She slipped off her robe and climbed naked into the other side of the bed, sliding down next to him, clasping her plump arm around his thigh. Her full breasts fell heavily against his hip.

"Now, don't be expectin' anything. My head is killing me." Billy rubbed his forehead as if that would help. "Any aspirin around this place?"

Neva reluctantly got out of bed and found a bottle of Bayer on the chest. She handed him three aspirins and climbed back in bed. He took them with a slug of coffee, praying he hadn't fucked up all the way.

"Did we...uh...get it on, last night?" he asked her.

Neva cuddled his arm. "No honey. You was too drunk. Jack Kelly had to help me walk you over here from the bar."

Oh shit, Billy thought. Could it be any worse? Well, yes. He coulda' fucked her. The bad news was that Jack knew she spent the night. He'd better get to him before he told anyone else on the railroad. If it got back to Lola... Billy got a little nauseous at the thought of her being hurt. And she would probably leave him. Things had just gotten back to normal with her since the awful scene with Hamburger. She'd almost forgiven him.

"Feelin' better now?" Neva asked as she stroked his limp penis.

"No, I don't. I feel rotten. I'm not up to anything right now," Billy said. "Why don't you go home, because I need to check-in and see when I'll be called." Billy picked up the phone next to him and dialed the station to see where he was in the lineup.

Neva took her hand away from his genitals, but didn't move.

When Billy hung up he realized she was still beside him. "Did you hear me? I'm goin' back in an hour. I need to get cleaned up. Git out of here." He spoke a little harsher than he meant to.

Neva started to cry, her hand covering her mouth.

"Now whatcha cryin' about? Come on, stop."

She continued to make little whimpering sounds like a lost puppy.

Billy turned over and loosely put his arm around her, patting her back. "For Christ's sake, Neva. Don't cry. I should have told you before. I have a girlfriend now, back home. I didn't mean for you to spend the night. I don't know how this happened."

Neva stopped crying and opened her eyes, looking up at Billy. Her wet lashes glistened as a ray of sun sneaked in through the blinds, flashing across her brown face. She was quite pretty, Billy thought. Long black hair and big black eyes.

"You mean you don't want me to stay over anymore?" her voice was thick with tears.

"Yes. That's exactly what I mean." Billy began to feel a little relieved. Perhaps he could get himself out of this mess, after all. He didn't want to hurt her, but he really didn't want Lola to hear about this.

She slipped from the bed and began dressing. When

she had put on her shoes and sweater, she left the room quietly and let herself out the front door. Billy released a big sigh, staggered out of bed, and headed for the shower.

Part 3
Losses and Gains

*R*onnie boarded the train in Needles and stowed his gear in the locker. His brakeman, Phil Horton, a long-time acquaintance and drinking buddy, climbed aboard and put his grip in the locker next to Ronnie's.

"Hey, man. How's it goin?" Phil greeted him.

"Hated to get out of bed this mornin'," Ronnie answered, remembering Sherry's sweet kisses as she flung her arms around his neck in a good-bye hug. Then she'd snuggled all sleepy warm under the covers, her eyes shut tight against the coming dawn.

"Yeah, know whatcha mean. My old lady was all ready, when the phone rang," Phil said with a wicked grin, interrupting Ronnie's reverie.

Ronnie grinned back as he zipped up his down-lined jacket and took his seat at the controls. The desert could be very cold in the early morning hours. Ronnie had opted for Barstow this trip, instead of Seligman. He figured Billy would probably be coming home from Seligman about now. The engine was already warmed up in preparation for heading out of the station. Pulling the train whistle twice, he waved to a couple of railroaders going off duty. His mind wandered back to the woman asleep in his bed. He was so in love he hardly cared about his life when he wasn't with her. He tried to let her know his feelings, but she wouldn't let him say the words. Every day he assured her she could stay with him as long as she wanted, while he built up the courage to ask her to marry him. But, he knew it was too soon; Sherry had only been living with him six weeks. He was a man smitten, no longer logical or practical. He only knew he wanted her with him, always.

He thought of Billy and Lola. They seemed to be very much in love and enjoying themselves, except for sometimes when Billy drank too much. He envied Billy. He had always admired and looked up to him ever since they'd started hanging out together. 'Course, Lola was mighty pissed off at Billy lately. It was a fact of life, that when you raised a steer for meat, it's gonna be your dinner. But Billy's rage had gotten out of hand that day. Yeah, that business with the steer had caused a lot of trouble.

Ronnie surveyed the rock formations that characterized the beginning of the high desert as dawn broke over the tops of the ridges. Up ahead, the tracks meandered between the foothills like a black ribbon. He sniffed the air. Besides the train smoke, he caught a whiff of wood smoke. Someone probably cooking an early breakfast over an open fire. He could almost smell the bacon.

Phil entered the engine cab and sat down behind Ronnie. He yelled over the chugging of the engine. "Checked the cables on the cars before we left. All's well." He pulled a joint from his pocket and lit up.

Taking a deep drag he passed it to Ronnie who took a long pull on it, then passed it back.

"We'd better be careful," Ronnie said. "I hear the inspectors' been boardin' trains in the middle of runs."

"Shitttt... I'll eat the joint before they get on board. They can't prove anything." Phil smirked as he took another hit.

Ronnie kept his eyes on the rails. "Just warnin' ya. Billy got stopped a week ago. Fortunately, no one was holdin'. You know, they can make you do a urine test."

"Don't think that would stand up," Phil said. "Pot stays in the urine 24 hours or more, so they couldn't prove anyone smoked on the job." He finished the joint and ate the roach.

"If they find grass in yer urine, you can bet your booty you'll get fired," Ronnie shouted over the engine noise. "Smokin' pot any time's against the law."

Suddenly, in the distance, Ronnie saw something on the tracks. A large, dark shape loomed against the early morning light. He shook his head, thinking it was a mirage. According to his dispatch information, the only other train headed his way was supposed to be side-tracked. At first he couldn't believe his eyes. Then, when he did believe it, he yelled, "Jesus, Phil! Look! There's another train on our tracks!"

Phil leaned forward and looked out the front window of the train. About a mile ahead, a full-loaded freight was barreling toward them. "Jesus Christ! What we gonna' do?" He stood up and held onto the back of Ronnie's seat.

Ronnie's first thought was of Sherry. He saw her as he had left her. Blond hair tossed across the white pillow, yellow as corn silk. Then his vision focused immediately outward on the tracks ahead. He knew he couldn't take a chance on a head-on. He put in a quick call to the dispatcher back in Needles, reporting the situation.

"Ron Webb reporting another train on tracks headed toward me. Time: 6:45 a.m. Gonna' avoid a head-on." Jumping the tracks wasn't easy, but he could do it. He knew he wouldn't get an answer in time. He pulled the cord and blew the high-pitched whistle of the train; its scream across the high plains a warning of the impending disaster. Even the vultures and crows seemed alarmed, circling above Ronnie's cab, as the two trains sped toward one another.

※

Billy Jim got off the train in Needles and headed for the station office. When he entered he noticed several railroaders bunched around the dispatcher. He reached for his time card and punched out.

"What's happening, Ben?" Jack Holmes, a brakeman addressed the dispatcher, Ben Hagan. "We heard the 215 went off the track to avoid an oncoming. What's the scoop?"

Ben looked up from his desk. "That's right. Looks like both trains are in bad shape. Got a rescue truck there and an engine on the way."

Billy's attention was glued to the board above the dispatcher's head, listing all trains that were on the track.

"Can you tell us what happened?" Jack persisted.

"Near as we can tell," Ben said, "the freight heading east that was supposed to be on a side rail, wasn't. The 215 was headed west, for Barstow. Don't know much more than that, right now."

Several of the railroaders going off duty watched the board silently. Others left the office and headed home. Train wrecks didn't happen often, but when they did, it was bad news for the railroad. The trains were delayed until the tracks were fixed and the debris cleaned up, and that meant time out of work, but more than that, it meant injuries and sometimes fatalities.

Billy pushed up to Ben's desk. "Is Ronnie Webb on his way to Seligman?"

Ben consulted his roster. He looked up at Billy. "No, Ronnie was on the 215."

Billy fell back in the crowd as the men pushed forward to find out the identity of the other men on the wrecked trains. Ronnie didn't often choose to go to Barstow. He must have wanted the extra money for the longer run. Jesus! This was the first wreck Ronnie was ever involved in, Billy thought. Hope he was all right. He remembered the one and only train wreck he'd ever had. They'd derailed in the desert southeast of Barstow. Only a few cars jumped the track, the engine holding fast to the rails. It was the carcass of a coyote lying beside the tracks that had caused the problem.

The second and third cars had struck the animal, spilling some of their contents, while the engine had missed it entirely. Not a particularly bad accident, but it had caused the usual inquiry, and he was lucky. Discovery of the coyote's body cleared him from any responsibility as the engineer.

Billy walked across the street, entered the Red Dog Saloon and found a seat at the bar. The bartender automatically placed a Bud in front of him. He'd have a few beers and then check with the dispatcher again to see if there was any more news. He remembered Neva, the Indian girl's tears as she'd left the trailer, and his intent to talk it over with Ronnie as soon as they were together. Now the possibility of Ronnie in danger overshadowed his peccadillo. He was worried about his friend. After his third Bud, he pushed away from the bar and walked back across the street to the Sante Fe office. As soon as he entered he knew it was not good news. The atmosphere was as thick as a sand storm. Several men were still seated or clustered around Ben's desk.

Billy stepped up to Ben. "What's the latest?"

"Not good," Ben said. "There were two fatalities on the 215."

Billy knew even before he asked. "Who?"

"I'm real sorry, Billy," Ben said. "Ronnie and one of the brakemen, Phil Horton. Ronnie took the engine off the tracks to prevent a head-on."

Billy felt as though he was in slow motion, his arms and legs moving through a thick sea of molasses. He couldn't seem to get control of his body, and several of the men gently pushed against him in their efforts to press closer to Ben's desk. He found himself being shoved to the back. His head was pounding, his mind was crying, no… no…! He staggered to a chair by the windows and put his head between his legs. It couldn't be. Not Ronnie, his buddy. There was some mistake. There had to be. But in his deepest heart, he knew there was no mistake. Billy let out a long, low moan like a wounded animal. All sound ceased in the crowded room.

Jack crouched beside him and put his hand on his shoulder. "Jesus, Billy. I'm so sorry." He tried to comfort him in the only way macho railroaders knew, by patting his shoulder gently, over and over.

Billy was openly sobbing, his body shaking.

Another railroader knelt beside him. "Its okay, Billy. He probably didn't feel a thing. Most likely he went fast."

Billy heard nothing. All that penetrated his brain was that his best friend was gone. The man that had stood by him in work, romance and trouble. Finally, Jack helped Billy to his feet and led him out to his car. He pushed him in the front seat and Jack slid behind the wheel.

When he drove into Billy's driveway, Lola was standing at the door, waiting. Ben, the dispatcher had called ahead and told her. She knew Sherry might be in need about now, but this was her first priority. She helped Jack bring Billy inside and they walked him to the bed. Lola pulled off his boots, and Jack removed

Billy's heavy down jacket and Stetson. After they'd tucked the blanket under his chin, she and Jack went into the living room, leaving the bedroom door ajar.

"He's in shock, right now. It most likely'll wear off by tomorrow," Jack said quietly.

Lola nodded. "Thanks for bringing him home. It was real nice of you."

Jack placed his hand on her shoulder. "Least I could do for a friend. Some of the boys will bring his truck by later."

Lola watched him climb into his car and drive away. Dear Ronnie. To have his life snuffed out like a match in the wind. And Sherry. She would need some expert TLC in the next few weeks. Lola took another peek at Billy from the bedroom doorway. He was laying quite still with his eyes wide. Her heart opened and she forgave him for what he had done to Hamburger. She felt tears stream down her cheeks.

※

Sherry dropped the receiver in its cradle and slid to her knees. The dispatcher had just called. My God! It couldn't be true! It was a cruel joke! She quickly dialed Lola's number. The phone rang several times, but no answer. Struggling up from the floor, she grabbed her purse, jumped in her car and backed out the drive. Her numb fingers were barely able to grip the wheel. Her brain had stopped working, frozen in the moment of hearing the dispatcher's words. "I'm sorry, Sherry.

Ronnie has been killed in a train wreck." Why would Ben have said a thing like that?

A few minutes later, she pulled into Billy's driveway. Lola's Beetle was sitting beside the garage, but Billy's truck was gone. She hurried to the door and knocked.

Lola opened it and put a finger to her lips. "Come in. Billy's sleeping." She stepped back for Sherry to enter.

The two women looked into each other's faces. Sherry saw the grief lines already etched in Lola's. It was then that it hit her. She walked to the couch and fell down on the cushions. Covering her face with her hands, she sobbed in loud moans.

Lola hurried to the bedroom door and closed it. Sherry let out a wail that disturbed Mr. P. outside. The flamboyant bird let out his usual shriek.

Lola knelt beside Sherry and pulled her into her arms, their bodies gently rocking back and forth.

Gradually, Sherry's sobs began to subside. "I couldn't believe it when Ben called," she said.

"I know, honey," Lola replied, continuing to hold her, rubbing her back as if she were a child.

Sherry lifted her head. Her face was blotchy red, eyes swollen. "He just left home this morning." She searched Lola's face for some assurance that it wasn't true.

Lola's arms hung loosely around Sherry's shoulders.

"We were going to Vegas for a long weekend next month." Sherry rubbed her wet nose with the back of her hand.

Lola handed her a tissue from the coffee table.

"Ben didn't say how it happened," she asked Lola. "Do you know?"

"Yes. Do you want to hear now?"

Sherry nodded. So Lola told her the details that Ben had related on the phone.

"You mean he de-railed the train on purpose to avoid a head-on?" Sherry asked, bubbles escaping from her mouth.

Lola nodded.

"So he probably saved the lives of the men on the other train."

"Yes, he did."

"That figures. Ronnie's so kind and thoughtful. Always thinking of other people."

"Yes, he was."

A fresh onslaught of tears engulfed Sherry. She cried in Lola's arms until her sobs became dry gasps. Lola laid her down on the couch and spread a blanket over her. Then she went to the kitchen and made a pot of fresh coffee. She returned with two cups, and Sherry sat up, wiping her nose and eyes.

"I'll never love anyone the way I do Ronnie," she said.

"I know," Lola replied. She handed a cup to Sherry and the two women sat in silence. Mr. P. continued to shout the news across the Valley, his raucous voice shrill and clear in the afternoon sun.

Billy opened his eyes and looked around the bedroom. He recognized his bed, Lola's guitar in the corner, and the reprints of Georgia O'Keefe's flowers on the wall. Shutting his eyes, he hoped it had all been a nightmare. The train wreck. Ronnie gone. Suddenly, the raw reality flooded his brain. It *had* all really happened. He shook his head gently, opened his eyes again, aware of the morning sun streaming through the half-open blinds and the tantalizing smell of fresh coffee wafting from the kitchen. He heard movement and knew Lola was still home. He couldn't remember if she had to work at the Tavern today. Throwing back the covers, he pulled his pants from the chair and stepped into them. Padding barefoot into the living room, he saw Lola standing at the stove, stirring something in a skillet. She turned and saw him.

"Morning. I thought I was being quiet." She smiled and continued stirring.

He shrugged and said, "Guess I was ready to wake up. What you cookin'?"

"Scrambled eggs. Want some?"

Billy nodded. He went to the coffee pot and poured himself a cup, then took a chair at the table.

"Want some sausage, too?" Lola asked.

Billy nodded again.

She opened the fridge and took out the homemade sausage that Billy had prepared himself. She made two patties and laid them in another pan. When the meat was cooked, she dished up the food and set a plate in front of him.

Billy looked down at the dish, steam rising from the hot sausage. He picked up his fork and began moving the food around his plate.

Lola sat across from him with her eggs and toast. She watched him take a few bites, then push the food away. He walked to the refrigerator, pulled out a can of beer, snapped the tab and took a long swig.

"Kinda early isn't it?" Lola said.

Billy walked into the living room and threw himself down on the couch. "Don't start! I just lost my best friend."

Lola followed, sitting beside him on the floor. "I'm sorry, Billy. I shouldn't have said that."

He looked at her. His face was blank; devoid of all expression. The pupils of his eyes were enlarged.

She put her hands on his knees. "I'm so sorry about Ronnie. I cared for him too. Sherry was here last night. She's really broken up."

Billy looked down at Lola and his voice was cold. "She's only known him a few months. I've known him for years."

Lola nodded, not knowing what else to say. She rose and went into the kitchen and began putting together a homemade vegetable soup, busying herself with cutting up celery, potatoes, carrots and onions. Billy continued to finish the six-pack of beer. When he threw the last can in the trash, he went to the bedroom and returned with a clean shirt and his boots on. He pulled his

Stetson from the rack. "I'm going down to the Tavern, where there's some company," he said.

She called after him. "Billy, stay here with me, please? I'll keep you company."

His face was hard and still. She didn't recognize this man; his eyes glittered like wet agate. He stared at her for a moment then headed out the door and got in his truck. Stomping on the gas pedal he slid out the driveway.

※

*I*t was Christmas week and the shops in Needles were decorated with ribbons, artificial pine boughs and brightly colored lights. The weather varied this time of year a few degrees but stayed pretty much around 80 degrees. The sun beat down on the dry land that rain had abandoned.

Lola had bought a small tree and put it up in Billy's living room. He passed it by without even a glance. She had decided not to buy gifts. Who was in the mood for celebrating? Certainly not the two of them.

The day before Christmas the Baptist church in Needles filled to capacity. Every railroader that wasn't working was in attendance. Every friend that Ronnie and Phil Horton had in the Valley was there. Marsh, Sherry, Lola and Billy sat in the second row. It was a double funeral and both Ronnie and Phil's caskets were closed. Ronnie's parents from Phoenix, and Phil's wife decided to have the double ceremony.

Phil had been honored first. Now it was Ronnie's turn. The minister began the eulogy by affirming that Ronnie was a hero in taking the train off the tracks and saving the engineer and brakeman on the other train.

"Ronnie Webb cared for his fellow man enough to give his own life," the minister's voice spoke dramatically over the PA system. "Wasn't that what Jesus did? Ronnie was one of our earthly saints. He chose in the moment between life and death, to save God's children. And because of his sacrifice, our heavenly father has taken Ronnie into his arms for everlasting peace and salvation."

Sherry felt like throwing up. Ronnie was not a saint. He had been a real flesh and blood man. Damn that preacher for making him something he wasn't. She wiped her eyes beneath the sunglasses. Her legs felt numb from the hardness of the pews and her head ached. When her shoulders shook, Lola squeezed her hand tightly.

Lola stole a look at Billy. He was slumped over with his head down and eyes shut. He had been almost a zombie since the accident. She'd gotten him to eat a little, but he mostly drank and slept and laid off the railroad.

Russell had been asked to play *Amazing Grace* at the close of the funeral. He suggested Lola sing it, and she had agreed. For once, she didn't ask Billy. In fact she didn't think he was aware of it when her soprano voice soared above the congregation. Russell blended harmony on the chorus. "Amazing Grace, how sweet the sound, that saved a wretch like me… I once was lost but now am found. Was blind, but now I see."

At the last chorus, she gestured for everyone to sing along and the entire church swelled in musical rapture. Billy never once lifted his eyes to the front where Ronnie's coffin lay. Lola gently touched the casket as she finished singing. "Good-bye, Ronnie," she whispered.

On the way home, Lola drove Billy's truck, and Sherry brought up the rear, driving Marsh's.

Billy spoke for the first time all day. "Let's stop at the Tavern."

"Not now," Lola answered. She skidded into Billy's driveway and Sherry honked as she passed by in a dust cloud.

As soon as they got inside the house, Billy headed for the refrigerator and took out a can of beer. He pulled a pint of Jim Beam from the cupboard. Several hours later, Lola spread a cover over him on the couch, turned off the tree lights and crept quietly to bed.

※

*L*ola poured an ample amount of vodka into a glass, waved the tonic over it and placed it in front of Marsh. Billy had gone back to work that morning, still grieving for Ronnie and being unresponsive to Lola's efforts to comfort him.

Marsh took a long swig from his vodka. "That's a mighty fine drink you poured, ma love." He grinned at Lola at the other end of the bar waiting on another customer.

She smiled back and placed a beer before the customer, then began her shift inventory as to what she needed to stock in the cold boxes. She filled one box with different brands of beer, another with cans of soft drinks, but her thoughts were on Billy. She knew that time would heal his pain; she just needed to be patient. But he was being so damn cold to her. They hadn't made love since the train wreck three weeks ago. When he climbed into bed beside her, he immediately turned his back. If she cuddled up to him, he pulled away, angrily. That had been a shock! Then she remembered she'd read somewhere that grieving can take on many facets. Sometimes the anger can be directed against a surviving loved one. Of course, that was it. She sure hoped he came around pretty soon. She was already tired of his constant drinking and spending hours at the Red Dog or Sweeney's Tavern. He'd be drunk and belligerent by the time he walked in the door. Then, he wouldn't speak to her, so she'd either go in the bedroom and read, or if he followed her in there and insisted on turning out the light, she'd move into the living room and curl up on the couch. Sometimes he would follow and start harassing her about leaving his bed, and sometimes he would just drink himself into a stupor. How could it have all fallen apart so quickly? They'd spent their first New Year's Eve together at home, Billy so drunk that she'd left him all night on the couch where he'd passed out. She thought she loved him. She thought for sure he loved her. He used to tell her all the time. Didn't it say in all the manuals that people needed to be there for their partners in times of crisis? Well, it sure wasn't working with Billy.

Lola looked toward Marsh at the end of the bar. Sherry had told her about Marsh's brain tumor, but Lola had kept it to herself. Poor old guy! Didn't seem to have anyone in the entire world to care for him, except her and Sherry. As if Marsh knew what she was thinking, he looked in her direction and winked. Then, before her eyes, he turned suddenly gray and then pale. His eyes grew wide and he toppled off the stool to the floor, flinging his arms out like a rag doll. Lola ran from behind the bar and knelt down beside him. Two old desert rats hobbled over and looked down at Marsh.

"He sure tied one on," one old man said to the other.

"Yep. He shoulda quit a few hours ago," the other one said.

"Someone call an ambulance, quick," Lola said, but when no one moved to the phone, she jumped up and ran back behind the bar, tossing a stack of clean bar towels to one of the old men standing beside Marsh.

"Put those under his head," she commanded. She picked up the phone and dialed the number of the ambulance posted on the wall.

"Needles Ambulance," a male voice answered.

"This is Sweeney's Tavern in Mohave Valley. We have a customer who passed out. I'm pretty sure he isn't drunk," Lola said, breathlessly.

"Be there in ten minutes," the man said.

Lola hung up, slung a clean towel under the faucet and came back around to Marsh just as he was opening his eyes.

She put the wet towel across his forehead,` brushing back locks of long white hair.

Marsh's bloodshot eyes focused on her. "Ah, there ya are, ma love. Guess I had enough fer today." He began to struggle to a sitting position.

"I happen to know you haven't drank much today, Marsh. You stay right here. The ambulance is on its way." Lola gently pushed him back down.

"Oh, hell, girl. Why'd you go and do that? I'm fine. Just a little anemic, I 'spect."

"You just stay quiet. I'm in the driver's seat right now. I don't like customers keeling over on my shift. Gives me a bad name." She tried to make him smile.

It worked. Marsh gave her a grin. "Okay, since you seem to have the reins of this ole horse, I'll be docile."

Lola went into the back room and found a blanket. She brought it out to the bar and threw it over him.

"Say, little gal, how 'bout givin' me a sip of my vodka while we're waiting for the ambulance."

Lola wanted to comply but with the bar watching, which consisted of six men, she didn't think it would be very professional. "I don't think so right now, Marsh." She suddenly felt a flash of guilt for fixing him such a stiff drink. Four of the customers left, and the two old men went back to bending their elbows on the bar, nursing their whiskeys.

The ambulance could be heard a mile away wailing its way down Hwy 95. It pulled up in front of the Tavern, siren still screaming. Two attendants rushed into the bar and over to Marsh on the floor.

One of them said to Marsh, "What happened old-timer? Did you fall?"

"I sure did," Marsh exclaimed. "Think I hit my head, 'cause it's shore achin'."

They began to unroll a portable gurney, and skillfully picked up Marsh, sliding him onto it.

Lola came from behind the bar again. "I'll be in to see you, as soon as I get off." She patted Marsh's shoulder, then leaned over and kissed him on the cheek.

"No need for that, honey," Marsh said thickly.

Lola was sure she saw tears in his eyes. She damn sure wasn't gonna let him go to the hospital without friends nearby. "You just hush. I'll see you later."

Marsh waved feebly as the attendants took him out the door. Then the siren began again and gradually faded away.

Lola went to the phone, called Pat and told her what happened. Then she hung up and dialed Sherry's number.

The next day Lola picked up Sherry at Ronnie's trailer and they headed into Needles Hospital to visit Marsh.

"Did you talk to the doctor?" Sherry asked.

"I did, last night. Marsh is doing as well as can be expected. He may be able to come home tomorrow." She looked over at Sherry. "How was the meeting with Ronnie's parents?"

Sherry's voice became quieter. "It was okay. They said I could stay there until the trailer was sold. They're listing it with a realtor in Needles. But I don't much want to stay. Too many memories."

Lola was silent.

"I may go back to Phoenix," Sherry said. "My old crowd's still there."

Lola took her eyes off the road and glanced over at her friend. "Why would you do that? You want to run into Greg?"

Sherry shook her head. "No, not really, but at least I would feel more at home. I've never felt accepted here in this Valley. Even when Ronnie and I were together. It was as if they tolerated me because of him."

Lola nodded. "I know what you mean."

"You felt that way too?"

Lola nodded again. "It takes a whole lot for the locals to accept new people. You and I are outsiders. But, you know, if we stayed long enough, we'd probably be let in. Billy was from somewhere else before he came here."

"Isn't everyone from somewhere else?" Sherry said.

"Yeah, everyone except Marshmallow. He's been here so long no one remembers when he wasn't."

The girls both laughed as Lola pulled into the hospital parking lot.

Marsh was in the back on the first floor. Sherry carried a bouquet of flowers and Lola had a half pint of vodka hidden in her purse.

When they entered the room, Marsh was sitting

up in bed, a green hospital gown draped around his shoulders. His usual deep weathered tan, the color of old cowhide, was several shades lighter. His eyeglasses were balanced across his nose and he had a crossword puzzle in front of him on the tray. "Damn it! I knew I shouldn't a started this dern thing! Never kin finish 'em." He looked up and saw the girls. "Well I'll be darned, my two favorite women are here. Just in time." He threw the folded sheet of newspaper viciously at the wastebasket, missing it by several inches.

Lola picked it up, deposited it in the basket, then took a seat beside him. Sherry took the chair on his other side.

"Hey, Marshmallow," Lola said. "I'm sure glad to hear your usual disposition's back."

"Me too," Sherry said. "Look, we brought you some flowers." She held up the bouquet.

"Damn sweet of you two. I ain't seen a flower since I been here."

"You've only been here overnight, Marsh," Sherry said, laughing.

"Yeah, but at home I always look at the flowers and the cactus most everyday."

"Well, I'll go find a vase," Sherry said, giggling as she left the room.

Lola took one of his gnarled hands in hers. There was black around his short nails and the knuckles held ancient desert dirt in each wrinkle that no amount of hospital washing or antiseptic could change. "When did the doctor say you could come home?"

"He said prob'ly tomorrow. Ain't nothing they can do mor'n they have. I don't like them pain pills they give me. Makes my head dizzy and I stagger worse than being drunk. Just give me my vodka." Marsh laid back against the pillows and grinned for the first time.

Lola opened her purse. "That reminds me. Here's a sleeping aid for tonight." She covertly slipped the bottle into Marsh's hands.

He looked at the label. "Smirnoff's. Wow! How come I rate this?"

"Because you're such a dear. Let's put this away before the nurses see it."

"Put it in the back of the drawer, behind the Bible," he instructed her. "They never move that. Prob'ly against the rules to disturb the Bible."

Lola giggled, as she tucked the pint behind the Christian epic.

Sherry came back with the flowers in a vase and set them on the bedside table next to Marsh.

"Thanks for the flowers, girls. You two are a couple of pretty flowers yourselves."

Sherry leaned down and kissed Marsh on the cheek. "You say the nicest things."

Marsh was beaming, feeling better than he had since he'd keeled over in the Tavern yesterday.

"If you get released tomorrow, I'll come and get you," Lola said.

"You ain't workin' tomorrow?" he asked.

"Pat said I could take the day off if you were coming home."

"Well, it don't take the whole day to carry me home."

"When I get you home, I thought I'd make some soup and stay with you for a while."

"Now honey, you got Billy to take care of. You don't bother 'bout me."

Lola looked down at her lap. "Billy doesn't need me these days as much as he did. Besides, I want to take care of you the first day you're home."

Marsh reached for her hand, his forehead filled with furrows. "Whatcha mean, darlin'? About Billy?"

"Billy's been drinkin' a lot since the train wreck. Sometimes he's not so great to be around."

Marsh lay quietly for a few moments, his deep-set dark eyes staring out the window. "Well, I shore hope that scallywag don't fuck up and mistreat you. If that should ever happen, you come right over to my place, you hear?"

"Don't you worry, he hasn't mistreated me. Just doesn't seem to want my company anymore. But, I'm hoping he'll get over it. He's still grieving." She looked at Sherry on the other side of the bed.

Marsh turned to Sherry. "Some folks grieve and don't turn against the ones they love." He took Sherry's hand in his other one. "Now don't be gettin' my temperature up. The doc won't let me go home tomorrow."

All three of them laughed and Lola stood up. "I'll call the hospital in the morning and find out when they'll release you. See you then, Marsh." She leaned down and kissed him on his cracked, old lips.

Sherry kissed him too.

"Lord Almighty! I think I've died and gone to heaven!"

They turned at the door and saw Marsh grinning, flashing his nicotine-stained teeth, his eyes gleaming with moisture, and his cheeks a deep shade of rose.

≋

*P*aul put aside the rubber vagina, slid *Hustler,* the girlie magazine, under his bed, and leaned back against the pillows. His flaccid penis rested against his left testicle, refusing to come to attention. Gloom flooded his face and his shoulders drooped. He was hoping that the combination of the magazine and the sex toy would give him an erection. Honey stepped tentatively on Paul's bare thighs, looking for a cozy place to curl up. Paul brushed her off impatiently.

"Get off me, you lazy dog."

Honey wasn't to be put off so easily. She accidentally placed one soft paw on his genitals and shifted her weight. Paul yelped and struck the animal. The Pekinese landed in a heap on the other side of the bed. She jumped off and scurried underneath.

He quickly dressed in dirty overalls and a rumpled shirt. Without combing his hair or washing up, he left the apartment and walked the twenty yards to the back door of the Tavern.

Inside, Lola was working behind the bar. Six customers were scattered along the stools. When Lola saw him, she stopped smiling and her eyes became cold.

"Howdy," Paul said, nodding to her. He took a beer from one of the coolers and, careful not to brush against her, walked around the bar and sat on a stool.

Lola merely nodded back but said nothing. Two of the customers laid money on the bar and left.

Sunlight flashed across the bar floor as the door opened. Sherry bounced in, her blond hair dancing. She took a seat at the other end of the bar, away from Paul.

"Hi," she said, as Lola put a napkin in front of her on the bar.

"Want a beer?" Lola asked.

"No. Just a coke. Thanks."

Lola filled a glass from the fountain. "What's up?"

"I just left Marsh," Sherry said. "Got him up and dressed and fixed him breakfast. Then he made me leave. Said he was getting too attached to me. He's such a sweet ole guy. How come they don't make young guys like him?"

Lola laughed. "That would be too easy. Men are a challenge that women have been trying to figure out since the beginning of time."

"Well, I for one don't like the challenge. I want a man that appreciates me. When I finally found one..." Sherry's eyes began to tear up.

Lola reached across the bar and covered her hand. "Just remember, some of us never find one like Ronnie. At least you had him for a little while."

Sherry nodded, wiping the corners of her eyes.

Paul got up and moved down toward Sherry and took the seat beside her. "How ya doin?" he asked.

Sherry spoke without turning to look at Paul. "About as good as can be expected." She finished her coke and slipped off the stool. "Gotta go, Lola. See ya later." Sherry turned and quickly walked to the door. Again, shafts of afternoon sunlight spilled into the bar, briefly warming the cool interior.

"She's kinda unfriendly, don't you think?" Paul said, slurping his beer.

Lola began wiping down the bar. "No, I don't think so," She kept her head and eyes down.

"Well, I do. I was talkin' to her and she up and left."

Lola looked straight into his eyes. "You can't expect people to like you when they know who you really are."

Paul stared at her for a second, then his eyes slid away. "Up yours, girl." He got off the stool and headed for the front door, hitting it hard with the palm of his hand.

The Arizona sun burned his eyes and stung his white, pasty face. 'Damn that bitch," he muttered under his breath. His whole body ached with hatred for her. If he could think of a way to get rid of her for good, he'd do it. She had been a thorn in his side since the day she'd walked into the Tavern.

*B*illy bellied up to the bar and slammed his empty Bud on the counter. "Hey, babe, give me another." He tossed the can behind the bar. It fell short of the bucket, landing on the wooden floor slats.

Lola slowly walked toward him. "Billy, don't throw your cans and don't bang them on the bar." She reached into the cold box, opened a Bud and placed it in front of him.

Billy threw back his head and took a long swig. "I'll do what I damn well please." His brow had long furrows running in horizontal lines and his face revealed a couple days of beard growth.

"Not on my shift you won't." Lola spoke with determination. She had to keep Billy to the same rules as the other customers.

"Don't I get some leeway here, 'cause I'm your lover man?" Billy gave her a lopsided grin.

Lola thought about reminding him he hadn't been her lover man since Ronnie's death, but now wasn't the time. He hadn't touched her for four weeks and Lola had stopped trying since the last time he pushed her away. Today he'd been drinking in the Tavern all afternoon, since he'd come in off the railroad at eleven. She was going to have to cut him off, but first she'd suggest he leave, to save face.

"Why don't you go home and feed the animals and collect the eggs for me. I'll be home at six and then I'll fix us some dinner."

"Fuck the eggs. That's women's work. The animals can wait. I'm not through here yet." He drained the Bud and slammed it on the bar.

"You're quite through here, Billy. Go home." Lola grabbed the can, wiped the bar down angrily, and tossed the empty in the large barrel in back.

"Give me another," Billy demanded, his words slurring slightly, his red eyes staring her down.

It seemed to Lola that all the customers were riveted on the two of them. Their heads turned toward Billy, waiting to hear Lola's answer.

"I said no, Billy. Go home." She spoke slowly and clearly, as if she were addressing a child.

"Are you fuckin' refusin' to serve me?"

"That's right. I should have cut you off hours ago." Lola stood straight, she and Billy eye to eye.

Finally he stood up, swaying from side to side. "You bitch! I never thought you'd do this to me in public." He turned and shuffled to the red door, opened it, then slammed it as hard as he could.

Lola hoped he didn't end up in the ditch somewhere between the bar and the three blocks to his place. Or maybe she hoped he would.

☒☒

*L*ola and Sherry climbed into Betsy after having dinner at the Sports Lounge.

"Let's go by the Sundancer for a beer," Sherry said.

Lola hesitated as she knew Billy hated for her to

drink in a bar without him. "Okay, just one. I want to check on Marsh before it gets too late."

Five minutes later they pulled into the Sundancer parking lot and entered the club. Judd was behind the bar. The room was full and several railroaders greeted the girls.

"What'll you have girls?" Judd laid down two napkins.

"Two Buds," Lola said.

"Sure 'nuff. On the house. What you two up to?"

"Thanks," Sherry said, acknowledging the beer.

"Nothin' much," Lola answered.

"Did ya get permission from Billy to go out?" He grinned at Lola.

"No, she didn't." Sherry said. "And I think she's worried about it getting back to him. Billy may throw a shit fit when he hears we're in here havin' a beer."

"You know, I'm still my own boss. I make my own decisions," Lola said quietly.

"Hey, I was just kiddin' ya. Didn't mean no harm," Judd said.

Lola smiled. "No harm taken."

The jukebox was blaring and one of the railroaders came over and asked Sherry to dance. She joined him on the sawdust floor. No one approached Lola and she was relieved. She was off-limits. Billy Jim's girl.

After the second beer, Lola said, "Let's go."

Sherry didn't put up a fuss. They waved to Judd and were about to open the door when a customer pushed through. Lola immediately felt his presence like a cold splash of river water. Paul stood facing them just inside the door. He stared at her for a moment, his eyes wide in surprise. Then a tiny smile pulled down one corner of his mouth, his lips parted and yellow teeth came into view. Lola stepped aside and waited for him to pass by. He went inside, and the girls left quickly before he could speak.

The two of them jumped into Lola's VW. "Damn, he'll spread it all over the valley that we were in there tonight," Sherry said.

"Probably," Lola said as she backed out of the parking lot.

"Don't worry about it. We were together and we're on our way to Marsh's now. He can't get mad about that." Sherry lit a joint.

Lola glanced over at her. "You'd be surprised what he can get mad about."

"You don't talk to me, Lola. Is he being an asshole?"

Lola nodded. "Sometimes."

"Why do you put up with it? You don't have to."

"I keep thinking he'll go back to the way he used to be when we first got together. He can't grieve his friend forever. I'm trying to be patient." She took a toke of the joint that Sherry handed her. "And I feel I have to try harder this time, so I can make this one work." She glanced over at Sherry. "Do you understand?"

"Yeah, I understand Lola, but what if he doesn't go back to the way he was? You know, you helped me get away from Greg. You gave me some good advice. Maybe you should think about that."

Lola nodded again. "I hear you," she said, as she pulled up beside Marsh's trailer.

They knocked and pushed open the faded door. The interior was dim but the girls could make out Marsh asleep in his chair in one corner of the tiny room. His glasses were resting on his chest and the newspaper had fallen across his lap. A glass of vodka was half empty on the side table.

Sherry picked up his glasses and the newspaper and laid them on the table. Lola knelt down and started untying Marsh's shoelaces.

"What the fuck…!" Marsh jumped and his eyes flew open.

"It's just us," Sherry said. "We came to check in on you."

"Well, ya don't have to scare a man to death."

"Sorry, Marshmallow," Lola said, gently slipping off his shoes.

"What you two up to, besides botherin' me?" He sounded cross.

"We went to dinner and had a couple of beers at the Sundancer," Sherry said. "Did you have any dinner?"

"Well, I don't rightly remember." Marsh sat up in the chair, rubbing his eyes.

Lola went to the refrigerator and looked inside. The soup she had brought two days ago was still in its container. She poured some into a saucepan and heated it up on the stove.

"Don't you worry 'bout me, now. I'm just fine. I'll eat if'n I'm hungry."

"We do worry about you, Marsh," Sherry said. "Whose gonna if we don't?"

"Well, you got a point there." The old man scratched his head.

Lola brought a bowl of vegetable soup to Marsh. "Eat this."

"God, you two women are getting' bossy with me."

Lola grinned. "Yes, I guess we are. But we care, so humor us and eat."

Marsh gave a big sigh and slowly dipped the spoon into the soup, raising it to his mouth. After the first spoonful he continued to eat the soup, making slurpy noises as he sucked it up. The girls exchanged smiles. When he'd finished the bowl he handed it to Lola. "That was pretty good, after all. Thanks honey." He winked at Lola.

"Now, are you ready to go night, night?" Sherry teased.

"Hell, yes, if it means I get you two to come with me."

Lola and Sherry giggled. "In your wildest dreams," Sherry said.

"Can't blame an ole man for tryin'." Marsh struggled up from the chair. Once upright he staggered and put his hand to his head.

Lola grabbed his arm. "What's wrong?"

"Just one of my dizzy spells. Nothin' important."

With Sherry and Lola on each side, they walked

him through the narrow trailer and sat him down on the green spread. Sherry pulled his shirt over his head and started unbuckling his belt.

"Better not start somethin' you can't finish, honey," Marsh joked.

"Now Marsh, Lola and I've put you to bed half a dozen times. Why you giving us such a hard time tonight?"

"I don't know. Maybe this is my lucky night." The old man's eyes twinkled.

Lola slipped off his pants and slid his thin legs under the covers, gently pushing his upper body down on the bed. Before she pulled the blanket up to his chin she noticed his raggedy, gray boxer shorts.

"Bring me my vodka off the table, would ya honey?" He squeezed Sherry's hand.

She went to get the glass and handed it to Marsh. He raised his head and swallowed it in one gulp, then laid his head back and took Sherry's hand in his.

"Ya know how I feel 'bout you two, don't ya?" He held Lola's eyes.

Lola nodded. "We know, Marshmallow. We feel the same."

The old man's eyes glistened with tears. "Haven't had no one care about me in years."

"It's okay, sweetie," Sherry said.

"Now git, 'fore I say or do somethin' I'll regret tomorrow." Marsh wiped his mouth with the back of his hand.

Lola leaned down and kissed him on the cheek. Sherry kissed his lips. "See you, Marshmallow."

The two women turned out the one light by the couch and let themselves out of the trailer, climbed into Betsy and drove away into the quiet desert night.

※

*P*aul set another Budweiser in front of Billy and picked up the five lying on the bar. He deposited it in the cash register, placing the change on the counter.

He leaned close to Billy's ear. "They was dancin' with some guys. I didn't recognize them. Not from around here. I think they were sittin' with them too, in a booth."

Billy's eyes were red and he needed a shave. The brim of his Stetson was damp against his brow. "When did you say you saw them in the Sundancer?"

"It was last night, while you was out on the railroad. They seemed to be having a real nice time. You know Billy, I wouldn't told you 'cept I think you can do better than her. She ain't your type."

"Yeah, I don't give a shit what you think, Paul. You swear you saw them in the bar last night?"

"I swear on my mother's honor." Paul held three fingers up as if he was giving the scout's pledge.

Something in the back of Billy's mind reminded him that Paul was not trustworthy, but he immediately forgot it, as he'd had quite a few drinks since coming in off the railroad. He left the change on the bar and climbed off the stool, walking unsteadily down the dim hallway to the can. Using the urinal against the wall, he peed a steady stream, gave it a shake, then zipped up his fly and went back to the bar. Picking up his grip, he turned to leave.

"I just thought you should know, Billy. Hope yer not pissed at me," Paul called after him.

Billy hit the swinging door of the Tavern, walking into the hot evening air just as the sky blazed pink, blue, gray and mauve above the mountains. But the beauty of the Arizona sunset was lost on him. He jumped into his red truck, skidding out of the parking lot. Charging down the dirt road to his house, the dust trail the Ford kicked up looked like a small twister. He turned sharply into the circular driveway, hit his brakes so fast he slid sideways, scaring Mr. P., who had recognized the truck engine and was waiting at the front gate. He squawked, wings flapping as he flew eight feet to the right, out of harm's way. Billy jumped from the pickup, slamming the door, and stormed into the house. Lola was in the kitchen standing at the stove.

"Hi. I called the trainmaster and he said you got in at three."

Billy took off his hat, hanging it on the bull horns on the wall. He sat on the couch and pulled off his boots.

Lola walked over and leaned down to kiss him. "Where were you?" she said lightly.

Billy pushed her away. "What you doin', checking up on me?"

Lola pulled back. "No. I just wanted to have dinner ready when you got home."

She went back into the kitchen and started dishing up rice and beef stroganoff onto Billy's plate and placed the sautéed vegetables and rice on hers.

Taking two bottles of beer from the refrigerator she put them beside the plates. "Want to eat?" She inquired gingerly. When Billy didn't answer, she sat down at the table and picked up her beer.

Billy joined her and sat down. He looked down at his plate. "What's this?"

"Beef stroganoff. You said you liked it."

He picked up his fork and tasted it. "Not bad." He looked over at her plate. "Yer not havin' none?"

Lola shook her head.

"How come?"

She met his eyes. "You know why."

Billy laughed meanly. "If I knew why, I wouldn't be askin' ya."

Lola looked down at her plate. "Because of Hamburger."

"Ya mean you don't wanta eat him."

Lola looked up; searching his eyes for the man she loved.

He shook his head and laughed. "You're stupid. Everybody that raises their own meat eats it."

"Well I don't," she said, rising from the chair and rushing to the bedroom.

"I ain't finished talkin' to ya, come back here, woman," Billy yelled after her.

Lola slammed the door and leaned against it, tears running down her face. He'd never called her stupid before. She was wiping her cheeks when the door flew open, throwing her forward a few feet to the carpet. Billy stood in the doorway, clutching his beer in one hand, his eyes wild.

"I said I wasn't through talkin'."

Lola got to her feet and retreated to the bed, sitting stiffly on the edge.

"You was in the Sundancer last night," he stated accusingly.

Lola looked at his face. "Yes. Sherry and I stopped in after dinner and had two drinks. We were there a total of twenty minutes."

"Twenty minutes, huh? I heard you was dancin' and sittin' with some out-of-town guys."

"Well, you heard wrong. I didn't leave my stool. Sherry danced with one guy. No one talked to me except Judd who was behind the bar." Lola wondered why she was explaining.

"Where'd you two have dinner?"

"The Sports Lounge."

"Anybody talk to you there?"

Lola started to laugh. "Listen to yourself, Billy. You are pathetic. I can have a life when you're not here."

Billy threw the glass of beer. It hit the bed beside her thigh, splashing beer across her lap. She jumped up and ran past him. He reached out to grab her arm, but wasn't quick enough. She picked up her keys and purse by the door and ran out to Betsy, started the engine and drove out the drive, managing to avoid Mr. P., who was still standing guard at the gate. Her thoughts were jumbled and troubling. His rage was escalating. Why did she stay? Of course, she knew the answer. She loved him and she felt this relationship deserved more work than she had been willing to give the others. But his jealousy was getting to be too much. Every day he was pushing her further away. Who would have told such a lie to him? She knew instantly.

※

*P*aul turned on the faucets of the bathtub, then sat down on the toilet seat, picked up the pink plastic sex toy from the floor and stuck his semi-erect penis into the rubber vagina. He started pumping slowly, then a little faster. After a few seconds his penis slid out and fell against his thigh. Pissed off, he threw the apparatus against the bathroom wall. Shit! He couldn't even keep a hard-on long enough to get off. Maybe a magazine would help. He got a sex magazine from beneath the bed. Sitting back down on the toilet he began stroking himself as he turned the pages. Finally he came to a wrinkled and much-used page. Small spots of dried liquid were scattered across the steamy picture of a naked brunette with fingers buried deep in her pubic hair. She reminded him of Lola. Had the same big tits and long legs. But, while she had a come-hither look, Paul could never quite conjure up that look on Lola's face. By God, he'd fixed her, for good. After what he told Billy the other night, she was probably out on her ass, by now. She'd be gone from the Valley soon and he'd never have to see her again or be reminded of his rejection and failures. He reached over and turned off the faucets, the tub almost brimming over.

Back on the toilet seat, finally achieving an erection, he picked up the plastic vagina. Inserting himself inside again he started pumping. He kept this up for nearly ten minutes, straining and grunting, his face flushed, his eyes glassy. Leaning back, he pushed as hard as he could against the soft, slightly sweet-smelling sex toy. Turning up the controls helped. The thing squeezed his penis even harder, increasing the pleasure. Finally it was working.

"Oh yeah, yeah, baby," he crooned to the little pink object.

His face suddenly became very red, the color creeping down his neck and shoulders to a deep maroon, and just as he climaxed, he let out a long wail, then rose up slightly from the seat, knees bent, eyes bugged. Dropping the sex toy, he clasped his hands to his heart and fell sideways, losing his balance, slipping head first into the full tub. The weight of his body caused the water to rise up like a geyser, cascading onto the floor. The last thought to flash across Paul's mind was that the water was too damn hot. His final breath sucked steaming liquid into his lungs. For a few seconds the water bubbled above his head and roiled around his shoulders. His arms jerked and splashed a few times, then everything became quiet, legs dangling over the side.

In search of her master, Honey appeared at the bathroom door as the water seeped onto the rug. The little dog saw Paul's legs and picked her way across the soaked floor. She reached up and licked his toes, whining as if she sensed something was wrong. Standing on her hind legs she put her front paws on his knee, then looked into the tub. She leaned over and licked some fluid stuck to the top of Paul's thigh. Then she jumped down and turned to leave. Noticing the rubber vagina lodged against the wall, Honey went over and smelled it. She saw white liquid seeping from the opening. Her pink tongue darted out and tasted the substance. Whimpering she went back into the bedroom, curled up on the bed and began cleaning her wet paws.

※

*M*arsh opened his eyes and tried to figure out what time it was. Probably near dawn. He thought he heard Billy's rooster crowin' down the road. Maybe not. Could just be the ringin' and clickin' goin' on in his head. He sat up slowly so the dizziness wouldn't come, put his legs over the side of the bed and stood up. Holding on to the wall he limped to the tiny bathroom and sat down on the stool. He remembered the two girls comin' in last night to put him to bed. Shore was nice to have such sweet things hoverin' around. Sherry had fallen head over heels for Ronnie. Too damn bad that life dealt them such a crappy hand. They both deserved more. He wished Billy Jim would treat Lola better. A man don't find such a treasure easily in this world. It's natural to grieve losin' a best friend, but not to the exclusion of yer woman.

Lola reminded Marsh of that special woman from his past. They had similar coloring but it was the earthiness and innate sweetness that they both shared. He thought of the one woman in his life that he'd never forget, Uma. Musta been sixty years ago. He'd never married her but he'd meant to. It was up north near Fort Mohave that they'd first met at a church dinner in an outdoor tent. He'd gone because his mother had insisted and when he saw the lovely Indian girl, he was glad he had. She had the long, black shiny hair of the Yavapai's. Big, doe eyes and skin the color of honey. She'd lost both her parents in a smallpox epidemic on the reservation and was being Christianized by the family that had taken her in. He didn't care what religion she was. He was smitten. He'd ridden over on his horse several times to pay her court, and her foster family seemed to like him. Then the damn Marines beckoned. He didn't know why he joined up and was almost immediately shipped to Central America to put down a rebellion there. Even though she said she'd wait, by the time he returned, she had married someone else; a half-breed Mohave. It hadn't been long before he'd heard through the grapevine that her husband was beatin' her. Jesus, he didn't know what to do about that. Indians weren't allowed to drink in the bars in those days, so her husband got liquored up down by the river with the other winos. He'd taken to runnin' into Uma when she came into town to get her supplies, often helping her load up the wagon and then accompanying her back to her place. Even kissed her a few times, but she wouldn't be unfaithful to her husband. He begged her to come away with him, but stopped short of just taking her when she told him she was expecting a baby. When he realized she'd never leave with him, he cried.

About a week later one of the church deacons told him the half-breed had beaten Uma to death in a drunken rage. The police turned him over to the Indian court on the Reservation and they had fined him and released him. It took Marsh a goodly while to mourn Uma and return to the living. When he did, he made his plans carefully. One night down by the river, when Uma's husband was real drunk and staggerin' toward home, he lay in wait behind a tree. He beat the man to death with a tree limb, bashing in his head. The authorities decided it was a drunken fight among the winos, and let it go at that. He had never regretted that act. Why the fuck did he remember that crime he'd committed all those eons ago? He hadn't thought of it in years. He'd never married. After Uma, no one seemed worth it. He stood up and hobbled back to bed, climbed in, and slowly pulled the covers over his shriveled body.

His head really hurt now, no longer thinking he heard a cock's crow, but more like a coal-burning train engine racing through his brain. The pressure was fierce, the front of his forehead felt like a balloon, ready to burst. The damn tumor was wantin' out. "Well, damn it, get on with it, then," Marsh mumbled.

He wished he could have one last vodka, but it was too much trouble to go get it. He thought he heard the night winds singing and then he saw her. She was dressed in a buckskin dress with leather fringe and beads on the front. Her long black hair billowed out behind her as she beckoned to him to follow. It was time. By God, she'd come for him.

"I'm comin', love," Marsh said, as he closed his eyes.

※

There were two funerals in one week in the Valley. Sherry, Lola and Billy made an appearance at Paul's, out of respect for Pat, but left as soon as the first shovel of sod was thrown on his casket. Death by drowning, the coroner said, even though Paul apparently had had a heart attack and fell into the tub.

Pat had closed the Tavern for a few days after the funeral. Offering to work more shifts when Pat reopened, Lola was very glad she hadn't told her about Paul's attack in the motel room. An appropriate ending for an evil man, she thought. Remembering her own father's death confirmed her feelings there was sweet justice in this world, after all.

Marsh's funeral was different. The sun was beginning to heat up in the perfect-blue Arizona sky. The cemetery was next to an old Mohave burial site. Long ago the Indians had given permission for the locals to be buried next to their own sacred ground. Mesquite and Tamarind trees intermingled with scrub brush among the headstones. Jackrabbits bounded across the dry earth, and sidewinders slinked under the rocks.

Lola lifted her chin and smelled the sweet aroma of the desert, mixed with the few bouquets of flowers brought by Marsh's friends. Flowers were sparse in the Valley and very expensive. Many of the flowers resting on Marsh's coffin had come from people's gardens. Lola had cut a bunch of oleanders from beside their gate.

Several people chipped in, and Lola, Sherry and Billy dug in their pockets to give Marsh a graveside ceremony. Privately, Lola arranged for a plot and small headstone for Marsh. All the customers from the Red Dog and the Tavern as well as the Sundancer were there. His old drinkin' buddies, including Ole Dewey, brought their own bottles and had a nip while the Baptist minister said a few words.

"Jonathon Marsh was a member of this Arizona community for eighty years. He made many friends in his eight decades. He was baptized at Fort Mohave in 1922 and lived with his parents on a ranch, nearby, until he joined the Marines in 1938 and went to Central America to keep the peace. Later on in his life, he became part-owner of a gold mine. Some say he made quite a bit of money from it before his partner took it over. He could always be found at the local bar and made it his business to feed half the starving dogs and cats in the valley. If anyone needed a friend, Marsh was always there."

Lola listened to the minister talk about parts of Marsh she had never known. Events that Marsh had never mentioned. Only thing that was important was that she had loved the old man. She rarely let herself get attached to anyone, least of all a man nearly three times her age. She wondered if he'd ever been in love and with whom. Hell, yes. A man of his wisdom and character hadn't lived all these years without falling in love, at least once. With his wise-cracking ways, he'd probably loved lots of ladies. Lola smiled in spite of her tears.

Billy gave the minister two twenty dollar bills after the ceremony. Lola and Sherry dropped the oleanders on top of the casket just before Billy threw the first shovel of dirt. The three of them stayed until the grave was nearly filled in.

"He'll sure be missed," Billy said. "Can't imagine goin' into the Tavern and not seein' Marsh sittin' on a stool."

Lola wiped her eyes as they headed for Billy's truck. Billy'd been very sweet and considerate to her since Marsh had died. They had even made love, which surprised her. She had almost made up her mind to leave him. But now he seemed to be getting past the heavy grieving phase for Ronnie. Four deaths in the Valley in the last two months, including the brakeman on Ronnie's train. That was pretty unusual.

Sherry had discovered Marsh the next afternoon after he'd died. She'd walked in calling his name, but got no answer. The hair on the back of her neck stood up and she knew. She went to the back of the trailer and saw him lying beneath the dirty-gray sheets, white and still. Marsh's eyes were closed and the corners of his mouth were turned up. She fled to Lola's and they had called the sheriff, who then called the coroner.

"I'm goin' by Marsh's place and tidy up," Sherry said as they climbed in the truck. "Would you come with me?"

"Sure." Then she turned to Billy. "When you going to work?"

"Soon as I call in," he said.

Lola paused. "Do you mind if I go with Sherry?" She didn't want to disturb the fragile truce between them.

Billy shook his head. "No, I think you two were as close as anyone to Marsh. He'd want you both there."

"A lawyer from Needles called yesterday and asked for us to come into his office next week," Lola said to Sherry. "He said it had to do with Marsh's will."

"Well I can't imagine what Marsh could have, besides the trailer and that acre of land," Sherry said.

"Me either," Lola agreed. "Maybe a few personal items he wanted us to have."

"Poor ole Marsh. I think he lived on his social security. Always seemed to have enough dough to sit all day at the bar, though," Billy said, as he pulled into the drive.

They all piled out and went inside. Lola and Sherry changed clothes and assembled some cleaning supplies.

Billy was at the table reading the paper and drinking a cup of re-heated coffee. She leaned down to kiss him on the cheek. He turned his head and caught her lips with his. It was a nice, lingering kiss.

"Bye, love. See you when you get in," Lola said.

"Will you be home, when I get back?" Billy asked, pointedly.

She hesitated. That meant she'd have to call the

trainmaster several times to track his return so she'd know exactly when he'd be coming in. She nodded. "I'll be here."

><

Pat went in the back door that she always left unlocked, threw her purse on the table and dropped onto the couch. Boy, what a relief that was over! Funerals were awful. An exercise in dishonesty. At least this one was. She'd had to stand there and accept condolences from half the Valley, all the time delirious with her good luck. The son-of-a-bitch was finally gone. No more lies, or fumblings in the night, no more excuses, no more limp dicks. She laughed out loud. Would he ever be shocked if he knew how she really felt, had felt for the last few years. But she'd played the game, same as he did. Only she hadn't known how sick he really was, how desperate, that he would actually use one of those nasty contraptions to get off. She'd known about the sex magazines beneath the bed, had just ignored them, figuring that was the best way to handle it.

When he hadn't come into the bar to help her close that night, she figured he'd gone out. He'd often taken to goin' out late at night. When she found him, Honey was whining and crying and licking the feet that hung over the tub. She leaned over and saw his head and shoulders underwater and knew immediately he was dead. She threw down a couple of bath towels to soak up the water on the floor. That's when she spotted the pink object jammed against the wall. Picking it up, she saw a trickle of white liquid still trapped at the opening. The sex toy was attached by a cord to a control box. She remembered she began laughing... well, he'd finally got off, the poor bastard. She took it to the kitchen, placed it in a plastic garbage bag and hid it under the sink. Honey was whining and wrapped herself around Pat's ankles.

"Stop, Honey. He's not here anymore. You only got me now." Pat reached down and stroked the small dog until she quieted. Then she went to the phone and called the Sheriff. Del pulled up in front of the Tavern about a half hour later and Pat let him in the office door.

"Where is he?" Del asked.

"Back here." She led him to the bathroom.

The sheriff took one look and shook his head. "Real sorry, Pat. Were you here?"

She told him how and when she had discovered Paul in the tub. Del called the coroner and the body was picked up about an hour later.

That was the other night. Now that the funeral was over, she'd close the Tavern for a few days and then life would continue, nearly as before. She hadn't realized how much she disliked Paul until he was gone. She slipped off her pumps, and unbuttoned the top button of her skirt. This called for a drink. She went to the dining room cabinet and poured two fingers of Jim Beam in a glass and raised it in a toast.

"Here's to sweet justice," she said, and drank it down in one gulp. She poured another shot and settled on the couch. Maybe she could even close the Tavern for a couple of weeks in the winter and go to the Caribbean or Mexico. Yeah, now there's an idea.

※

*T*he sun was low in the sky, just above the mountain ridge. Lola and Sherry were riding Dobbin and Apache along the gravel road.

"We'd better turn back," Lola called to Sherry over her shoulder. "It'll be dark soon and Apache gets skittish at car headlights."

"Okay."

Ahead, a lone horseman was riding at a trot toward them. He came abreast and reined in his horse. "Hi, Lola, Sherry," Russell said. "What you two up to?"

"We were just out riding," Lola said. "How about yourself?"

"I've been down at Ole Sam's place looking at his bull. Thinkin' about breeding him to some of my stock. Say, why don'tcha stop by my place tonight. We're having a jam. We'd love to have ya sing with us." His big, dark eyes smiled at her.

"Uh, thanks, but Billy's out and I really can't. But I appreciate the invite."

"Well, bring Sherry along. That way no one can talk."

Lola looked down and stroked Apache's neck. "You know, it wouldn't matter who I brought along." She glanced up and caught Russell's look.

"It's none of my business, Lola, but we all have to live our lives with a certain amount of freedom and independence," Russell offered. "Seems like you've given up a bit of yours."

Lola nodded. "You're right. I'm working on that."

"She can't do jack, when Billy's out on the railroad," Sherry blurted. "He hardly likes her to be with me."

Lola glared at Sherry. "It's not that bad. He's getting better."

"Well, I shore miss yer singin', lady. Wish there was some way we could rehearse so you could sing with us on stage."

"Thanks, Russell. Right now, I'm working on my relationship with Billy. Maybe singing with you guys can come later."

At that moment the sun disappeared behind the ridge. "Gotta go, Russell," Lola said. "See you." Lola turned Apache around.

Russell tipped his cowboy hat. "Sure sorry about losin Marsh. See ya later, girls."

"So are we. Thanks, Russell," Lola said.

Sherry and Lola hurried their horses back down the road, past Marsh's empty trailer.

"Yer dreamin', Lola, if you think Billy will ever let you rehearse with Russell and the band." Apache and Dobbin were nose to nose as they rode into the gate at Billy's.

"I have my priorities, Sherry. I think getting along with Billy is more important, right now."

"You know, I think Russell's got more than a casual

interest in you." Sherry grinned at her friend.

"Oh, I don't think so. He's just being nice."

"Lola, he's a man, and yer a good-lookin' woman. Of course he's interested in you."

Lola turned toward Sherry. "All the more reason to stay away from him." Lola could just see Billy picking a fight with Russell.

They dismounted and led the horses into the corral. Lola put the saddles in the tack room and Sherry rubbed down Dobbin.

"It's a waste of talent. You not bein' able to sing with them," Sherry fussed.

Lola threw a chip of alfalfa to the horses and fed them each a dipper of grain. She rubbed her hands together, brushing away the hay. "I can always sing, when the time is right."

The girls fed the various animals and collected the eggs. It was still dusk and the chickens were just beginning to roost for the night. Lola reached under a soft white hen that pecked at her hand, and decided to leave the eggs. "This hen's been sittin' on her eggs for two weeks. Guess she wants some little ones." Lola laughed.

"Speakin' of little ones, do you ever wish you had a baby?" Sherry asked.

"Oh maybe, with the right man," Lola answered. "But my life has been so haphazard and unpredictable these last few years that I couldn't raise a child." She looked over at Sherry. "How 'bout you?"

"Sometimes I get a yen for a child and a family. I even daydreamed about it after I met Ronnie. But now……. I don't think so. Not anytime soon." Sherry put all the eggs she'd collected in the basket Lola was holding. "You know, Lola, I've been thinkin' about movin' on. Now that Ronnie's place has been sold, I have to be out next month. Maybe I'll go back to Phoenix."

"What's in Phoenix, Sherry?" Lola gave her an intense look.

"Nothin' much, just old friends. I grew up there. Guess it represents a kind of security for me."

"I'd sure miss you."

Sherry turned to Lola. "I'd miss you too, honey, but we could visit each other, couldn't we?"

Lola nodded.

"Or if things don't work out here, you could come to Phoenix," Sherry suggested.

"I don't think Phoenix holds any attraction for me."

"Yeah," Sherry said, cleaning chicken manure off her boots.

"Wanta come in and have some supper with me?" Lola asked.

Sherry nodded. "Thanks."

They cleaned their boots on the metal rungs of Billy's tractor. The moon was out and Mr. P.'s evening call rang crisp on the clear air.

≳≲

*M*artin Fellino placed the gas pump back in its cradle and closed his gas tank cap. He climbed behind the wheel of his '75 Cadillac and drove out of the station heading across the river for the Tavern. The Arizona community had tried to make him think Lola had left the area. That only confirmed what he'd already figured; that the locals were trying to protect her. Then he'd spied her car parked on a gravel road in the vicinity, just a few blocks from the Tavern. He was checking out the houses, when he spotted her distinctive VW. The little adobe house was pretty with blooming cactus in the front. She'd found a place to hide, but not from Martin. He knew he had to off Tony's girlfriend in case she had been there that night. The night he'd killed Tony Ricco. He hadn't found anyone in the house, but she could have been hidden well enough that he and his partner had overlooked her.

He hated killing women. It was always such a guilt trip. He didn't mind killing the ones that deserved it, but when it came to the opposite sex, he didn't take any pride in doing his job. But the bosses had told him it was necessary. So he had no choice.

He picked a piece of hamburger from his teeth with a toothpick he had taken on his way out of Denny's in Needles. Crossing the narrow bridge between California and Arizona, he turned on the air conditioner and pulled a cold beer from his six-pack cooler. He hated this desert. It was so inhospitable. Only fit for rattlers and scorpions and an occasional body that might need dropping off.

He'd soon be at the Tavern and he knew she was working the late shift. Lola would be closing up, so he'd catch her when she was alone and vulnerable, do what he had to do and be done with it. Make it look like a robbery. Then he could high-tail it back to Vegas. There was a special meeting next Monday and he would report his completion of the job. One of the big bosses had implied that he would have a special assignment next time. Something about getting rid of a local politician that was troublesome. He looked forward to that kind of job. The new assignment would be a man.

Martin looked at his watch. The glowing dials told him it was 1:50 a.m. Lola would be closing the bar right about now. He pulled into the back of the Tavern and parked, closing the car door silently and walked to the front. Then he pulled his 9 millimeter semi-automatic from the satchel he carried, his face grim.

※

*I*t was three minutes before two when Pat came in the back door of the Tavern to help Lola count the day's take in the till. She noticed a strange car parked in the back of the bar. Maybe someone was leaving their car overnight. Pat sat down at the desk in the backroom to check her ledger. Everyone had left. Ole Dewey was the last and Lola walked him out to his truck.

"Drive careful now," Lola said, as she waved to him

and walked back into the bar. She stooped down to slide the lock closed at the base of the door when someone pushed it open knocking Lola on her butt.

"Sorry we're cl...." Lola didn't get the last word out. Standing above her was the white haired man with a gun in his hand. In spite of her shock, she looked up at him and noticed the ragged cuticle and chewed nail of his forefinger clenched around the trigger. She felt faint and couldn't catch her breath. This was her worst nightmare coming true. Tony's killer had found her.

"Thought you'd fooled me, eh? Get up." Martin Fellino motioned with the gun. "Stand over there." He pointed to a spot away from the door.

Lola did what he said. She glanced around but couldn't see or hear Pat. Her legs were trembling so hard she could hardly walk.

"Now I don't know if you was in Tony's house or not. I'm just cleanin' up loose ends."

"Lola swallowed. "I wasn't," she lied. "I don't know anything."

"Yeah? Then why'd you run?" His pale blue eyes squinted and his lips opened, showing a broken front tooth.

"Well, I...was scared. I didn't know why Tony was...killed, and since I was his girlfriend, I panicked." She took a deep breath.

"The way I hear it, you was with Tony every night you had off. And I did find a woman's nightgown on the floor. Can't blame me for coming to the conclusion that you mighta' been there."

Lola could only shake her head. "Well, I wasn't… that night."

"Then who do you suppose was in Tony's bed? Think he was screwin' somebody else?"

"I honestly don't know." Lola raised her voice a little. If she could keep him talking, maybe Pat would hear and call the sheriff.

"Ya see, it don't matter to me, one way or the other. It ain't personal. You get it?" Martin lied, trying to keep a neutral attitude.

"Yes, I get it. You're nothing but trash. You don't care who you hurt." Lola was suddenly angry. If he was going to kill her, she'd get her two cents worth in. "You kill innocent people as well as the guilty. I hope you burn in hell," she spat at him.

"Well…the little lady's showin' some gumption. I like that. But not enough to spare your life." Damn these kinds of jobs, Martin thought.

"Can you tell me *why* Tony was killed?" Lola's voice shook, trying to stall for time, so Pat would hear them. "He always seemed like a good casino manager."

"Well, he wasn't. He was skimmin' and you know the Family don't look kindly on stealin' from them."

"That's kinda' ironic, when the Family does their share of stealing."

"Can't deny that. I think we've said everything we have to say." Martin raised his 9-millimeter Beretta to within a few inches of Lola's head.

"Get on your knees." He clamped his teeth together hard in preparation for what he had to do. His concentration wavered slightly.

Tears poured from her eyes. She wished she'd listened to her intuition and left the Valley when the killer first showed up. But hindsight wouldn't save her life now. She shut her eyes and prayed. Prayed for forgiveness for all her mistakes as she knelt before the killer. She wondered if her life would flash before her eyes as the pundits claimed. Her last thought was… where the hell was Pat? At that moment, her instincts kicked in. She rolled to the right and screamed, just before she heard the gun go off.… three shots. The noise was so intense, it made her ears ring. She waited for the force of the bullets to tear into her brain. She waited… but felt nothing.

Her eyes flew open and she saw the white-haired man stretched out a few feet away on his back, his arms flung wide as if he were welcoming his transition to the afterlife. Blood was already seeping from his chest through his blue rayon shirt. There was also blood on his forehead, surrounding a small dark hole. Lola saw the gun near the man's right hand where it had fallen. The killer down still didn't register on Lola's brain.

Pat came running from behind the bar. "Lola, are you all right?" She reached for her, helping her up.

Little wailing moans came from Lola. She couldn't believe she was still alive.

Pat pulled Lola to her chest with her left arm, still holding the .38 caliber pistol in her shaking right hand. She had never killed anyone before, but she always knew she could do it if necessary.

Lola continued to sob on Pat's shoulder until the full impact finally hit her. "My God, Pat! You shot *him*."

"I sure as hell did!"

Lola pulled away, bent down and felt the side of the killer's throat. There was no pulse. "He's *dead!*"

"I shore hope so. I ain't considered a good shot for no reason. Now, this here man tried to rob us. That's what we'll tell Sheriff Del."

Lola wiped the tears from her face on the sleeve of her blouse. "But Pat, he *didn't* try to rob us."

Well, as soon as I put the day's take on him, it'll look like he did. Now don't worry darlin'. Sheriff Del will buy it."

"Half the Valley knows this man was askin' about me. Don't you think the sheriff knows that, too?"

"Even if he does, it don't matter. Ain't nobody to contradict us. And you forget, honey. We protect our own here in the Valley. Now let me git this money into his pockets."

Pat laid the .38 on the bar, went to the register and scooped out all the bills, carried them over to the dead man and stuffed the money into his jacket pockets. She felt less shaky now. Then she went to the phone.

When she'd finished talking to the sheriff, she picked up a clean towel, ran warm water over it and carried it to Lola, who was sitting in a booth by the door, her hands covering her face. She wiped her cheeks and hands trying to erase the last few minutes. She looked at Pat, whose face was blotchy, both cheekbones still flushed red. "Pat, you okay?" Lola placed her hand on Pat's cheek.

"I'm fine, honey. Ain't everyday I shoot somebody. But I kin take it in stride. It's good to know my aim's still accurate."

In spite of a dead man lying on the floor, Lola had to smile. "You are something else, lady."

"Now here's what happened, honey." Pat took the wet towel from Lola and tossed it on the bar. "He forced his way in just as you was lockin' up, and demanded all the money in the till. After you gave it to him, he said he was sorry he'd have to kill you. I had just come into the back door and overhead him say he'd have to kill you. That's when I shot him, three times. Can you remember that?"

Lola nodded, "I'll never forget it. I counted the number of times the gun went off."

Pat put her arm around Lola's shoulders. "Nothin' else happened or was talked about. Okay?"

Lola looked up at Pat. "Why you doing this for me?"

"Cause you're a good girl and you don't deserve to have this happen to you."

"I can never repay you for saving my life and getting me out of this jam."

"No need, darlin'. We women have to stick together. By the way, is Billy Jim in or out?"

"He's in Seligman right now. I expect him home tomorrow morning."

"When he gets home, it'll all be over."

"Only you and Billy know what happened in Vegas," Lola said. "I never even told Sherry."

"The official story will be just what we tell Sheriff Del."

Lola put her arms around Pat and hugged her. "Thanks Pat. You're a real good friend, and a fine woman."

"Now don't be making my mascara run," Pat said, wiping beneath her eyes.

Sheriff Del showed up in half an hour with a Mohave County deputy. The Kingman Coroner arrived an hour later. Del listened to Pat's story, checking the pockets of the dead man.

Del picked up the killer's gun with a plastic glove. "This here's a nine-millimeter semi-automatic. Did you hear his gun go off?"

Pat shrugged. "Well, I don't think so. He threatened to kill Lola. I couldn't let him do that, could I? I think I shot him before he got a shot off."

"Looks like you got him once in the head and twice in the chest." The Sheriff looked at Pat hard. "Well, I'll have to take your .38 with me, too."

"Sure," Pat said, nonchalantly.

Lola felt her face burning when Sheriff Del asked her, "You ever seen this guy before?" She shook her head and managed a credible "No."

"I'll have to have your word, Pat, that you won't leave the state while the investigation is in progress. And you and Lola need to come into the office tomorrow to give your statements."

"Of course, Del. Where the hell would I go with a bar to run?"

"It's just a formality, Pat. Do I have your word?"

"You got my word, Del."

The Coroner and the sheriff put the body in a canvas bag and carried it out to the Needles meat wagon. Ten minutes later, the body was on its way to the mortuary. The deputy drove the Cadillac parked behind the bar into town and Sheriff Del left in the police car.

After the sheriff left, Pat drove Lola home, leaving Betsy in a parking place beside the motel. Pat followed Lola inside and poured them both a stiff shot of Jack Daniels that she'd had the foresight to grab from behind the bar. They sat and sipped their whiskeys until Lola's eyes felt heavy. Pat led her to bed, helped her undress, and tucked her under the covers. Lola's eyes closed just when dawn opened hers as she peeked over the eastern ridge.

"Try to sleep, honey. I'll talk to you later today."

"Thanks, Pat..." Lola mumbled as she heard the front door close.

⋛⋚

Billy Jim was shook up when he heard how close Lola came to being dead.

"Damn, I shoulda' been here," he said.

"Pat took care of the situation real fine. I owe her my life."

"It's a pity she don't know what Paul tried to do to you."

"I don't need to tell her now. It's water under the bridge. Let's leave her with what good memories she might have of him."

He leaned back on the sofa and pulled Lola into his

arms. "So, now you're safe. No need to worry about any more hit men from Vegas."

Lola wasn't sure. "I hope you're right."

"Whadayamean?"

"What if someone else comes looking for me?"

"Now don't be worryin' about that already. We just got rid of this hit man."

Lola smiled. What he should have said was…Pat got rid of the hit man.

That afternoon, Lola and Pat went to the Mohave County Sheriff Station in Bullhead City, gave their statements and signed them. Lola was edgy about lying, but Pat was so terrific, the deputies called her a heroine for saving Lola's life.

When she told Sherry about the robbery, Sherry wasn't convinced.

"Lola, I know you're not tellin' me the whole story. I've always known you was scared of somethin', since you first came here. But I'll wait till you're ready to tell me."

"Thanks, Sherry," was all Lola could say.

Two days after the shooting, the *Needles News* had a short paragraph on the front page.

> Early Tuesday morning Pat Sweeney shot and killed a hold-up man that tried to rob Sweeney's Tavern. The dead man is identified by his driver's license as Martin Fellino of Las Vegas. No next of kin was located so he'll be buried in Potter's Field next to the hospital.

Lola closed the paper and got up to feed the animals. Thank God that was the end of it.

*L*ola and Sherry entered the door with black lettering which read, **Samuel Taylor, Attorney-at-law**. His office was on a side street in Needles across from the Claypool's supermarket.

Mr. Taylor motioned for them to sit down. "Good afternoon, ladies. Thanks for coming in." He reached over and shook hands with both Lola and Sherry. "I'm Sam Taylor, executor for Jonathon Marsh's estate."

"Nice to meet you," Lola said.

Sherry smiled.

"How long have you known Mr. Marsh?" He looked at the two of them.

"Well, eleven months or so," Lola answered.

"I've known him since I came to the Valley two years ago," Sherry added. "He used to come into the bar where I worked."

"You probably are surprised that Mr. Marsh had anything that could be called an estate?" Mr. Taylor raised his eyebrows.

"Yes, we are," Lola said.

"Well, he had a reasonable sum of money that's accumulated interest over the years. About a month ago he came in and made out a will, making you two the beneficiaries. He knew he didn't have much longer, so he decided to tie up some loose ends. I'm certainly glad he did, otherwise the state would have received his money."

Both Lola and Sherry stared at the lawyer.

"Neither of us knew he did this," Lola said.

"I know. He didn't want you to know until he was gone. He told me you girls took care of him these last few months, and he was immensely grateful."

"Didn't Marsh have any relatives?" Lola asked.

"No, he didn't. He was an only child and all of his relatives are gone."

The girls were silent and the lawyer paused.

"So in keeping with the terms of the will, I'll read it to you. 'I, Jonathon Marsh being of sound mind give all of my earthly possessions, including my trailer and my truck, to Sherry Brown and Lola Raines. I leave a third of my money to my lawyer, Samuel Taylor and the rest to the above mentioned, Sherry and Lola.'" Samuel looked up at the girls.

Sherry and Lola were speechless.

Finally Lola found her voice. "That was so sweet of him." She had tears in her eyes and she clasped Sherry's hand.

"Jonathon's initial investment was quite small but it totals over $30,000 now. So each of you will get a little more than $10,000." The lawyer looked at the girls over the rim of his glasses.

"My God! Who could guess that Marshmallow had that kind of money?" Sherry exclaimed. She looked at Lola. "I can hardly believe this is happening."

"We are certainly surprised, Mr. Taylor. Everyone thought Marsh had only his social security to live on," Lola said.

"Apparently he did live on it. He never touched

this money."

"Where did he get the money originally?" Lola asked.

"He was part owner of a gold mine many years ago. The story I heard was that his partner cheated him out of his half, but before that, they had taken quite a bit of gold out of the mine. Jonathon saved his share and let it accumulate."

"The minister at the funeral mentioned the gold mine, but Marsh never talked about it," Lola said.

"I've known Mr. Marsh for forty years, and he never talked about it to me, either." The lawyer picked up a pen. "If I can get you two to sign these papers stating you accept this bequest, I'll get your checks printed out. Or I can have them deposited in your accounts at the bank."

Both the girls signed the papers silently. Then Lola spoke. "Please forgive us, Mr. Taylor. We are still in shock. But I don't want mine deposited." She looked at Sherry.

Sherry nodded. "Me either."

The lawyer looked at them and frowned. "Isn't that kind of risky? Do you plan on cashing them right away?"

"Probably."

"Well, all right. Give me a minute, and I'll have my secretary make them out." He walked down a hallway into a back office.

Sherry leaned over and whispered to Lola. "Why don't we want the checks deposited?"

"Because we don't want anyone to know we have

the money," Lola said quietly.

Sherry took a minute for that to sink in. "Okay. But what will we do with $10,000 in cash?"

"Put it in a bag and hide it," Lola said.

Sherry looked at Lola and started laughing. Then Lola started. They were both howling when Mr. Taylor came back with the checks.

"I see you're warming up to your good fortune." He smiled at them, his eyes twinkling.

Lola sobered. "Mr. Taylor, could we ask a personal favor of you? That you not tell anyone of our windfall. It will make our lives less complicated."

"Of course, dear, my lips are sealed." He handed the checks to Lola and Sherry.

Lola looked down at the check. $10,317.00 was typed on the voucher. "Thank you, Mr. Taylor."

"May I ask what you will do with Mr. Marsh's trailer and truck and the acre of land?"

The girls looked at each other. Sherry shrugged. "We haven't even thought of that yet. When we decide, we'll let you know."

Mr. Taylor again offered his hand. "It was a pleasure, ladies."

Both Lola and Sherry carefully placed the checks in their purses. "Bye, Mr. Taylor," Lola said as they left his office.

When they got into Betsy, Lola rolled up the windows and let out a yell. "My God, Sherry. Do you believe that old rascal, Marshmallow?"

"He sure was a sweetheart. I loved him to pieces."

Sherry choked up.

"Me, too," Lola agreed.

Sherry looked over at her best friend. "But why are we bein' so secretive, Lola? Please explain this to me. It's not like we did anything wrong to get this money."

Lola kept her eyes on the road as she maneuvered the bridge over the Colorado River. "I'm not sure. It's just a gut feeling I have. I don't want anyone to know about this."

"Not even Billy?" Sherry asked.

"Not even Billy," Lola repeated.

※

*I*t was Thursday and this was the first day the Tavern was open since the shooting. It had been quiet; mostly regulars and locals wanting to gossip about Paul, the funeral and the robbery and the shooting of the hold-up man. Lola was working the ten-to-six shift.

At five, Russell and the band came in to do a practice session with lights and their sound equipment. Russell's long black hair hung loosely around his shoulders as he tuned up his guitar. He came off the stage and walked to the bar. "Why don't you stay a while after you get off, we could run through a few songs together." His intense dark eyes stared into hers.

She liked Russell and always enjoyed singing with him. "Well, I don't know if that's a good idea."

"Look, we're all here in a public place. He can't object to that."

Lola paused. "Okay." She let her desire to sing with the group override her concern.

Lola stocked the bar and cleaned up the dirty glasses. Pat came in at six and took over.

"Not very busy, today, huh?" Pat said as she came behind the bar.

Lola shook her head. "Pretty quiet." They counted the money in the till together, and Lola picked up her tips in a jar at the end of the bar.

"You goin' home?" Pat asked.

"I'm going to do a little rehearsing with Russell and the band," Lola said, smiling, and heading for the stage.

"You be careful. You know who won't like it," Pat called after Lola.

Lola turned around. "I'm here with you and in a public place."

"You know that boy ain't always reasonable. Especially if he's liquored up."

Lola shrugged her shoulders. "Pat, I have to do my own thing."

"Okay, honey. You don't have to convince me, but don't say I didn't warn you."

Lola made a face at Pat and joined Russell on the stage.

"What would you like to do first?" he asked.

"How 'bout, "Help Me Make It Through the Night." You sing real nice harmony."

"Okay, babe." Russell gave her key to the band and they launched into the song. Lola sang melody and when she forgot the words Russell placed them in front of her. Lola felt the mournfulness of the song and got lost in the music. When they were finished, the few customers at the bar clapped.

Russell beamed his smile on her and the drummer and bass guitarist whooped their approval. They worked on a couple of other songs, started one, and then changed the key, until they had it down. Lola looked at her watch and saw it was nearly eight o'clock; but there was still some light. She knew she was late feeding the animals; Billy liked them to be fed before dark. She thanked the guys in the band.

"I'll walk you out," Russell said.

Lola grabbed her purse from behind the bar, waved goodbye to Pat, and she and Russell left the Tavern.

The sky was a soft pastel pink with swirls of blue-gray and lavender.

"Thanks for asking me to stay. I really enjoyed it." Lola said.

"Think you can sing with us on our Saturday night gig at the Sports Lounge?"

"I don't know, Russell. You know how Billy is. If he's in, he may go for it. If he's out, probably not."

Russell nodded and lit a cigarette. "You know, Lola, if you ever need any help you can call on me. I don't know what your personal life is like, but I just want you to know I'd like to be here for you, if you need me." He reached out and took her hand.

"Thanks, Russell. I appreciate it." Lola moved away and got into Betsy.

He leaned in her window, his eyes resting on her mouth. "Besides, we make beautiful music together. We oughta let the public hear that gift."

Lola laughed. "We'll see. Thanks again."

Russell's intense eyes followed her as she backed out of the Tavern lot and headed home.

Maybe Sherry was right. Was Russell making a pass at her, or was she just imagining it? She suspected she'd been out of action too long.

⋈

*L*ola was watching television when she heard Billy's truck pull in the drive. She hadn't worked at the Tavern today, nor was she scheduled to work tonight or Saturday night. Pat had hired a new man for part-time and was breaking him in. Instead, she'd spent the time doing odd jobs around Billy's place. She wanted to ask Billy if he would mind her singing with Russell and the band tomorrow night. Picking the right time to talk to him was crucial. Maybe after he'd had dinner. There was a casserole warming in the oven. She hoped he'd be home tomorrow, so they could both go to the Sports Lounge together.

Billy stamped his feet loudly on the porch mat and opened the door.

"Hi, honey," Lola said.

Billy hung up his hat and jacket and sat down next to her to take off his boots. "Hi," he grunted.

Lola could smell the whiskey. She looked at his

eyes. They were puffy and half-closed. His face was flushed and his hair was matted. He'd been doing some heavy-duty drinking. Lola felt a slight queasiness in her stomach.

"You been in long?" she ventured.

"Wha's it to you?" he slurred.

Lola shrugged and was silent.

"Been at the Red Dog all afternoon." He fell back on the couch.

She wished she could keep her mouth shut, but she asked anyway. "What's wrong?"

Billy leaned his head back and closed his eyes. "Nothin," he muttered.

She got up and removed the casserole from the oven, took the salad from the refrigerator and placed them on the table. She opened two cans of beer. "Dinner's ready," she said. No answer from the couch. She sat down and dished up some salad.

Billy stood and lurched over to the table. "Whatcha do today?" he asked, slumping into the chair.

"Well… I cleaned the house and the corrals."

"Ya' didn't work at the Tavern?"

She looked at Billy's bloodshot eyes and shook her head.

He picked up his beer and held it up to his lips. "What else ya do?"

"Let's see. I played my guitar and brushed Sedona and Apache."

"Did ya see Russell?"

"No," she said calmly.

"You fuckin' sure?" Billy said, his lips pulled back, showing his teeth.

"What's on your mind, Billy?"

"You fuckin' bitch, you been seein' him!"

"No, Billy, I haven't."

It happened so fast Lola didn't see it coming. Billy's free hand curled around the salt shaker and threw it across the table. It hit Lola hard in the chest and fell to the floor. She jumped up and ran through the archway into the living room. "Billy, you hurt me." She crossed her arms over her breasts, tears welling from her eyes.

He followed her, but Lola kept several feet between them.

"I heard about you and him at the Red Dog. Playin' music together and the two of you outside the Tavern." Billy's fists were clenched at his sides.

"Yes, I practiced with the band the other night and Russell came outside for a cigarette when I was leaving. Billy, you're getting carried away over nothing." Lola felt like a boa constrictor was uncurling in her abdomen, its circumference swelling as it moved up her torso.

"And what else, bitch?" Billy spat the words at her.

Lola turned to get her purse. She was getting out of here right now. But Billy seemed to read her mind and cut her off. He grabbed her by the shoulders, dragging her down to the rug, his hard body falling over hers.

"You ain't goin' nowhere!"

Lola panicked. She pushed against his muscular chest but he didn't budge. She tried to knee him in the groin but aimed too high and got him in the stomach.

"Bitch," he swore and placed his hands around her neck. He started squeezing as she wrestled against his large hands. He was cutting off her air, and she was gasping for a breath. Just before she passed out, in a moment of instinct, she stopped struggling and went limp beneath him. He took his hands away from her neck, and shook her by the shoulders. When she didn't respond he got up, stumbling into the kitchen.

Lola felt groggy but watched him between the slits of her eyes. Her throat ached and her tongue felt parched and stiff. She knew she had to get out while she still could. As soon as Billy was at the sink filling a cup, she crawled to the door, grabbed her purse and car keys, pulled herself to her feet, and was out the door. She ran to Betsy, jumped in, and started her up. When she drove out of the drive, she saw him standing in the doorway.

"Lola, don't go," he cried.

≳≲

She sobbed all the way to Sherry's place. Ronnie's double-wide was dark and Lola pulled around behind it and parked Betsy under some trees. She walked around in front to the door, looked under the mat where Sherry kept the spare key and let herself in. It was dark inside and she didn't turn on a light. She slumped down in the first chair she came to and leaned back in Ronnie's recliner. This was really the last straw. He'd tried to strangle her; had he really meant to kill her? No, but she knew for sure she would never trust him again. She had wondered how it would end. Why were all men such assholes? Couldn't they just accept the love from a good woman without fucking everything up?

It had all begun with her father. She should know after all these years; men were not to be trusted. She had adored her father when she was very young, then when he started sexually molesting her, she feared him, and then one day, maybe just before she threatened to tell her mother, she realized she hated him. His end had been one that he'd deserved. Back then, when she was seventeen, Jack — Jack Morales, that was her father's name — had arranged with the next-door neighbors to take their little girl to a carnival. Lola had seen him helping her into his car. She went immediately to her mother, Claire, and told her the secret she had kept for so long. Her mother was horrified, calling her a liar, and forbid her to ever repeat such a lie against her father to anyone.

"But Mother, aren't you going to do something about the little girl? Stop him," Lola cried.

Her mother poured herself another shot of bourbon and said, "It's not your business. Stay out of it."

Lola could hardly believe her mother's behavior. She went to her room and slammed the door. When her mother left for her job that evening waiting tables in the local diner, Lola packed her suitcase and left home. She'd never returned. Later she heard that her father was killed in a fire with other firefighters. She didn't go to the funeral or contact her mother. A few years later, her mother died in a rest home from TB and cirrhosis of the liver. Sometimes, she wished she'd been a better daughter. But at the time, she couldn't forgive her for her neglect. Now, all these years later, she did forgive her. As for her father, well she knew he was sick, like Paul. They were sad, half-people, moving through life with a film covering their hearts. Billy too, was sick, in his own way. Lola knew instinctively that when people let go of their fear of things in this world, they can love. Apparently Billy still had a lot of fear to deal with.

She wiped the tears from her face. She knew now it was time to move on. Not run away, just get on with her life. This Valley was no longer the place for her. Like the song went, she'd been looking for love in all the wrong places.

She heard a car drive up, a door open and then close and the car drive away. Sherry opened the unlocked door.

"Who's here?" Sherry sounded a little unsure. "Lola, is that you?"

Lola reached up and turned on the light beside the chair.

Sherry saw her tear-stained face. "Are you okay?"

Lola nodded, not trusting her voice.

"What happened?" Sherry asked, putting down her purse and coming to Lola's side.

Lola told her. She started to cry again when she told

how Billy strangled her.

"That bastard!" Sherry swore. "Look at the red marks around your neck!"

Lola brought her hands to her neck in a protective manner. "It hurts too," she croaked.

Sherry reached for her, holding her by the shoulders, letting Lola sob. Finally her crying subsided.

"Lola. Let's leave. Tomorrow."

"Yes."

"Have you cashed your check yet?"

"No," Lola said, wiping away her tears. "Have you?"

Sherry shook her head. "It's still in my purse."

"Mine, too. We can cash them on our way out of town."

"We'll leave this damn valley in our dust," Sherry said, as she opened her stash box and started rolling a joint.

※

The next morning, the girls kept a low profile, not answering the phone. They saw Billy drive by several times but he didn't stop. At two in the afternoon, Lola called the trainmaster and was told Billy was on his way to Seligman. The girls immediately loaded Sherry's suitcase in the backseat. Lola tied a blue scarf around her neck to hide the black and blue marks that had appeared overnight. They climbed into Betsy and drove over to Billy's place.

The little adobe house looked forlorn. Sedona,

Apache and Dobbin all whinnied at the sight of the girls. Lola threw them some alfalfa and petted Apache, kissing her on the nose.

"I'll sure miss you, girl." She stroked her sleek neck. Apache seemed to sense this was goodbye. She nuzzled Lola's hair and cheek, getting slobber on her face. Lola laughed. "I sure hope Billy takes good care of you."

"God, Lola, I wouldn't worry about that, we got enough else to worry about," Sherry said. "Let's get your packing done and get the hell out of here."

Lola left Apache reluctantly and went into the house. She'd been gone a day and the place was a mess. On the table was a note from Billy.

She picked it up and read it aloud.

> Lola — Please forgive me for what I did to you last night. I was out of my head. If you can forgive me I promise to never hurt you again. I realize now there wasn't any reason for me to freak out like that. Call me in Seligman at the trailer. I don't want to lose you.
> Love, Billy

"What an asshole. He thinks you'll just overlook his strangling you?" Sherry snorted in disgust.

Lola wadded up the note in her fist and dropped it back on the table. The girls went into the bedroom and Lola pulled a suitcase from the closet and started packing. She picked up a few things from the bathroom; a toothbrush, her makeup. When the suitcase was filled, she took it out to Betsy and stowed it on top of Sherry's bag in the backseat. She'd come with one suitcase and she was leaving with one. The last thing she loaded was her guitar wrapped in a blanket.

Sherry was sitting on the couch rolling a couple of joints. Lola took a last look around the place, trying to store up the happy memories for later and to forget the bad ones. But she couldn't get the last scene out of her head. It seemed to play over and over like a broken reel of an old movie. She shook her head as if to shake it loose from her mind.

"Come on, Sherry. I'm outta here." She dropped Billy's key on the table and slammed the door. They got in Betsy and drove out the circular driveway on which Billy Jim had dragged Hamburger.

Lola headed for the Tavern. "I'm telling Pat we're leaving."

Pat asked no questions, and paid her for the last few days.

"We'll sure miss you two around here. The Valley won't be the same." Pat squeezed Lola's hand and hugged her affectionately.

"I have a feeling this Valley's seen a lot of changes through the years and one more isn't going to matter too much," Lola said.

"Come back and see us sometime, honey."

"I'll make it back someday, Pat. Thanks for everything." She held the older woman at arm's length and looked into her eyes. Then Lola wrapped her arms around Pat's shoulders and hugged her tightly. She stepped away, blew her a kiss and waved good-bye as she let the swinging door bang behind her.

Back on the road, they stopped at the Bank of America in Needles and went in to cash their checks. The teller was in shock at two checks over ten thousand dollars each, being cashed the same day and called over the bank manager, Cora. She, in turn, called the attorney, Samuel Taylor, and got his okay.

The two tellers and the bank manager were gathered around Cora's desk, helping Sherry and Lola count their money. There were several stacks of one hundred dollar bills. The tellers were laughing and joking, like it was a holiday. Nothing like this had happened since two robbers held up the bank ten years ago. The thieves got caught on their way out of town when their car broke down just outside Needles on Interstate 40.

Sherry packed her money in an overnight case and Lola stashed her loot in a saddlebag.

※

*L*ola knew by tomorrow word would have traveled across river to the Valley that the girls left town with a lot of money and there would be speculation as to where it came from.

"You know how gossip gets twisted," Sherry said. "We could end up being bank robbers."

They both giggled at the thought of becoming outlaw legends in the Valley.

Their last stop was at the attorney's. Lola left the keys to Marsh's trailer and truck, with instructions to sell them and the property. They left Sherry's parents phone number in Phoenix as a contact, getting his promise not to give it out to anyone.

Five minutes later they were cruising toward Blythe down a two-lane blacktop. Prickly Cactus and Ocotillo bloomed along the road. On their right, a ridge of blue mountains outlined the valley. On the left, the Colorado River flowed urgently toward the Gulf. Jackrabbits darted across the road, daring Betsy to run them down.

Lola's heart was going through a spring thaw regarding Billy. She no longer despised him, but hoped he got his shit together and had a decent life. Perhaps he would learn too, from this experience. She vowed she would not exercise such poor judgment about men in the future. In her deepest consciousness she always knew the difference between ordinary good men, and those like Tony and Billy Jim. They were outlaws, or slightly dangerous, and that appealed to the adventurous side of her character. But it got her into trouble when she ignored the signposts. Men like Marsh made her feel good about herself. He must have had confidence in her and Sherry that they would choose the right path in their lives.

Even in the face of her recent losses, Lola felt the quickening of the lust for travel, the desire to move on, deep in her bones. Seeing new and exotic places had always been in her blood; like a gypsy, she could pick up and just go. Dear Marsh. She would miss him so very much. What a sweet, loving man. Her heart hurt remembering how she first saw Billy Jim at the Tavern, his cowboy hat tilted back, his eyes smiling across the room at her. Well, she'd made her bed, slept in it, and when it didn't fit anymore, she'd go looking for one that did. She'd find a lasting love no matter how long it took.

"Where are we goin'?" Sherry asked, breaking into Lola's reverie.

"I know a little town in Mexico just outside Chihuahua. Old friend of mine lives there."

Sherry's eyes grew wide. "Wow, go to Mexico? I don't know. Can you speak any Spanish?"

"Si, Senorita. Would a girl named Lola Morales not speak Spanish?"

Sherry laughed, her fine blond hair blowing out the window. "All right, Lola. Let's *do* it." She clapped her hands.

Lola flipped on the radio and found a station playing Ranchero music. She kept time with her fingers on the steering wheel. Sherry pulled some chocolate-covered malt balls from a bag and handed some to Lola.

"Lola, what are we gonna' do with all this money?"

Lola turned toward her friend and grinned. "Oh, we'll find some way of spending it."

Sherry giggled and lit a joint, inhaled deeply and passed it over to Lola. "Here's to the first day of the rest of our lives, girl."

Lola took a deep hit. "Amen," she said.

EPILOGUE

𝒫at wiped down the bar counter and turned to the customer that had just come in.

"What'll ya have?"

"How about a cold bottle of Bud," the stranger said.

"Comin' right up." Pat went to the cooler and pulled a bottle of beer, filled a glass with ice and put it before the man. She noticed his dark suit, dirty nails and his white, pasty skin.

"Just passin' through?" she asked.

"Kind of," the stranger said. "Actually I'm looking for an old friend from Vegas."

Pat felt a tightness in her stomach. "Yeah? Who's your friend?"

"I'm looking for Lola Raines. Heard she was a bartender here."

"Well, you missed her by about a couple of months. She worked here briefly, then moved on."

The man slurped his beer. "Have any idea where she went?"

"Nope. She didn't talk much and I didn't ask questions."

"Do you know of anyone she was friends with?" the man persisted.

"Nope. Like I said she was a loner."

"Are there any other bars here in this Valley she mighta' worked in?"

"Well, there is a couple on this side of the river and then there's the Red Dog in Needles. I don't think she worked at any of them but this one. But you could ask."

The stranger drained his glass and left a fiver on the bar. "Thanks. I'll do that." He slipped off the stool and let himself out the swinging door of Sweeney's Tavern, the bright Arizona sunlight spilling into the darkness of the bar.

Pat went to the phone. She'd call Clyde and Leila at the Red Dog and Judd at the Sundancer and Bill at the Sports Lounge before the stranger from Vegas got to any of them.

To order additional copies of this book, contact Colleen Rae at: raecol@i2k.com